THE TOWN THAT LAUGHED

The TOWN THAT LAUGHED

a novel

MANU BHATTATHIRI

Happy reading!

ALEPH

ALEPH BOOK COMPANY
An independent publishing firm
promoted by ***Rupa Publications India***

First published in India in 2018
by Aleph Book Company
7/16 Ansari Road, Daryaganj
New Delhi 110 002

This is a work of fiction. Names, characters, places and incidents are either the product of the author's imagination or are used fictitiously and any resemblance to any actual persons, living or dead, events or locales is entirely coincidental.

ISBN: 978-93-87561-41-0

1 3 5 7 9 10 8 6 4 2

Printed and bound in India by Parksons Graphics Pvt. Ltd., Mumbai.

To Amma and Achoy
for always lighting up my path
without ever trying to change it.

Contents

1.

Joby

Over the past few years much has changed in the small south Indian town of Karuthupuzha.

The first change, the one you see even as you are travelling here, concerns the only bus to Karuthupuzha. It has been repainted. The bright new coat of paint came after numerous meetings of the municipal council, urgent letters, strings being pulled, political muscle being flexed and even some secret bribes paid out of town funds. As always, every day the bus puffs to a halt at the marketplace, sneezes once from its underside, offers up a brief prayer of gratitude at yet another eventless trip made and falls silent with a happy tiredness. It rocks involuntarily with each passenger jumping off, feeling lighter and happier as its load lessens. All this is as it has always been. What is new is its pride in the wavy green and blue lines interspersed with red astral designs that now adorn its body. The shiny paint brings back memories of the young bus it once was. The new design invokes some admiration for the unknown artist at the bus body-shop in the city from onlookers in the Karuthupuzha market. More importantly, for one and all, it heralds the fact that Karuthupuzha is different. The very way you arrive here has changed.

There are other indicators of change. Now you might find the odd tobacconist muttering words like 'trend' or 'changing mindsets' under his breath as he sprinkles water on the betel leaves stacked up in his shop. You will also certainly hear heated discussions on technology and foreign cities and the youth of other lands under banyan trees and behind rustling newspapers. In a certain toddy shop that we will visit presently, arguments rage every evening about Western clothes versus Eastern culture, with participants growing steadily more violent as they down more and more arrack. Everywhere in the town you will see its residents endeavouring to keep up with the world as it changes around them.

People in Karuthupuzha now listen to weather forecasts on the radio. Where grandmothers shielded their eyes with withered palms and squinted at the skies to predict rainfall, people now turn to the Meteorology Department. Though significantly less dependable than the forecasts of the grandmothers, no one would dream of going back to that practice—it was so retrograde. They had figured out that if you kept your radio facing west, it was more likely that the predictions would be accurate. Moreover, everyone knew that it wasn't all that vital to know exactly when the rain would descend from the skies. The people of Karuthupuzha had the patience and the time to wait until it rained to know that it was raining. Weather predictions had entertainment value, no more.

The change sweeping through Karuthupuzha had spread beyond its human populace. If you took the first side lane after the bus stop, you would pass by a barren jackfruit tree that no one had spared a second glance for. In all the years that it had grown to adulthood the tree had never yielded a single fruit. Even the birds deemed it not significant enough to alight upon, and its meagre and stingy shade had never been used by a single traveller for a moment's rest throughout its history. But now, after centuries of an incredibly useless existence, the tree had started to bear fruit! It seemed to have realized that when you suck life-giving goodies from the soil and pluck sunlight from the air, it was important to give back. It seemed to have finally absorbed the principle that politicians and philosophers couldn't stop talking about. That it was important to give back was something that was taught in the town's only school.

It was an axiom that even irked the otherwise impermeable consciences of some of the very rich businessmen like Eeppachan Mothalali and Moydeen Mappila, who would from time to time engage in frantic but incomplete acts of social responsibility. Having abruptly realized its inadequacies in this department the tree had borne, the previous season, its first intensely sweet, perfectly shapeless and rather heavy jackfruit. The fruit had stuck out from among its thick, hitherto selfish leaves like the bulge of a pregnant woman. Ever since, it had been insanely fertile across seasons. Birds, squirrels, flies, ants and humans were beneficiaries of the jackfruit tree's new resolve. But the tree had taken the philosophy so much to heart that nobody could keep up. Even though everyone ate their fill, there was still much left over. These fruits ended up on the roadside and lay there, crushed by the fall, sticky and messy.

Now, it is important that when you try to capture the ethos of a place you must be completely honest if you are seeking to give the reader a true picture. You can't just highlight one aspect; so in the interests of accuracy it is necessary to point out that change had not reached every corner of Karuthupuzha. There were some holdouts. One such throwback lay comfortably on the steps leading up to Sureshan's barbershop, oblivious to the fact that it was day now and the establishment would soon be open for business.

This unchanged element of Karuthupuzha was Joby the town drunk. He now lay sprawled on the steps, feet on the lowest step, head lolling on the uppermost. By one slightly swollen foot lay the bitch Lilly, her tail curled beneath her safely like it was the most precious part of her. Still swimming in yesterday's arrack, Joby was in no mood to make way for the day. From under his dirty shirt a hairy bellybutton showed. Although from the way he was lying on the steps you would think the man was dead at last, succumbing to a lifetime of toddy shop food and crude alcohol, a lifetime of being a buffoon who burned himself out to make everyone laugh, a lifetime of trying and failing to find anything at all that deserved his sobriety, Joby was very much alive. No sooner had Poulose the grocer—who had his shop two doors away and was opening its shutters for the day—commented on how some people belonged in an ocean of arrack, the drunk let loose such a volley of classic abuses that the dew on a nearby shrub quickly evaporated. Poulose looked around to check if anyone had heard. When he realized that half of Karuthupuzha had heard, he rushed into his shop, pretending that nothing had happened. It's one of those days, Poulose thought, when Joby the drunk decides to recite the morning prayers for the whole damn town.

From the grocer Poulose to Manikanthan of the stationery shop further down, to Chacko the electrician who was tinkering with something while perched on a nearby electric pole, to Abu who bought old newspapers, everyone was now eagerly anticipating the arrival of Sureshan. Everyone knew that Sureshan would be particularly distressed to find the town drunk fouling up his front steps. The barber was a neat, methodical man who never got drunk and kept his shop as if it were a temple. The first thing he did every morning after opening his shop was to splash a bucket of water on the steps so the way to his shop would be clean and welcoming for customers. A cruder man might not have deviated from his routine this morning as well, and would have washed down his steps as always. But Sureshan was a fine person who hated to cause anyone any pain. Everyone waited to see what he would do when he arrived.

Sure enough, here was Sureshan, his umbrella tucked under his arm, carrying a crisp morning paper that he occasionally glanced at as he walked towards his shop. Sureshan glowed with vitality, fresh from a cold-water bath, his hair well-oiled and combed, his forehead ablaze with turmeric paste. The last was on account of the fact that every morning he worshipped at the temple before going to work. There was a smile of contentment on his face which owed much to the tasty boiled tapioca his wife, Meenu, had made him for breakfast. This smile is what all the onlookers thought would abruptly vanish as soon as he saw the prostrate form on his doorstep. Electrician Chacko giggled silently, making the whole post shake precariously and causing the electric wires to shiver for some distance. Poulose looked from Joby to Sureshan and back at Joby again. Abu the recycler sang some lines from an ancient film song—'You've got a visitor'.

Barber Sureshan walked up to the recumbent Joby and exclaimed: 'Here you are!' He then switched his umbrella to his other arm and said: 'You're here!'

Joby's eyes moved behind his tightly shut eyelids, but he said nothing. Lilly the bitch opened her eyes a little, and finding nothing worth getting excited about, curled herself into a new position and went back to sleep. When Sureshan prodded Joby with his umbrella, Poulose shut his ears, bracing himself for another volley of abuse. Everyone liked to begin the day with some sort of entertainment, but no one wanted Sureshan to be showered with expletives. Luckily, Joby just lay there and slowly his snoring picked up again.

Sureshan again prodded him. 'You got drunk again! And here you are at my doorstep. Dearest Lord Vishnu!'

'W-what's so s-s-special about your doors-s-step?' slurred Joby, his eyes still shut tightly to fight off the inevitability of sunlight. Sureshan gently adjusted the man's shirt with the tip of his umbrella, covering Joby's bellybutton.

'And your gentle lover will shield your alluring skin from the very winds,' sang Abu, but Poulose motioned for him to shut up. No one had ever seen Barber Sureshan angry, but it would be awkward to witness the first time.

'Do you remember anything of what we spoke about last noon?' Sureshan was asking Joby. 'Even if you don't, you will have to get up. My customers will be coming soon.'

'Oh, what a big city,' Joby muttered. 'Customers rushing in for a s-s-shave every morning. What a bu-bus-busy business.'

'I can see you haven't forgotten our conversation,' Sureshan said. 'That's why you decided to fall dead on my very own steps.'

'What's so s-s-special about your s-steps?'

'Forget that. Do you remember what we spoke of yesterday?'

Sureshan asked, but seeing that Joby had begun to snore again, he turned to Poulose: 'This man was supposed to come see me this morning, freshly washed and decently turned out, and we were to go somewhere.'

'Ha ha,' laughed Poulose. 'Joby, fresh and decent? If that happens, it will appear in that newspaper you're holding.'

This brought forth a fresh salvo of abuse from the comatose figure. This time the water in a nearby puddle began to sizzle. Abu hummed a tune, then fell silent.

'Well, get up,' Sureshan said, moving one of Joby's slippers that had come off closer to his feet. 'I need to clean the place.'

'Yes, of course,' Joby murmured, opening his eyes momentarily only so that the tears he'd been holding in could come streaming down his face. 'Clean away the f-f-filth. Sweep me away; at least your s-steps will be free of dirt.'

He began to weep noisily, his chest moving up and down in giant heaves, tears dribbling from under his tightly shut eyelids. Empathetically, Lilly licked his feet. Sureshan was at a loss to react to this exhibition. Abu leaned out of his little store and sang a song about the harsh world inflicting pain on a hapless heart and tearing it apart. From where he lay, through his violent sobs and with his eyes still shut, Joby responded to Abu's song with a third great eruption of abuse, stunning everyone with the profundity of his vocabulary. The electric post was vibrating with Chacko's suppressed laughter. Karuthupuzha had woken up to another very normal day where change and constancy were threads of the same rope.

After what seemed like ages—during which time Abu kept singing fresh songs to make Joby break into abuse—Barber Sureshan made up his mind. He beckoned to his friend Poulose to help. The grocer hurried over and the two tried to lift Joby off the steps. For someone so slim and emaciated, he was incredibly heavy. But luckily he kept completely still (except for the occasional involuntary sob) and even seemed to be trying to help the men who were picking him up. The greatest problem was in getting his foot into the one slipper that had come off. Joby simply wouldn't open his eyes and Poulose and Sureshan could not free their hands. Finally Abu came over and shoved the slipper onto the foot, and then walked away humming. Somebody shooed Lilly away and she walked up to a nearby shrub, made a bit of water, and then curled up again to finish her nap.

There was a bit of confusion when it looked as though Sureshan and Poulose were pulling the drunk in opposite directions. The grocer was trying to get Joby off the steps, which was the obvious thing to do. But Sureshan seemed to want to take him up the steps and into his shop. Puffing and panting he made his intention clear to Poulose. Reeling under the weight of the drunk, Poulose didn't waste time questioning the wisdom of this and helped move Joby into the shop. The two men lowered the man onto the big old salon chair that groaned deeply under the dead weight.

The grocer coughed twice and then gathered enough breath to exclaim: 'Why in the name of the holy goddess Chinnamma would you bring this container of arrack into your salon?'

This was met with only a couple of pungent profanities from Joby.

'I have some plans for our man here,' replied Sureshan, panting but with a gentle smile.

'Dear goddess, what plans can you have with this drunk?'

'Quiet, Joby,' said Sureshan as the man began on yet another profane word. 'Don't use that kind of language in my shop. Particularly not now, for I'm lighting the lamps.'

Joby feebly opened his eyes a crack. He saw Barber Sureshan light three lamps and an incense stick before the pictures of deities on a shelf, so that the day would start auspiciously. The barber prayed briefly before the gods. Then he filled a plastic pot with water and began washing the steps that had recently been occupied by Joby. Poulose followed him around.

'I hope you know what you are doing. The man will likely vomit all over your floor and quite certainly drive away your customers.'

'Oh, I won't have him in here for long,' Sureshan replied. 'Just need to work on him a bit. There was a time, after all, when he was one of us, don't you remember?'

Poulose shrugged. 'He's your headache. I'm off; the vendors from the city will bring in some goods soon. Call if you need me.' Then he yelled from the doorway: 'Will come later for tea.'

'I won't be in,' Sureshan yelled back, getting his salon equipment out of a neat little box. 'See you for evening tea, maybe!'

Alone with Joby, Sureshan became aware of a frightful battle that was being waged between two conflicting smells inside his salon: the thick, overbearing stench of decay and arrack from the lips of the snoring Joby versus the holy aroma from the incense stick. It reminded him of the eternal war between good and evil which, as all our tales tell us, resulted in the victory of the righteous. But you could never tell in real life, Sureshan thought. He lit another incense stick to muscle up the forces of the good.

Taking his blade and soap, Sureshan gently lathered the sleeping man's cheeks. Under the ministrations of his long, bony fingers, Joby's head moved around like a small boat on the gently bobbing waves of the Karuthupuzha river. As he delicately stretched Joby's skin with his fingers and effortlessly sliced away hair, he saw into the man. A lump rose in his throat as he looked into the emptiness within Joby, the absolute lack of glory in his life, his painfully mundane days and nights where arrack was the only thing that stood between Joby and his hurt at having never amounted to anything.

Slowly, carefully, Barber Sureshan groomed the sleeping drunk, first smoothening his stubbly cheeks, then working on the long, ropey hair on his head, now wetting it, now shaping it, now cutting it. He was creating a new man out of the sodden ashes of the old, in spite of the fact that terrible curses still rose from Joby's sleeping soul and escaped from his near-paralyzed lips. Sureshan ignored this and lost himself in the hair before him. Every now and then he would turn to the clock, murmur that they had plenty of time, check Joby's face in front of him, then in the mirror, and set to work again.

After an unusually long time—much more than the time he

spent on his most distinguished customers—Sureshan stood back, satisfied. Joby was presentable, if you limited yourself to looking at his face and ignored the deep furrow on his forehead, stamped there by last night's heavy drinking, and if you were deaf and couldn't read lips enough to decipher a bad word. *And* if your sense of smell was totally dead.

Well, this would have to do. Sureshan went out and yelled to Poulose to arrange for some fresh buttermilk. The sour taste of the drink would wake Joby up. There wasn't much else he could do. Joby would have to make his own way home, take a bath and put on some fresh clothes, without falling asleep in between. Sureshan prayed to the deities on the shelf that they might help Joby with these tasks. And that they might help Joby start afresh.

He noted with pleasure that in the war of the aromas the incense sticks seemed to be winning.

2.

A Life of Retirement

The same sunlight that had washed the town drunk lit up the little bedroom on the first floor of ex-Police Inspector Paachu's home. It bathed his ancient bed, projected the intricate shadow of his half-undone mosquito net onto the whitewashed wall opposite, and was reflected in the long mirror in a corner. Ex-Inspector Paachu, who was also known—increasingly rarely now—as Paachu Yemaan (meaning Paachu the Boss, or the Chief) was looking thoughtfully into the mirror. It was a ritual that took place every morning. He would regard himself in the mirror for a long time, as if to convince himself that it was he and none other who had just woken up on his bed.

Today, Paachu said to himself, I don't have much to report as I'm retired. But I'm still in good shape, except perhaps for a hint of sagging in my cheeks. Paachu was shorter than he would have liked, stocky yet hardened, with proudly hairy arms and chest, and a short, almost non-existent, neck. His face was perfectly round with very little hair to hide its curvature. In fact, he had generous hair growth everywhere except on his head. The few strands of hair he had left were plastered across his scalp in a vain attempt to cover his baldness. At the very summit of Paachu Yemaan's hairless pate a grotesque tuft had suddenly begun to sprout, around the time of his retirement. Ever since, he'd had to regularly trim this tuft of hair because it made people laugh at him and there was nothing that Paachu hated more than to be laughed at. As he looked into the mirror, he felt for this tuft to see if it was time to pay Barber Sureshan a visit. It wouldn't do to have his little niece, Priya, giggle at the breakfast table, or to see his wife, Sharada, suppress her mirth when he came out after his bath.

No, the tuft hadn't grown back yet. The ex-Inspector inspected his oppressively large moustache next. He ran his palm down either side of it, smoothening it out, testing its strength and rejoicing at its stiffness. In its time, this colossal moustache had terrified many a lawless crook, straightened out numerous self-styled anarchic revolutionaries, and made several arrogant subordinates at the police station fall in line. He never had and never would dye his moustache; the streaks of grey in it only added to the gravitas and seriousness of his face. It was only the weak and vain who dyed their hair and moustache. Suppressing a yawn, he patted the moustache once, like a fond father. He thought with satisfaction that all he needed to control his wife or, in special instances, his niece, Priya, was to make his moustache bristle, whereupon they would instantly come to attention and do his bidding.

The need to control Priya was new. When he was still Inspector of Karuthupuzha Police Station he had never even once felt the need to make his little niece fear him. Yes, he had made sure that the whole town feared and respected him, but had granted Priya the right to actually laugh with him, sometimes even at him. The little girl was allowed to come running and jump on to his lap when he was in the station behind his desk. She could ask to ride on his shoulders when they were walking in Paachu's small orchard at the back of his house. Even at the time of his retirement, when that awful tuft had popped up on his head, she was the only one who was allowed to twirl it and laugh at it. But of late he had started to feel that her bubbly laughter, especially when it was directed at him, needed to be curbed. He had begun to notice changes in the relationship between them. A certain distance seemed to have grown between them. This hurt him in a place in his heart that he had not known had existed before. There was good reason why Priya meant so much to him. Her parents had died when she was very small. Ever since, Paachu and Sharada had brought her up, never giving her any reason to feel sorrow or loneliness. Being childless themselves, little Priya had filled as big a void in their lives as they had in hers. It was all perfect.

But children grow up, Paachu now thought, as he continued to regard himself in the mirror. And as they grew older it was necessary to change the way in which they were parented—as he was doing now. His wife, Sharada, would never learn this. To her Priya would always be little Priya. She would always chase after the girl with her morning glass of milk, sit behind her and tie her hair, tell her the same stories over and over. And so it was left to him, Uncle Paachu, to change the way she was brought up. It was Paachu's dream to make Priya the Police Inspector of Karuthupuzha one day. And in order to achieve that, it was necessary for him to change the way he dealt with her as she grew. It wouldn't do for her to remain his baby always. Her girlish laughter, her innocent pranks and chirpy mannerisms would have to be reshaped into character traits that would be appropriate to a tough police officer. He knew that for a woman it would be particularly difficult to be acknowledged as a law enforcer, especially among an ignorant crowd like the one in this town. It was Paachu's dream that in the last lap of his life he would see Priya occupy the place he once had—a strong police officer whom her male subordinates would be terrified of.

'Coffee,' said Sharada, gliding into the room. Her husband muttered something under his breath, his eyes still fixed on himself in the mirror. Sharada placed the cup of steaming black coffee on the stool next to the mirror and began making the bed. She usually left her husband to meditate on his own image in the mirror, but today she said, 'They'll be here soon. Sureshan Barber with…'

'Hmm,' he muttered, this time audibly, his voice grating. For a fleeting moment he looked at her in the mirror.

Sharada was the most beautiful old woman you could imagine. Graceful, slender and mild of manner, she seemed to grow more attractive with age–the grey of her hair, the few wrinkles at the corners of her mouth made her seem not just good looking but also kind and empathetic. Of course, it wasn't all in her appearance. Her fluid movements, her deep, mellifluous voice reflected a personality that charmed everyone she met. It was almost as if the constant grating of her life against the hard stone of her husband was shaping her into a priceless diamond with each passing day.

Neatly folding the bedclothes and tying up the mosquito net, Sharada then walked over to the cupboard and performed a most curious act, part of her daily routine. She took out Paachu's police uniform, washed and starched as always, and laid it neatly on the bed, the way she would have done had he still been Inspector. There was the stiff-collared khaki shirt and the perfectly fitting khaki pants, the polished leather belt and a neatly ironed cotton handkerchief. The cap, the decorations and the police baton would not be required. Sharada then turned, gently touched the cup of black coffee to remind him to drink it before it got cold and glided out of the room, noiselessly pulling the door shut behind her.

Meanwhile, Paachu Yemaan continued to stare at himself. He was beginning to get angry. Like a locomotive warming up where it stood, not moving an inch though its powerful engine was beginning to roar. There was nothing spontaneous or impulsive about this anger. Paachu could work it up anytime, anywhere, at anyone and to any degree. Even when it was at its peak, a marvel of destructive wrath, everything about his behaviour and speech would still be totally under his control. For all the burning in his eyes and the murderous rage in his every muscle, he would do nothing or say nothing that he might regret later. So powerful was Paachu's will, and such was his mastery over his own anger, that it was a weapon that he could wield at will and use to destroy to the desired measure. And just to keep it in good nick, every morning he would practise his anger in front of the mirror.

It was several decades ago that Paachu had joined the police department as a young constable with scarcely any facial hair. That was in a distant town, and what he sought from his employment was clear to him—money, success and worldly status. His elders and friends had told him that a police career could fetch him all of these. While the pay would be modest, there were enough opportunities to make money on the side. If he diligently kept to his career, time would bring him success. And, as an enforcer of the law, the world would respect him. All this sounded like a pretty good deal and Paachu wasted no time in finding himself a job as a policeman.

Shockingly though, the reality of being a policeman was very different from what he had dreamt about. His job was largely to ensure that the inspector in his station got his coffee without sugar and that certain thick ledgers reached the right tables at the right times.

However, right from the outset, Paachu showed that he was not one to be cowed down or thwarted in his ambition. Having spent a great deal of time thinking about how he might get ahead in his career and secure everything he was denied, he came up with a strategy. One day, when he was off duty, he caught hold of a pickpocket right in the centre of a busy market and planted a fist in his belly. To his horror the pickpocket gave it right back, smashing his fist into Paachu's belly. He then dusted off his hands on his dirty pants and strode away as people looked on! Thankful that he wasn't in uniform, Paachu raced to the police station and narrated the incident to the inspector, sure that every man on the force would be deployed to find and arrest the pickpocket who had dared to attack one of their own. But the inspector laughed heartily and advised him not to indulge in police business while off duty. Many months later Paachu learned that a lot of the pickpocket's stolen stuff made its way into the pockets of the inspector and his senior colleagues. Awed by this insight, Paachu began to understand the true nature of a policeman's work. He could now begin to fashion his future with confidence. He started cultivating just the right amount of stubble on his cheeks so he looked older and more menacing without appearing dishevelled.

By the time he was transferred to the small town of Karuthupuzha,

Paachu was well on his way to becoming a tough, corrupt cop. There was still a hint of the callow, sensitive youth in him, though. However, one incident erased that from his character and made him the policeman who now stared back at him in the mirror.

Around the time Paachu joined the Karuthupuzha Police Station as a constable, a petty thief named Gopalan, who specialized in stealing women's underwear from backyards where they were hung out to dry, was wreaking havoc in town. He was no pervert, really, only he thought it was quite funny to have the womenfolk of Karuthupuzha wake up in the mornings to see their bras and panties missing from their clotheslines. Everyone knew Gopalan was the culprit but the women themselves were too ashamed to discuss the items they had lost and specifically told their men not to report the stolen undergarments to the police. Consequently, Gopalan's crime spree continued unchecked. He would steal underwear of all shapes and sizes, wash them thoroughly, iron them and sell them in the black market in the nearby city. He made sure he didn't steal from the same locality too often, so that his benefactors wouldn't suffer significant losses and decide to overcome their modesty and make a formal complaint to the police. In the absence of any official complaint, the police and everyone else gave Gopalan a free pass and he continued with his crimes.

If Paachu hadn't joined as constable, Gopalan would have continued his antics indefinitely. But Paachu saw Gopalan as an easy target, one he could use to make an impression on this town. When someone changes a longstanding practice, he knew, a lasting impression is made. Besides, there was nothing funny about what Gopalan was doing. The underwear belonged to the women and what Gopalan was doing was illegal. For the first time since his ill-advised run-in with the pickpocket, Paachu worked up some righteous anger and decided to put an end to the Gopalan menace.

One evening he did not change out of his khakis after coming from work. He drank the coffee that his young wife, Sharada, had made, told her that he would be back soon and went out into the twilight. Around midnight, he spotted Gopalan stealing underwear belonging to a very fat woman who was the wife of a local treasury official. He caught hold of the petty thief by the hair and began beating him. Even as he was being punched, Gopalan tried to point out that the whole thing was a joke and that every policeman before Paachu had laughed it off. This flimsy attempt to explain away his crime helped Paachu muster even more anger. He began to slap Gopalan's cheeks repeatedly and loudly. No one witnessed the show as it was past midnight, except the treasury official who decided not to embarrass his wife by waking her up. The official's witnessing of the event would have consequences later but we will come to that in a while.

By the time Paachu had finished thrashing Gopalan, the thief was so distraught that he seemed to have lost his reason and fled in a direction opposite to the one he would otherwise have taken. Indeed, it was the only route anyone getting out of Karuthupuzha, whether in a hurry or at leisure, could take—the road to the city that the newly painted bus had arrived by. But Gopalan had been so wounded in body and mind that he reflexively wished to hide from the world like the big bad bandit that he wasn't. He fled to the western border of Karuthupuzha where the puzha, or river, flanked the town, separating it from the nearby forest and hills. Having meted out his form of justice, Paachu went home with a sense of accomplishment. He took a cold water bath under the full moon and then went to sleep beside his still-awake wife without offering her any explanation of what he had been up to.

It was only the next afternoon—much after the treasury official had spread word all around of Paachu's law enforcement techniques (adding much embellishment)—that Gopalan was found dead by the river. There were three theories about what had caused the petty thief's death.

Some people connected it to the rumoured appearance of a leopard in the vicinity of Karuthupuzha. It seemed that the animal had often swum across the river and made off with poultry and sheep over the last month. It is surprising how a rumour takes shape with retrospective effect when something unusual happens. No one was sure if such a leopard had ever been discussed before, really, but now everyone had something to say about it. Muthu, the milkman, suddenly claimed that a calf of his had had its throat ripped out only the week before. A young housewife in quite another part of town made it known that she had lost her oldest hen (for whom she'd harboured a deep affection), some days ago. By way of proof she claimed she had immediately narrated the incident to her neighbour, another young housewife, who acknowledged the fact after only a bit of initial doubt.

Apparently this leopard, whose existence was now established beyond doubt, had mauled Gopalan in the dark of night, found him unpalatable (he was only a petty thief, after all), and had left him to die without eating him. This was why the body was found whole, only bruised and bleeding from the mouth. A surprisingly large number of people believed this story and began discussing what must be done about the leopard now that it had started attacking humans.

The second theory about Gopalan's death was scarier. This stemmed from a legend that was so flexible in its construction that every narrator changed it some to suit his penchant for fantasy. It was the legend of Karuthu, a pretty, dark-skinned girl from whom the town had apparently derived its name. Karuthu had been cruelly drowned by her father-in-law in this very puzha centuries ago and was now a banshee who eternally longed for life's unrequited pleasures. She haunted the river and its banks, usually in a form thinner than air so that she wasn't visible to mortal eyes. But when she came across a lonesome young man, as troubled with the world as she herself was, she would turn into the lovesick maiden she had once been, and approach the young man with the intent of fulfilling her centuries' long thirst. She hadn't the powers to force anybody to do her bidding, but she could turn infinitely desirable and almost impossibly tempting.

On the night he was to be loved to death, Gopalan—a low thief of feeble intellect and feebler power of will—had seen the beautiful Karuthu materialize out of a big tree. Against his better judgment he had yielded to her wooing, letting himself be caught in the beautiful illusion. As lust bloomed in his mind, the giant tree had turned into a palace of pleasures. The thorny grass on the forest floor had turned rich velvet. The star-studded sky was transformed into an ornately decorated ceiling. At the end of a timeless act of lovemaking in which all of nature participated, Karuthu the banshee pressed her lips to Gopalan's. She first sucked his blood out, then his life, and then his very soul.

Believers of this theory demanded that Gopalan be buried up in the hills across the river, where there was a graveyard for such deaths. This graveyard was surrounded by totems and talismans of all religions, so that whatever evils had caused such deaths would be contained and would not cross the river to haunt the people of the town.

But prowling leopards and bloodthirsty banshees notwithstanding, it was the third theory about the man's death that was the scariest. It was so scary that no one said it aloud for perhaps a decade! After Gopalan's body was discovered, the treasury official of that night lapsed into a shocked silence. All over the small town, people telepathically sent into each other's heads a horrifying theory that was worse than any nightmare. Everyone knew that everyone knew. But not a lip moved.

However, as a result of the third theory, wherever Paachu went, people gave him a wide berth and hushed each other. Even within the police station the change was marked. The inspector gently explained to Paachu that he should not worry about bringing him his tea; it would get to him anyway. He was not to carry the big ledgers from table to table. The more challenging and difficult cases (such as the ones that never graced the eventless town of Karuthupuzha) would be handed to Paachu to investigate. The inspector even wrote to headquarters as a result of which Paachu was promoted to senior constable long before it was due to him.

Paachu himself understood what was going on. The boyish stripling in khaki was being transformed into a raw, tough, merciless policeman. Hair grew on his forearms and out of his ears. His moustache began to spread across his face. In time a bald spot appeared on top of his head. The politicians and businessmen of Karuthupuzha began to take note of him and then work to have him on their side. He grew far more powerful than the inspector himself, and began to be talked about with awe in the circles that mattered. He acquired the reputation of being a law enforcer who stopped at nothing; he made it known that he couldn't be bought for a pittance. To appease Paachu, the bribes had to be colossal.

After analysing all the events that had led to this change in perception, Pachu realized that it was the fake anger he had worked up that night against Gopalan that had been the most effective. He realized that power was best expressed in anger. He saw that all our gods were deeply revered when they got angry. There were, in fact, entire temples devoted to angry gods. Who did not fear and worship an angry god? The very demons and rakshasas bowed to the power of a god who was out of sorts. Likewise, it was their fiery temper that made the heroes in films awe-inspiring. Paachu took in the clenched fists, bulging muscles and bloodshot eyes of heroes on film posters. He started to keep a scrapbook in which he glued newspaper advertisements featuring movie stars on the rampage. He still had the book somewhere on the top shelf in his room, although it was all dusty now because he no longer needed it But at the time he had studied the art of anger from the expressions of movie stars in a fury—from the way they made their veins pop on their foreheads, and had just the right amount of moisture glistening in their bloodshot eyes so that they looked very angry but not sad. From his deep study of his role models Paachu gained a precious insight. It was not enough just to look angry. You had to *be* angry and *think* angrily. It was beyond human ability to perfectly orchestrate all the muscles and glands in the body to simulate anger without actually feeling it. You needed to be able to turn your anger on, so that your brain switched on the automatic mechanism that coordinated all the physical manifestations of a fiery temper. It wasn't easy, of course, but Paachu practised in front of his mirror, morning after morning, his scrapbook open before him and eventually perfected it.

Meanwhile Sharada, as devoted a wife then as she was now, was horrified to the point of distraction when the idea that her husband had killed a man was telepathically planted in her head. But not being stupid, she got herself under control. She watched the hair grow on his forearms, saw how he was fathering a moustache and generally noted all he was doing to get a hold on this town; she could live with all that. But at times she would think that she'd have no option but to run away if there was definite proof that he had indeed killed a man. She had always been a little scared of him, she thought. Beneath his hard exterior she did sense that he loved her, but she could never get over her fear that he might suddenly hit her. She had always felt, and felt to this day, that he was capable of suddenly smashing his concrete arms into her face. Although it was true that far from hitting her he had always been quite gentle with her, she could never get over her fear that he would suddenly turn violent—not sustained violence, but there was always the lurking fear that she might receive a slap that she hadn't seen coming.

In the years following Gopalan's death she could not bring herself to directly approach him and ask: Did you really kill that man? Instead, she resorted to quietly observing him and letting the passage of time unearth the truth. Gradually, as the years went by, the sound of his voice, especially during moments of happiness, his living warmth, his clothes hanging limply on hooks, his small tantrums at the dining table, all these combined to tell her the truth about her husband Paachu—he would do anything to own this town and townsfolk except kill a man. Before she knew it, the subject seemed so silly that she never felt the need to risk his anger by trying to approach him with it. It could be that she preferred not to have a final answer to whether Paachu had killed Gopalan so that her life could carry on rather than risk a radical confrontation that could change everything. That is as it may be. However, all that needs to be said at this juncture is that over the next decades, the gentle Sharada stayed faithful and devoted to her husband as he went on to become the most feared and powerful man Karuthupuzha had ever known.

As part of his career advancement, Paachu did all that was necessary to keep the fear and reverence accorded to him by the townsfolk from diminishing. Periodically, he would exhibit bursts of accurately graded anger before select audiences who he knew would exaggerate the events when they described them to others. Occasionally, he would catch people for the pettiest of misdemeanours and beat them up. A favourite activity of his was to round up men who played cards under coconut trees, slap and punch them, and then let them go with a lecture about the evils of gambling. In the thick of his reign even the most unemployed of men tried to look busy so his eyes wouldn't fall upon them. People remembered the times when unemployment was quite a pleasure. The times when young men woke up early in the morning, bathed, shaved, put on well-ironed and starched clothing, smeared turmeric paste on their foreheads, and then stood in groups under big banyan trees at nodal points in town, their arms on each other's shoulders, judging and evaluating passers-by. Unemployment had meant day-long gatherings even as the shadows of the trees (nature's own clocks) moved around them. When maidens passed by they made edgy and radical suggestions, as evidenced by the coy smiles on the girls' faces as they hurried away. But once Paachu gained power he swept up such groups in his dreaded police jeep, took them to the station, and told them to do some work. Very soon such young men actually began looking for work, because they knew that a repeat offence would entail more than just a lecture.

Sharada did not approve of a lot of this, of course, but she knew better than to interfere in what her husband called 'police duties'. She also knew that he extorted massive bribes from businessmen for strictly unfair favours and she sometimes stayed up nights worrying about the wrath of the gods. She prayed for her husband, prayed that age would soften him and make him more loved than feared. When Paachu influenced higher-ups in the department to prevent transfers so that he could always remain in Karuthupuzha as its most powerful inhabitant, she secretly wished that something, some quirk of fate, would take them away from here.

Over the last decade when Priya arrived in their home, Sharada's worries eased a little. She saw how the child had created a soft spot in Paachu's heart and how she snuggled into it. Of course, Paachu was unchanged as far as the rest of the world was concerned, but with Priya he was uncle, father and sometimes grandfather rolled into one. Very quickly he took to the child, loving her more than anything in the world, playing with her, spending time with her in ways that Sharada would never have thought likely. His kindness towards her seemed, in Sharada's eyes, to somehow mitigate all his other failings, even his cruelty and corruption. It seemed to complete him, centre him and bring him the kind of happiness that was more fulfilling than ambition.

But that was what was changing now, she thought on the morning of our story, when the serene rays of the sun lit her little kitchen as she was stirring the batter for breakfast. All around her were the pleasant sounds of the small town yawning and stretching before fully waking up, but they failed to cheer her up. The temple music from far away seemed to lend the very air a holy aroma, like camphor, but Sharada continued to worry. She worried that her husband was deliberately, definitively and rapidly changing his relationship with Priya. He no longer allowed her to laugh openly at him. He no longer told her funny police stories—anecdotes of how he himself had bungled while trying to be a hero. He did not let her play anymore with the comical tuft on his head. He no longer even bought her the kind of toys she liked—no dolls, no cotton-stuffed doggies, no tiny plastic kitchen sets. Instead he bought her guns and jeeps and soldiers, which a little boy would have found interesting.

The change had begun, she knew, some months after Paachu

had retired. Sitting at home he had been sunk deep in thought. It always portended something bad when he was like that. Then one day he had called Priya to him, put her on his lap and lectured her long and hard on how she needed to grow up to be a policewoman. He told the stunned child how he would still hold enough sway in the department when she was old enough to get her a posting in Karuthupuzha itself. He delivered an emotional thesis on how the good men and women of Karuthupuzha were waiting for someone from the Paachu family to one day take charge again. He railed about how the present inspector—Inspector Janardanan—was grossly inept and inadequate and how there was no hope of the team having someone who would be as hard on lawlessness as Paachu Yemaan, unless he groomed his heir, Priya, for the role.

It had been a matter of concern that Priya, a girl, was the only heir, but Uncle Paachu had then reasoned that in today's day and age that did not matter. Nowadays girls flew planes and climbed mountains as easily as men did. Though Priya's journey from sweet little girl (this was said with a quick kiss on the cheek) to tough policewoman would be a long and arduous one, Uncle Paachu would ensure that one day his little Priya would sit at the desk he had once occupied, and the crooks and ruffians of Karuthupuzha would once again have no option but to fall in line.

Inside her kitchen Sharada had listened to every word, going red in the face with the effort to suppress her laughter. But what Sharada had not foreseen was that Paachu had been dead serious. Little Priya had gone around dazed after her uncle's talk for a long time that day. That evening she had come to Sharada and told her that she wished to be a giant wheel operator when she grew up. Sharada had kissed her and given her some fresh butter to eat from the clay pot that hung from the ceiling of the kitchen.

But Sharada's worry was not just about Paachu's plan for Priya. That, she hoped, would have to change as the girl grew up. More worrying was the fact that her husband was not taking retirement the way he should. Paachu was obsessed with his Yemaan status, and he wasn't letting go. So much so, that Sharada sensed many in Karuthupuzha were actually laughing at him behind his back. She wished he would now grow old gracefully, not remain stuck in the past. She wished he would do some gardening, help those in need, spend his days with men his age, gossip a little, laugh with his niece, and generally be a pleasant old man for the rest of their lives. But once, when she had broached the subject of a peaceful retired life, he had merely said: 'Once a policeman, always a policeman.'

The finality of his voice did not just disappoint her; it scared her.

At the time our story begins, she was thinking that there was something she must do, or things would get uglier. Already there were men like Photographer Varky, Inspector Janardanan and others who were turning ex-Inspector Paachu into the joke of the town in his pension years. It was almost as if the town was determined now to laugh at the man who had terrified it and held it in his clutches for decades. And that worried Sharada more than anything. She knew that her husband would not take kindly to being laughed at when he eventually came to know about what was going on. She must do something, but she did not know what.

Meanwhile, the subject of her worry still stood directly above her head in his bedroom on the first floor, staring at his own angry face and quivering moustache in the mirror. Slowly, expertly, he let go of his anger as his practice for the day came to an end. Once a policeman, always a policeman.

When Paachu finally took his eyes off the mirror, he looked at the cup of coffee in front of him. In any other circumstance it would have long gone cold, but it was almost as if the blast of anger in its vicinity had kept it warm. With a practised motion he drank exactly half of it and then laid the cup down. He was satisfied that he was beginning to feel the rumblings in his belly. Nevertheless, for the perfect and complete emptying of his bowels, he would have to move on to the next step in his morning ritual. Quickly, he slipped out of his lungi. Then he carefully unfolded the khaki pants that Sharada had placed on the bed, laying the shirt aside. The shirt was just an add-on, in case the pants alone didn't do the trick—he needn't slip into it except on days when he had constipation. Then he would need almost his whole uniform. On the worst mornings, he even needed his police cap on his head, his medals on his chest and his baton in his hands before he could go to the toilet. But today he had already felt the rumblings, so the khaki pants would suffice. He slipped into them and then drank the rest of the coffee.

All this was necessary because, immediately after retirement, Paachu Yemaan had discovered that unless he practised the same morning routine as he had for decades, unless he fooled his system into believing that he was still the busy policeman who needed to quickly finish his ablutions and rush to the police station, his bowels would not empty themselves to his satisfaction. Ever since, Sharada had kept his uniform ready each morning, so that he could slip into it and kick-start his bowels.

As the pressure in his belly mounted to a pleasurable high, he quickly slipped out of the pants and wrapped his lungi around him again. The pants and the unused shirt of his old uniform he flung to a corner of the room so that Sharada could wash and iron them for the next day. Then Paachu hastened downstairs and out the back door towards the toilet outside the house, which only he used.

3.

Barber Sureshan

Two days before the morning we found Joby drunk on Sureshan's steps and ex-Inspector Paachu staring at the mirror in his upstairs bedroom, on a markedly windier day, Barber Sureshan had opened the windows wide in his shop. He usually did so because he liked the fresh air to come in first thing when he opened for business.

He had just lit a lamp before the gods and begun to pray for a day of good business when the wind blew the lamp out. Thankful that it hadn't upset the lamp itself, Sureshan relit the wick and joined his hands in prayer once again. This time the wind swirled around the incense sticks and smashed them to the floor. On its way it also upset a tin of talcum powder and some bottles of shaving lotion. This is what the wind did to him sometimes.

Among themselves the wind, the rain and the sun played a little game to see who could annoy Karuthupuzha's calmest man. This was why sometimes when Barber Sureshan was walking down the road it would suddenly start to rain, when there had not been the slightest hint of a cloud until then, on account of which he was without his umbrella. Then again, sometimes a calm and pleasant sun would suddenly turn scorching hot because Barber Sureshan was drawing water from the well near his home and there was nothing to cover his head with.

Now the wind blew his lamp out again and wondered if it

shouldn't just dislodge the big mirror and make it shatter on the floor. Before that could happen, Sureshan quickly went to the big mirror and adjusted it more securely on its nail. But by then the wind had blown about some cut hair that was neatly piled in a corner. Now there were bits of hair everywhere—on the salon chair, the blades of the small table fan, the open bowl of shaving water, Sureshan's own eyes and nostrils. The wind howled in silly glee as it banged the door to and fro.

'Why don't you just shut the door and windows?' Poulose the grocer had appeared at the door, momentarily blocking the wind.

'Oh, it'll die down soon,' Sureshan said. 'It's just giving me some additional work in the morning.'

He started sweeping up the clumps of hair. Poulose came in, shutting the door behind him. In spite of Sureshan, he shut the windows as well. Now the lamp, which Sureshan had lit yet again, stayed lit; the wind angrily banged some dry leaves against the windowpanes.

'What a storm!' said Poulose, who liked to exaggerate. 'You know what, Chacko is up on a post which is swaying dangerously in this wind.'

Sureshan looked up from his cleaning in concern, but Poulose only laughed. 'He can't come down when the post is swaying so! Occasionally the high-tension wires touch and bolts of electricity shoot out like lightning. Ha ha! Hope the old man doesn't fall and break his bones. He must be thinking it's better to be swallowed by the Wound in the Earth! They're looking for a ladder for him, last I heard.'

'It'll die down soon,' Sureshan repeated.

'Hmm. Our Chacko is a strange bird. He climbs posts even when nothing is wrong with the lines. Says he likes it up there.'

Sureshan smiled. The wind seemed to be dying down outside, so he opened a window. Then cautiously he opened the other window and then the door, careful not to inadvertently send out a challenge to the wind. It slithered like an invisible snake through some branches but did not pick up again. Barber Sureshan made a mental note to always clean up and dispose of cut hair in the evenings and never to leave it for the mornings. Then, suddenly, he turned to Poulose who was still standing by the door, and proclaimed, 'The climate is God's most direct way of reminding people that their plans are small and insignificant compared to His.'

Barber Sureshan sometimes thought that it was because he spoke in this manner, splicing deep philosophy and feel-good theories into his speech, that he lived the way he did. He spoke beautiful and profound sentences to his friends, often without even thinking. Later he would ponder what he had said and strive to live up to the standards he had voiced. The result was the calm, level-headed and honest Barber Sureshan who loved everybody and was loved by everybody. Even the wind, though it often played with him a little.

'Now if that isn't Purushan Vaidyan deciding to get himself a shave,' Poulose was saying. Sure enough, the Ayurvedic physician and Karuthupuzha's sole medic was approaching, dry leaves crunching under his feet. His black umbrella had been wrecked in the wind; it looked as though he was carrying a deformed, dead crow. Sureshan quickly wiped the ancient salon chair with a wet cloth to mop up any bits of hair. Under his ministrations the rusty, ancient springs of the chair giggled, as though they were being tickled.

'Ho, what wind! By the good spirits of Ambalakkavu, I almost got blown away,' exclaimed Purushan Vaidyan, coming in and greeting the duo with a nod. He slumped on the chair, held up his broken umbrella and said: 'Now I've got this thing to be repaired! Uh, Suresha, I haven't come for a shave. Just wanted to talk to you.' He began to get up hurriedly, remembering that he ought to leave the salon chair empty for any customer who might walk in. There was a heavy wooden bench drawn up parallel to one of the walls of the room for those waiting for a cut or a shave. Poulose had already settled on this. But Sureshan motioned for the doctor to sit down on the salon chair. He began to give the man a head massage.

'That Chacko, he's gone into shock,' Purushan Vaidyan said

excitedly. 'The idiot of a man had to climb a post just when it was getting all stormy! You know our posts. They hardly hold the wires up, instead I sometimes think *they* hang from the wires! This one shook like a tree in the wind. Poor man! And electric currents were flying all around him. I thought he would fall.'

'Oh, then?' Sureshan asked. Poulose looked up from the newspaper he was reading. He had made himself very comfortable, one leg up on the bench.

'Must have done something particularly pleasing to the gods in his last life. It isn't in this life, no. We know Chacko,' the doctor continued. 'They got him down. Held a ladder up for him when the wind had abated a bit. And guess who went up to fetch him? Ha, you won't believe it. Joby! Of all the idiots who were standing around watching, it had to be our man to go to the rescue, even though he was swaying without the help of the wind. I was saying that the post would break with all that swaying. And all the while that bitch of his stood under the post yelping its heart out like a panicking wife! But finally he reached up, drunk to his nose with last night's arrack, got hold of shocked old Chacko, and brought him down. Then he started laughing and laughing, his mouth full of the most scalding obscenities I've ever heard, walked up to a bush on the side of the road, and vomited massively. I am a physician, and I am yet to see a man vomit like that. What he brought up seemed more than anything the human stomach could hold. And all through he was still laughing and cursing. It was a sight to see!'

'Serves him right!' Poulose exclaimed. 'To be drunk like that and then go climbing electric posts. Besides there were others around too, right? Why did he have to do it? Climbing heights with a hangover can be very traumatic.'

'No, wait,' said Purushan Vaidyan. He caught hold of Barber Sureshan's hands to stop the head massage. 'I walked straight from there to you, Suresha. I decided that it is you that I needed to speak to. Only you can do something. It's about Joby.'

Sureshan nodded into the mirror. It was in the mirror that all three of them saw and spoke to each other.

'If he goes on like this, Joby will die soon.'

There it was, spoken out loud at last. The uncomfortable thought had been in Sureshan's mind for some time now, but he hadn't voiced it, not even to himself.

'Last month he had a fever and came to me,' Purushan Vaidyan went on. 'One touch on his upper belly and I knew. What else was to be expected? He has been drinking steadily for decades now. He is almost past middle age. I think he will be what—fifty, fifty-five, soon?'

'Forty-nine, I think.'

'Yes, you should know. You were friends once, am I right?' the doctor asked, and both Sureshan and Poulose nodded. 'Seems like a century ago, but I know. All of you, Suresha, Poulose here, Eeppachan Mothalali's driver Velu and some others, am I right?'

'Yes sir,' Sureshan said, beginning slowly to massage the back of the man's head again. He had decided that Purushan Vaidyan was his first customer of the day and he would serve the man whether he asked for it or not. 'We were very close friends, the five or six of us. We were all young then, and we used to sit by the river every evening and drink. *Every* evening.'

'Even at that time Joby was the greatest drinker among all of us,' Poulose said, smiling. 'The man used to amaze us with his capacity.'

'Yes, yes,' Purushan Vaidyan said. 'Well, I'm not trying to say this is your obligation or anything because he was once your friend. It's just that though Joby has had different groups of friends at different times, I could only think of you to say this to. Perhaps you, Suresha, could do something to help. Otherwise, all that we will be doing is silently watching Joby drink himself to death.'

'I understand, but what can I do? Once, I tried to get him a job at Eeppachan Mothalali's mill through Velu. Joby arrived drunk at the mill on his first day of work and couldn't lift a single sack of grain. He tried and tried and then fell asleep hugging the sack. The Mothalali was more than justified in sending him away.' Sureshan paused. 'B-but, I never thought at the time that he was dying.'

'He is,' Purushan Vaidyan said. 'Unless he stops drinking now. *Now*, you understand? The reason I am taking so much trouble in his case is because I have never looked upon Joby as the sort of hopeless drunk you find asleep in gutters. I know his past. He was a decent man once. Used to ferry children to school and back. It was a long time ago, I don't know if you remember. He used to have his sessions of debauchery even then, but that was only on holidays, I think. At least he wasn't given to sleeping by the road then, as far as I know. Everyone trusted him with the children, and never once did he falter in his job. He had an autorickshaw first, then a small tempo. Then he got married, but his drinking only increased. Through all this, though, he was never a nuisance, you'll agree, until recently.'

'In fact, I believe that has something to do with Paachu Yemaan's retirement,' Sureshan said, thoughtfully. 'When Paachu Yemaan was Inspector, Joby would never sleep drunk on the streets. He would never go about shouting obscenities. I think a couple of times Paachu Yemaan even pulled him up and bashed him some. It did him good. But now! Now he is scared of no one; there's no one to check him.'

'Yes, the man is free with the bottle,' Poulose said, a ghost of a smile on his lips. He found this whole thing quite amusing.

'Hmm,' muttered the doctor. 'But I only got really alarmed when I examined his belly. It's like a rock, his liver! Karuthupuzha has watched a good man destroy himself for no apparent reason. Now, are we ready to watch him die an untimely death and leave his wife a widow?'

'Let me think about what I can do, doctor,' Sureshan muttered, thinking deeply. 'The thing is, Joby is not the friend we once had. You know, even at that time I used to wonder about him sometimes. We were all very young, and drinking was like a sport. It was almost a matter of pride to down the maximum amount of arrack at one go. We used to think it was very amusing to say we had got so drunk that we couldn't see our own feet, or that we had a hangover until the next evening when we opened a fresh bottle. I remember Velu always said that he had drunk so much that he didn't recall who carried him home. But when we spoke like this I believe we were all exaggerating some. You know, we just said these things for the sake of saying them. We exaggerated to sound like young men having fun. But not Joby. He *really* drank like that. He wasn't exaggerating when he said he couldn't see his own feet! Never spoke much, like the rest of us, but *did* those things that the rest of us only spoke about. It was not a sport to him, drinking. It wasn't masculine or even amusing in the least. It was an obsession. With liquor, he was like one possessed. He would never waste time. Just put the bottle to his lips and gulp like the liquor didn't have any taste at all! No one could drink like him. He was the only true alcoholic amongst us.'

'I would guess he drinks that way even today,' Purushan Vaidyan said, getting up from the salon chair and sitting down on the bench. 'That's why he is dying.'

'As we all grew up, we went our different ways. Poulose started his grocery store, Velu became a driver, me a barber. And Joby stayed right where he was. Drinking by the river.'

'Yes, that's the sign of a true drunk,' Poulose said authoritatively.

'He got married and bought his wife a sewing machine!' Sureshan suddenly exclaimed. He had come over to the bench now and continued where he had left off with massaging Purushan Vaidyan's head. 'So that she could work and bring in the money for his drink. That's when he had really grown apart from the rest of us.'

'It's an illness, Suresha,' the doctor said. 'I hope you aren't going to blame the poor man. He was ill. He *is* ill. And now he is dying.'

'No, I won't blame him,' Sureshan replied, 'Not really. Yes, it isn't his fault. He is ill.' He looked askance at Poulose who was smirking. 'It's not his fault. Poor Joby. When we all moved on he made newer, younger friends. Ha! He had that Madhu and gang for some time, all rich people and yet some of them milked him—made him pay for their drink too. Then he made friends with all the taxi drivers. I remember he used to rush towards the taxi stand every evening. They would make him dance and recite his poetry. Poor Joby.'

'The last bunch he hung out with was George Kutty and others,' Poulose said. 'Old Joby and a group of young men. After George Kutty married Chacko's daughter and joined that music troupe, that gang moved on as well.'

There was silence in the room. The wind howled again, as if considering another visit. Poulose shuffled his newspaper awkwardly. Purushan Vaidyan seemed to have briefly fallen asleep under Barber Sureshan's soothing hands. Sureshan was thinking of how, at some point, Joby had turned into the town buffoon. Everyone tolerated him because he was harmless and funny. His huge drinking capacity had long ceased to be heroic or manly. It was merely funny and a cause for comment.

'Know anything about that love affair in his youth?' Purushan Vaidyan asked suddenly, his eyes shut and his face sleepy.

'Oh, that was nothing much, I think,' Sureshan said, his reply so prompt that it seemed he was thinking the same thing. 'There was some murmuring about him and that music teacher—what was her name? He used to take some children to music classes in the evenings. He hardly ever spoke to us about it.'

'Saraswati Teacher,' Poulose contributed. 'She used to teach classical music to children. Still does, in her home south of town. She's old now and still unmarried, you know.'

'Oh, I really think he just used to love listening to her sing, that's it,' Sureshan said. 'He wasn't in love or anything. He never even proposed to her. Never spoke about her much. Perhaps once or twice in his most drunken moments.'

'So a failed love story isn't behind his wasted life, then,' Purushan Vaidyan said with a sigh, getting up. He jerked his head this way and that. His neck made loud cracking noises. 'Look Suresha, I can't pay you now for the massage. I only have enough money to repair this.' He held up the broken umbrella.

'I didn't ask for payment.'

'But here, keep this,' Purushan Vaidyan said, giving Sureshan a bottle wrapped in an old newspaper. 'It's a thailam for muscle pain. Use it when winter comes. And see what you can do to help Joby. I don't think he belongs in the drains where he is sleeping nowadays. And I think he might still live a long time if he stops drinking immediately.'

'Yes sir,' said Sureshan, putting the bottle of medicinal oil away in his bag. 'I know that friendly advice will not help. He is too far gone for that. Let me think about what I can do.'

'Find him a job, perhaps. Not one that involves lifting heavy sacks. Something he might like to do.' Purushan Vaidyan bid them goodbye and left.

'I'll go too,' Poulose said, looking out to his shop. A customer had arrived and would need to be attended to. 'I would say don't break your head too much and don't get involved too much. He was a friend long ago, not anymore. Now he is the town drunk, that's all. Besides, you cannot save him.'

Poulose walked out, leaving Sureshan alone. The barber wiped his hands on a cloth and looked out at the dried leaves.

◆

That evening Barber Sureshan walked to ex-Inspector Paachu's orchard, which was at the back of his house. A few bats hung upside down from giant branches and looked at him accusingly. The soil here was like white powder and it stuck to his slippers but it muffled his footsteps. This was important as Sureshan did not wish to run into Paachu Yemaan. At least, not yet. Not until he'd had a chance to discuss the plan with Paachu's wife, the good lady whom he called Sharadechi (meaning Sharada, the elder sister), though she probably wasn't much older than he was. Barber Sureshan continued on his stealthy way to the back of the house.

He gently tapped on the kitchen window. Sharada's grey head appeared at the window and she was about to shoot out a greeting to him when Sureshan put a finger to his lips. Her head disappeared and the back door opened.

'Is Yemaan there?' Sureshan asked quietly. 'I need to speak to you alone first.'

'Oh, he's in the front, snoozing. You have nothing to fear.' She smiled and Sureshan made himself comfortable on the steps near the kitchen door.

'Sharadechi, I wished to speak to you first about this. It's a request. And if it can't be granted I will understand, and the Yemaan need not know.'

'What's worrying you?' she asked, placing before him a plate full of hot banana chips that she had been frying.

'It's Joby. I'm worried about him.'

'Joby, that drunk?'

'Well, yes. He was once a friend,' Sureshan was almost apologetic, 'Purushan Vaidyan says he is dying.'

'What else would you expect,' Sharada asked, stirring the chips in the pan. Sureshan was relieved that the hissing oil would keep the Yemaan from hearing them. 'The man has been a drunk ever since I can remember. So what about him? What can we do for him, then?'

'He doesn't belong in the gutter, Sharadechi. He is not a beggar. It is this town that has reduced him to that. In fact, it is only after Yemaan retired that Joby has been going around town miserably drunk and shouting and falling asleep on people's doorsteps. With no one to fear, he is more self-destructive than ever.'

He gave Sharada an account of his discussion with Purushan Vaidyan that morning. Sharada smiled wryly when Sureshan talked about how the town had made Joby into a buffoon. She knew how much the town liked to laugh at people who were on the sidelines. But she had no idea how she could help Joby. Perhaps Sureshan wanted Paachu to give Joby a sound lecture? She vaguely remembered the time when Joby drove children around for a living. But that was a long time ago.

'Perhaps Yemaan can give him a job, Sharadechi,' Sureshan said. 'I know it's much to ask to employ a drunk. But I thought about it a lot over the day. I strongly believe that if Joby found something to do under the supervision of Paachu Yemaan, he might actually mend his ways. Well, if not completely mend them, he might at least cut down on his wayward living. He fears and respects Yemaan. There's no one else who has that effect on Joby.'

From upstairs they could hear little Priya reading aloud from her Hindi text.

'But Suresha, what kind of job?' Sharada asked, 'And your Yemaan is not the person he once was, you know.'

'Yes Sharadechi, I know,' Sureshan said, 'That's another reason I came here. The Yemaan comes to me to cut his tuft, so I know. He is very unhappy about his retirement. Helping another man will do him good. This is his chance to save a man's life.'

That's something, Sharada thought. Setting Joby right, saving him from the bottle. She had often thought that what Paachu needed was to somehow discover qualities of kindness and charity within himself. Only that could save him as he transitioned from his life as a hot-headed police inspector to that of what would hopefully be a peaceful, happy retirement. But how? Was reforming Joby the answer? For the life of her she couldn't think of any job that Paachu could offer a man who was drunk all day long, all week long, all month long.

'Find him something to do Sharadechi, anything,' Sureshan was saying, reading her thoughts and munching the chips. 'Something to do around the house, perhaps?'

'No,' Sharada said immediately. 'The Yemaan will certainly not have a drunk around the house. I know this Joby is not your regular roadside drunk in spite of appearances. But still.'

'Well, something menial will do. But it has to be a regular job. Something that will take his mind off arrack. And I believe under the watchful eyes of Paachu Yemaan it is possible. I'm not sure, but I really do believe that this is Joby's last chance. Otherwise this town will laugh a man to his grave.'

Sharada breathed deeply, watching the round banana slices shudder excitedly in the oil like many suns surfacing out of a boiling ocean. Suddenly Priya's reading stopped from above them and a moment later she appeared in the kitchen. She rushed to sample the chips but stopped shyly when she saw Sureshan. He smiled warmly at her. Sureshan touched the chips on his plate to see if they weren't too hot, then motioned for her to come over and gently placed some on her little palm. The girl gave him a quick smile and vanished from the room. A moment later the Hindi lesson resumed.

'Sharada, is someone there?' came Paachu's gruff voice from the front porch. Sureshan stood up at once.

'It's Barber Sureshan,' Sharada called back, 'he's come to ask me something.'

'Tell him to come out front when you're done,' Paachu yelled. 'He needs to check if my tuft is ready for cutting.'

Sureshan ate the last of the chips on his plate and looked at Sharada. 'Just let me know Sharadechi. Joby needs help.' Then he thought a little before saying, 'And I think Paachu Yemaan needs help too.'

'Yes Suresha, I know,' Sharada replied. 'I know. I just cannot figure out where Joby will fit in.'

An idea struck Sureshan and he said to Sharada, 'Can I bring Joby along with me one of these days? Let him meet Paachu Yemaan.'

'Well, nothing bad can come of that,' Sharada said. A lizard began clicking its throat somewhere. The people in these parts believed that a lizard clicking meant that what was just spoken was the truth.

'I cannot find Joby today, it's too late,' Sureshan said, 'I'll find him tomorrow and persuade him to pay Paachu Yemaan a visit. I'll ready him for it.'

'Yes, you do that. But see that you really get him ready. Your Yemaan will not tolerate a drunken man here. He can still get very angry, you know.' And she smiled tiredly.

Sureshan smiled back. Then he bid her goodnight and went around the house to check if Paachu Yemaan's tuft was ready to be cut.

4.

A Crucial Meeting

That was how it came to be that on the morning Sureshan found Joby on the steps of his shop, the town drunk had made his way to Paachu Yemaan's porch by noon. He was an unusually fair-skinned man for these parts, and even when he was unkempt or dead drunk or badly hung-over (as he was now), you might mistake him for a foreigner if you didn't know him. Now, all shaved and bathed and perfumed thanks to Sureshan, he looked almost glamorous if you overlooked his forehead which still bore traces of last night's revelry. His face was flushed, particularly the tip of his nose which was quite red. He was fairly tall but bent over like he was working on becoming a hunchback. He was lean but you wouldn't call him thin. His belly rounded out the rest of him, hard and stubborn like a non-performing asset. People often called this belly Little Joby, the one who led Big Joby from the front. That was one of the oldest jokes circulating among those who had the ability to laugh afresh at the same joke every time.

Standing next to him was Barber Sureshan, who stood quite like an officer of the law, alert and respectful. Whenever Sureshan was in Paachu Yemaan's vicinity his body language was that of a police constable; he would subconsciously transform himself into Paachu's subordinate so he would never be guilty of upstaging the ex-Inspector. Every now and then Sureshan silently sniffed the air to make sure Joby's talcum was still beating the smell of arrack. They had been told by Sharada to wait for Paachu Yemaan who would see them in a short while. Standing behind the curtain of the front door was Priya, one of her little feet visible under it.

Every once in a while Lilly would trot in through the gates of the house to be near her master. She had been asked by Joby to wait outside and she understood him perfectly. It was just that she had an overwhelming urge to be beside her master, especially when it seemed as though there was some threat hanging in the air. Every time Lilly made her way in, her head stooped down in guilt and her tail wagged for disobeying her master's orders. A volley of abuse would gurgle up in Joby's throat but before it could well out of him Sureshan would say 'Shoo!' and the bitch would go back to sit by the gate, her tail making fresh arcs in the fallen leaves. This would be followed by a suppressed giggle from Priya behind the curtain. This routine went on for a very long time. The shadows on the ground became shorter and shorter as the sun took pleasure in burning Sureshan.

The delay was to be expected. You couldn't just come in and meet the Yemaan even if you had taken a prior appointment.

Finally, the front door creaked inward. It was like the doors of a temple opening. Sureshan stiffened visibly. Joby stayed the same—like a man sleeping with his eyes open. His eyebrows were slightly raised to counter the massive weight of his eyelids that was threatening to shut his eyes completely. Lilly yelped and lowered her head. Little Priya momentarily held the curtain aside to let her uncle and aunt pass and then quickly stepped behind it again.

Paachu appeared in a clean, almost-shining banyan and mundu. Slowly and deliberately he sat down on his easy chair. He then lifted one leg and put it up on the long armrest. Following this he looked at the two men on his porch for a long time in total silence. He did not return Sureshan's salute presumably because he was looking too intently at Joby. After being still for a very long duration, Paachu Yemaan grew even stiller, defying all rules of science and logic. Then he put his leg down and stiffened a little as if intending to speak at last. But he only cleared his throat with a giant, carnivorous roar and continued scrutinizing Joby. Joby looked back at the man, actually registering the other's presence.

'J-Joby and Sureshan,' Sharada announced unnecessarily. Sureshan saluted again and this time Paachu nodded at him.

'So we have the honour of meeting Karuthupuzha's great drunk and funny man, eh?' Paachu finally pronounced, his voice grating, the way Priya had heard him sound in the police station when he was Inspector. 'I hear you're dying?'

Joby's throat gargled something up and Sureshan was afraid he might spit a gob of phlegm on the porch. Thankfully he just stood there and, even better, lifted both his hands, crossed them at his chest and clutched his shoulders in a mark of submission. Sureshan was relieved that Sharadechi seemed to have briefed the Yemaan about the situation. He began in a feeble voice, 'Joby's ready to mend his ways Yemaan, he told me…', but Paachu held up his hand, still looking intently at the drunk.

'You drink, you die, that's your business,' he said, 'but you turn into a nuisance, you yell obscenities, you spend the night on people's doorsteps—that's not acceptable. Not while I am… not while I still have a part to play in keeping this town law-abiding. I might be retired, but I am not dead.' Then he looked up at Sharada who stood beside him, at Sureshan and then back at Joby. He waited to see if anyone would contest what he had just said. He didn't think so. 'When I was at the station I pulled you up several times, didn't I? DIDN'T I?' Sureshan nodded vigorously but Joby continued to look blankly at Paachu. His eyebrows crept higher. 'When I was at the station you weren't such a nuisance. You still drank yourself silly every night, but that's your business, as I said. But whenever I felt that you would turn into a pain around town I pulled you up, sometimes sank my fist into your belly, sometimes shook you up and you finally went back to making it just between you and your bottle. Am I right? AM I RIGHT?'

This time Joby nodded slightly and Sureshan heard the bones in the man's neck click.

'Now I know why you have turned into a troublesome drunk. Because there is nobody to check your antics. You are not afraid of the jokers at the station now. Yes, I call them jokers. For four decades I have been the law here and *I* am telling you—they are jokers, the ones in the station now. All they do is sit in the station all day long and play broker and middleman and tout, helping people sell what they don't need. And discuss women. They probably play rummy too (who knows?), right in the police station—probably actually gamble! Can you believe it? Oh, they're jokers all right. I should know. Things were different when I was around. For forty years I ensured that petty thieves and miserable drunks like you stayed off the streets of Karuthupuzha! Not a leaf moved out of turn when I was Inspector, you are all witness to that, each one of you. Oh, there were drunks and pickpockets and rowdies even then. But they stayed in the shadows. Out of fear. *I* was their fear. But let me tell you one thing. You would do well to fear me still.'

He looked up at Sharada and asked for a glass of water. This was one embarrassing side-effect of his age. His mouth went dry whenever he was saying something important with great vehemence. 'As long as I live there will be law and order in Karuthupuzha. I called you here, Mr Joby, to tell you that.' Nobody reminded him that he hadn't called Joby at all. 'There is still enough strength in these arms to straighten out a dozen louts like you. And mark my words, by the time I am dead there will still be someone from my side at the station. Someone from my family will still ensure the law rules in Karuthupuzha. Because this is *my* land, you understand?'

This last sentence was totally unplanned and sounded completely out of place. Paachu's voice faltered a bit in manly emotion. Joby's belly protruded even further than usual as he swallowed a yawn. It didn't look as if he understood what was being said. With the hot sun and Paachu's constant grating voice, his head was beginning to ache a little and he thirsted for the day's first drop of arrack. Lilly once again made as if to enter the compound and Sureshan once again shooed her away. Paachu began speaking again, his tone level and studied, 'Now, unfortunately, my friend Sureshan here and my own wife seem to think that my retirement is best spent trying to salvage an alcoholic. Inspector Paachu, on whom the town of Karuthupuzha bestowed the title "Yemaan" out of fear and respect, is now to offer his shoulder to a drunk! But let me tell you, each one of you, that is not how Paachu is used to doing things. That is not the way Paachu Yemaan straightens out lawlessness. You see this fist here? This is what I have always used, and this is what I will use the next time I hear that you have played the fool in your drunken stupor. IS THAT CLEAR?'

'Yes, Yemaan,' Joby pronounced loudly to the surprise of everybody.

Sureshan looked at Sharada. This wasn't going the way they had planned it at all. Far from discussing some job that he might offer Joby, Paachu was threatening him with violence. Why, a punch in the belly might kill Joby right then and there considering the condition he was in. Of course, a police-style lecture wasn't bad for a beginning, but Paachu did not seem to want to move on from there at all. Now that Joby had opened his mouth at last, perhaps the time was ripe to take things further. Sharada gave an almost imperceptible nod.

'Er...Yemaan,' Sureshan mumbled, 'can we discuss this with you a little?' He motioned for Paachu and Sharada to move to the side of the house. Paachu cleared his throat with an enormous roar and got up from his chair. He drank the remaining water in the copper pot Sharada had brought him and the three of them made their way towards the side of the house. Sureshan motioned to Joby to stay where he was. Joby did not nod but stood in the same pose, hands crossed over his shoulders.

Once out of Joby's earshot Sureshan began, 'Yemaan, he is not worthy of your fist. He will die if you so much as get angry with him. I think—'

'It's good that you put him in his place,' Sharada interrupted. 'He is humbled now. Perhaps now we could discuss some small job for him?'

'Oh yes! We can make him the Inspector of Karuthupuzha Police Station,' Paachu said loudly, making no attempt to stick with the plan he had discussed with his wife the previous night at the dinner table. 'Or maybe we can make him stand for next year's elections considering his popularity across town. Ha! Both of you will make me weep.'

Sureshan and Sharada set about trying to chip away at Paachu's worked-up wrath and consequent cynicism with the dexterity of sculptors. This involved agreeing with him initially so that they could gently begin disagreeing later, imperceptibly and gently moving him across to their point of view. It wasn't easy.

Meanwhile, on the front porch, a bat flew up and hooked itself upside down on a branch so that it could frown at Joby. Lilly howled at it and, using the distraction, crawled up to her master's side and sat down quietly. Behind the curtain the little feet stood still. All at once, a deep reverberation began to shake the air, like the groan of a faraway locomotive. The bat's eyes widened. From behind the curtain Priya moved to look out. It was Joby. He had fallen asleep standing, his snores emphatic yet almost soothing. The bat began to feel sleepy too and flew away fearing that it might fall straight down and give itself a fatal knock on the head. All around, Nature herself seemed to relax into the immensity of Joby's snores. Lilly soon stretched out though she kept one ear raised. Priya peeped from behind the curtain at the funny man who was standing erect and sleeping. Then she burst into peals of laughter and ran into the house, waking Joby with such a start that he almost fell.

Paachu, Sureshan and Sharada heard her laughter and that was what gave Sharada the idea. It was a brainwave, the kind of flash that wins you over immediately despite its impracticality, its difficulties, its very awkwardness.

But for the life of her Sharada did not know how to bring it up with her husband. She would have had no problem discussing it with Barber Sureshan if Paachu wasn't with them but that wasn't the case. As she stood there wondering what to do, her mind flitted over the various things that had contributed to the making of the idea. Her intuition told her that Joby was to be trusted, that he was a good man, totally harmless, perhaps even honest. Sureshan had corroborated all this. It was clear to her that Joby did not need police correction. He needed a vocation, just like Sureshan had said; something that he might enjoy doing, something that might bring out the best in him so that he might be tempted to stay off the bottle. But how could she say this firmly and convincingly to Paachu in his present mood? She came to a decision and told Sureshan, 'Take the man away for now. Let him rest. Come back some other time when he is…fresher. Let us (nodding towards her husband) discuss this a little. Maybe we can find some way to help him.'

Joby and Sureshan walked away after thanking the ex-Inspector profusely for his very helpful talk. Lilly followed them, head lowered, tail hidden between her legs. In a room inside, Priya's little body still rocked with laughter as she thought of Joby and his shadow sleeping while standing up. She muffled her face with a pillow and her sides ached.

◆

That evening, like every evening since he had retired, Paachu sat on his easy chair in the front balcony, his legs on the armrests, reading the newspaper from start to finish. This was his third round of reading. But rather than go into the specifics of each reading first, it might be more interesting to examine his day as a whole, in which we will see why he picked up the newspaper three times, dealing with it differently each time.

Paachu was busiest in the mornings, as we have already seen. In the early days of his retirement, Paachu's first difficulty was that he had nowhere to go after he woke up. The result of this, though he did not himself understand exactly how the two were connected, was constipation. Because he had nowhere to go, it might be that his body was in no hurry to relieve itself and be ready for the day. Then at odd times later in the day, usually when he was not ready for it—like when he was giving instructions to the men who harvested fruit in his orchard—he would feel his belly beginning to rumble. On other days he would not visit the toilet for an entire day. In an attempt to sort out the problem, he ingested bitter kashayams from Purushan Vaidyan and instructed Sharada to serve him boiled bananas with all three meals of the day. He even spoke on the phone to Doctor Ambookkan, an English doctor from outside town. Although sometimes the problem did go away it always came back. It was like his body wasn't entirely his own anymore and he was at a loss to make it understand that though he did not have a workplace to go to now, he would like his bowel movements to be regular as always. Worse, he sensed that Purushan Vaidyan and Doctor Ambookkan did not seem to take his case very seriously. Why, even Sharada had begun to look upon his constipation as a matter of routine. The fact that he was the only one worried about this alarmed him even more. And then he'd had the brilliant idea of putting on his old police uniform to fool his gut and that had solved the problem to a large extent.

Paachu still bathed in very cold water as he believed that this was a sign of good health. If you were a strong man you dipped the mug into a bucket of cold water on cold mornings and splashed your whole body without wincing. After his bath and breakfast Paachu would drop Priya to school on his scooter, then come back home and stretch out on the easy chair for the first time in the day and pick up his newspaper. He enjoyed the crackling, inky smell of the paper in his hand. On this reading he went over only the headlines mostly, except for front-page articles or articles that were of special interest, in which case he also read the first paragraph. Sometimes, though this was rare, he got up and switched on the radio and tuned into the news on some channel or the other. Mostly, he just read the paper until he dozed off. Although he called it 'a short nap', Sharada knew that he napped for a considerable time before lunch. After lunch Paachu would go into his room upstairs and have a proper siesta, his snores reverberating throughout the house. Upon waking up, he would fetch his niece from school, then read the paper again, sitting on the settee in the drawing room this time. Sharada would be in the kitchen and Priya would play with the boy-toys he had bought her as well as a few toys she had made for herself out of old pillows. This time he would read every word in the paper including the advertisements. He only skipped the obituaries and the sports pages because he hated these.

After tea, Paachu and Sharada would stroll around their orchard. Sometimes there would be men to pick the fruit and take them to the market in which case Paachu would discuss one of three things with them. The first was politics in which he was up to date thanks to his diligent newspaper reading. The next was his exploits in his police days; the aim of this discussion was to impress upon the poor labourers that he was still to be feared and listened to. The third topic, which was brought up rarely but was very dear to Paachu, was his bowel situation for that day. If this particular discussion was the one chanced upon, Sharada would gently drift away from the men and go to inspect the coconuts or check the water pump and pipes for rust.

Further into the evening, when the sun and moon were swapping their vigil, Paachu would wash up and once again sprawl upon his easy chair. He would now read the paper for the third time under a naked light bulb around which the fireflies buzzed in ignorant desperation. After dinner was cooked (dinner was the easiest meal for Sharada to cook, as it consisted only of some simple rice-water and butter so that Paachu's bowels would behave themselves the next morning, and a little rice and leftover curry from lunch for Priya and herself), Sharada would join her husband on the front porch, sitting on the floor and reading her Ramayana while he read his paper. Early into retirement, Sharada used to place the Ramayana suggestively on the arms of his easy chair. Each time, he would pick up the big book and put it down on the floor right where she came and sat after her cooking. He never opened it once because he associated reading religious texts with retirement and old age.

During his the third reading of the paper, Paachu would reread articles he found interesting. Sometimes he would even cut out certain stories and stick them in his scrapbook. In between readings he would sometimes put the paper down and listen to little Priya reading aloud from her textbooks from inside the house. At this time he would stare intently at an empty patch of sky until a star materialized. He had found out recently that if you stared long enough at any black portion of the night sky, a star, however faint, would eventually appear there. He would then pick up the paper and move on to another article. On some days, at this time, too, he would switch on his radio and listen to the news. He had always been interested in current affairs particularly regional politics. But his interest had grown manifold since his retirement. He fed himself on the news now with a kind of desperate hunger.

After they had retired for the night, husband and wife would speak about things immediate and distant; from the money their orchard had fetched them that year to Priya's future. When he talked about her joining the police force Sharada would point out gently that that was up to the little girl. Sharada would sometimes fall asleep mid-sentence and that would make him angry. But he would let her sleep and look out the window, staring at the sky and making new stars appear.

On the day of Joby's arrival and abrupt dismissal, when Paachu was on the third reading of his newspaper, Sharada appeared and stood at the doorway, not sitting down as usual with her Ramayana. After almost a lifetime together Sharada had still not found an appropriate noun or pronoun to attract her husband's attention. Sometimes she would begin by saying 'Actually…', at other times it would be 'Here…' or 'By the way…'. If she was close enough to him, as she was now, she would only need to clear her throat and he would know that she was addressing him. She cleared her throat mildly and Paachu responded by putting the paper down, though he did not look up.

'Er…I was thinking about our man Joby,' she began. He took

off his spectacles. 'I was thinking of a job for him. You know, he's not a bad sort actually. He is an honest man, though he lost his way at some point in life.'

'Hmm.'

'Well, I was thinking, perhaps we could have him take Priya to school and back.'

The crickets creaked away in the background as Paachu Yemaan sat there looking at his wife. Finally he managed to speak, 'Are you mad?'

Sharada sighed. His question admittedly did not seem out of place even to her. Her idea, which had seemed perfect when it first struck her, now seemed ridiculous—to actually entrust her little niece, a vulnerable girl who was too young to know good from bad, to Karuthupuzha's drunk and comedian who had lately begun sleeping by the roadside. There was no indication whatsoever that Joby would abruptly turn responsible even for a day if he had the little girl to take care of.

'Well, that's what he did a long time ago,' she said reluctantly, her confidence vanishing suddenly. 'He used to ferry children and there never was a complaint.'

'So therefore you decided that you could place in his hands a...,' he was about to say parentless but he knew Priya was listening, '... little girl's safety? Sharada, it has been centuries since he did a job of any sort around here.'

So there it was. It had been a bad idea from start though she had got excited about it. Her husband was right, of course. Though she had thought it might do Joby good perhaps she hadn't considered the risks. Even as she thought this it struck her that they were judging Joby unfairly. In all the years he had been drunk, he had never been caught doing anything remotely criminal. Though it was widely known that Joby had often drank away the little money he had, to the point of starvation, he had never once stolen or desired another man's money.

True, there had been rumours at one point of time that he had stolen slippers and shoes but then it had been later proven beyond doubt that these were just rumours—malicious rumours directed at a man too feeble to defend himself.

What harm had Joby ever done? He only made everyone laugh. He would make Priya laugh too, and God knew the little girl needed to laugh, particularly after she had grown apart from her uncle. Sharada recalled Priya's peals of laughter when Joby had fallen asleep.

That said, little girls did have impressionable minds. Joby had a loathsome vocabulary. What if he let loose a volley of abuse in her presence? That was unthinkable! Priya had been brought up with great care and delicacy. Good breeding was in her very gait. Wasn't Sharada putting all that at risk when she suggested an association between Priya and the drunk?

And what if Joby simply got drunk and did not turn up in the mornings? What if her husband then had to hurry up and get ready so he could take her to school? He would be furious with her!

All these doubts washed over her and yet, when her husband was picking up the newspaper again, she said, 'I really believe it's a new way of doing things. No one has given Joby a job, particularly this kind of a job, for ages. It-it's just that I thought we would do things in a new way.'

When she said this, all her doubts vanished. She was sure that, despite everything, her idea was a good one or she wouldn't have broached it with her husband. She was aware, too, that she had said 'a new way of doing things', as it was the one thing that always got her husband's attention. Paachu believed that trying new things, going against the current and all that, was what lent vitality to life. That's why he had used all his savings, even Sharada's jewellery, some years ago to buy their orchard. (That had been her suggestion, too, and it now fetched them a very welcome income.)

Although he had turned back to his papers to indicate that the discussion was closed she could see that he wasn't really reading. Paachu broke the silence after a while. 'Even if we do give him the job, he won't turn up in the mornings. He'll be asleep in the gutter when it's time to come and pick her up.'

From the absolute silence from indoors they knew that Priya was listening to every word.

'Initially you might have to fill in a bit,' Sharada contended. 'But even then he will surely be at the school to bring her back in the evenings so you needn't go.'

This was another big point. She knew how much Paachu hated taking Priya to and from school. When he was working it had been different. In the mornings they would go in the police jeep and Paachu would continue to the police station after dropping his niece off. In the evenings the jeep would be sent to fetch her to the station and from there they would come back home together. The whole routine fit well with his personality and style of functioning—misusing the police jeep for a family chore was just the sort of thing he could be expected to do. But after retiring the jeep had been taken from him (yes, forcibly snatched, in fact) and so he now had to ferry Priya on his old Bajaj scooter. Paachu Yemaan, the erstwhile terror of the town, had no option but to take his little niece across town twice a day on a rusty old scooter. The whole town seemed to mock him for it. Photographer Varky had found it particularly interesting. That one act of taking Priya to school and back on his antique scooter represented Paachu's ludicrous fall from power.

'But isn't there anyone else who will take Priya?' he said, as if the whole discussion was not about Joby but about finding someone to ferry the girl to and from school.

'Who else is as harmless as Joby? I mean, if you really think about it,' Sharada pointed out. She spoke casually as she didn't wish to sound like she was selling the idea too hard. 'During the day the man is as harmless as a fly. I don't think he starts in the mornings, to be fair to him. Besides, with anyone else we might have to pay significant money. It's twice a day, five and sometimes six days a week, you know.'

Paachu finally put the paper down. 'Hmm,' he said, and cleared his throat violently. He still could not visualize the drunk even coming close to his Priya. Why, the man stank! And Priya had been brought up like a princess. She was used to a lot of pampering. She had never even spoken a word to someone like Joby. Although Paachu could see there was something to Sharada's idea after all, it was impossible to accept it.

'Hmm,' he said again. 'I can give him a job easily enough in the orchard. Maybe pick up fallen areca nuts or something. Without pay, of course. We can give him one meal a day. But why should we put Priya at risk?'

At this, little Priya came marching out to the porch and proclaimed indignantly, 'I want Joby to take me to school. I don't mind.' The man who snored away standing up on her porch had made her laugh till she was blue in the face, and she wanted more of that.

Sharada smiled. Paachu lay back on his chair, took his reading glasses off. Of course, it hurt him that his Priya was so eager and open about replacing her uncle with a drunk for a chaperone during the school run. But he turned to her with a gentle smile, 'Your uncle and aunt will do what's good for you, little darling. Go inside and play.'

She pulled her pigtail and stretched it between her mouth and nose to imitate Paachu's giant moustache and said in a gruff voice that mimicked his, 'Go inside and play!' Then she ran inside. It was after a long time that Priya was indulging her uncle this way. Sharada laughed and Paachu smiled, too, though he continued to feel a deep hurt that he could not understand.

'Well, it's just that she hasn't been brought up to deal with drunks,' Paachu said, lowering his voice as if they were now exchanging secrets. 'Finding a job for this drunkard need not necessitate such a radical step. Same with finding someone to ferry Priya.'

'I just thought this is one job that might wean Joby from the bottle,' Sharada persisted gently. 'He loves the little ones. As I was saying, picking up and dropping off children was what he was doing some time ago. He will still drink if he picks up areca nuts but ferrying Priya might be his last chance of kicking his habit. Priya just might have that effect on him. And, who knows, if he's good at it more people might engage him and he might take up his old job again. We just might end up saving him and his wife.'

'I don't understand when *that* became your priority?'

The conversation seemed on the verge of changing into something nasty. It seemed that her husband might even get angry. Then Sharada had another brainwave; she was surprised that she could be so sly.

'I just thought interacting with a drunken man like Joby might also toughen up our Priya, you know, enable her to deal better with drunks and miscreants...we have discussed how she is growing up rather delicate, and sooner or later she has to face all this.'

She wasn't happy with herself for doing this but she could tell that it had the desired effect. That was apparent by the way her husband's lips moved under his moustache. Sharada watched him visualize Priya gradually growing tougher as she dealt with Joby, reprimanding him sternly when he used obscene language, threatening action when he smelt of arrack and moving to suspension and even dismissal when he did not turn up for work. Why, she would learn people management! As she saw his eyes light up, Sharada knew her husband now loved her idea but she also knew he wouldn't admit it for a while yet, because that would mean he had lost the argument.

Sure enough, at the dinner table that night Paachu suddenly announced, 'I think it's all right, what you suggested on the porch, ahem, a little earlier.' Then he cleared his throat and a tumbler of water shook. 'Joby can take Priya to school and back on a trial basis. We will try it out for a week, then two weeks, and then, if all goes well, for a month. Only after a month will we decide if it can become a permanent arrangement.'

Little Priya jumped off her chair, went around to her uncle and kissed him on the forehead, the way she hadn't done for months now. The funny man would ferry her to school! She was thrilled. Paachu again felt that ache in his soul, this time threatening to spill out of him, but he held it back. 'But,' he said, holding up his fingers. 'But...'

Sharada was about to transfer a ball of rice into Priya's mouth and she paused to give Paachu her full attention.

'I have some conditions. He is a drunk and this here is our little princess. I cannot just let him take her to school and back without changing some of his awful habits. My first condition, of course, is that he is not to drink during the day, before he has dropped Priya back here, COME WHAT MAY. I will have my sources to confirm this but if this happens, Priya, you are to report it to me the same day and his services will be terminated immediately. And not just terminated, mind you; he will be punished, police style.

'Second, Joby is not to demand a salary until we have tested him satisfactorily. He will take whatever we offer him, if at all, until we fix an amount as compensation. I think that's only fair. He is a drunken lout and no one would employ him anyway. Sharada, you can pay him in kind at the end of the month—fruits or grain or old clothes but not money.'

Sharada nodded. In any case money would only mean more arrack for Joby.

'Next condition: Joby will not ride his bicycle. He will seat Priya on the carrier and push it. He is not to mount the seat. Is that clear?'

They nodded. It would be a task for Joby to push the cycle from home to school and back but it had to be done. Sharada felt happy that her husband was thinking so clearly about the new arrangement. 'Lastly, I don't want him opening his filthy mouth to Priya. During the journey and back, you (he glanced at Priya) and Joby are not to speak. Not one word to each other. I expect you to stick to this.'

Priya looked at Sharada and then nodded. She was hoping for a lot of fun with the pot-bellied man and his pet mutt and she couldn't visualize how it would be fun if they never spoke a word to each other. But in her aunt's eyes she read a message that said: Just agree, and let's get this started. We can always improvise later.

This thought was instantly squelched by Paachu's next sentence: 'As I said, I will have my sources to see that my conditions are observed, and not just in the initial days but always. Priya, you will need to tell me word for word how it went the first few days. And even after, if anything unusual happens, or if any one of these conditions is violated, you need to report to me immediately.'

For the life of her Priya could not fathom what was so critical about this whole thing. The sleepy man looked safe enough to her. Besides, the roads from home to school were brightly lit by the sun and always had a fair number of people on them. In fact, her uncle had often told her that when she was a little older she could walk by herself to school. But again she read the instruction of compliance in her aunt's eyes, and she nodded.

Later, when they were stretched out on their bed upstairs, Sharada gently began, 'It's all fine except the last condition. How can they not speak a word to each other for the whole—'

'My conditions are not flexible,' her husband interrupted, cracking the joints on his fingers one by one. 'School reopens Monday, right? Hmm. I will find a way to ensure that these conditions are met and that she will be safe. Despite all your arguments, I am not for a moment going to trust Priya's safety to a drunk.'

That brought back all of Sharada's initial doubts. She stared into the dark, wide awake, hoping and praying that she wasn't wrong about Joby and that she wasn't needlessly inviting trouble. Her husband began snoring, while Sharada continued to look at the dark sky outside her bedroom window.

5.

The New Arrangement

Bats hung on branches outside Paachu Yemaan's house like dark clothes on door handles. The next morning some of them nudged the others awake for a very unusual sight had presented itself. They saw the little princess of the house sitting hunched over on a very rusty old cycle with partly deflated tyres that was being pushed by the town drunk, who seemed to be sleepwalking. Trotting cautiously beside them, as though she could smell gunpowder in the air, was the bitch Lilly. As the trio moved away from the compound a few of the bats, particularly the younger ones, flew up to another tree further away so they could get a better view. They could see Paachu Yemaan and Sharada waving goodbye to their little girl; Paachu was thundering out last minute instructions and warnings to Joby. None of them seemed to make any impression on the drunk whose entire focus seemed to be on making the cycle move forward without toppling over.

It was a bright morning, the kind that made you happier if you had woken up in a cheerful mood and cynical if you hadn't. Joby pushed the cycle with all his strength. His muscles ached. There was pain behind his eyes and every square inch of his skin cried out for a drink. He knew that very soon the pleasant morning would turn into a hot, sunny noon. By then he wanted to make sure that he was curled up in the comfortable shade of a big motherly tree, a bottle in hand. He would see about picking up this little girl in the evening; there was plenty of time for that.

School was reopening after a short festival break and the roads were full of little children going to school with their chaperones. The children were bursting with stories to tell each other about life-changing events that had occurred to them in the ten days they hadn't seen each other. The shopkeepers by the wayside were shouting out wares that were tempting to the children, from colour pencils and name-slips to ginger candy and home-made murukku. But everyone was riveted by the sight of Joby ferrying Priya. Most knew that Priya's uncle was ex-Inspector Paachu, a very exacting man. They knew that so far it was Paachu Yemaan who had dropped Priya to school and back. Everyone knew that Joby was a wretched buffoon who was most likely drunk. So what was going on here? Theories began to be formed. Some people said that perhaps Paachu was sick and this was an arrangement only for today. But then why had Joby been chosen of all people? Others said that the ex-Inspector had finally gone completely mad (they had seen it coming for some time) and had overthrown his good wife's better sense and gone and done something uniquely stupid. An old woman, who was in the habit of drinking soda for her gastritis at a small shop by the wayside, pondered deeply and then told the shopkeeper that this was what happened when a child's parents weren't around. 'Uncles and aunts can never take the place of fathers and mothers,' she said with feeling. 'Do you think if that little girl's parents were around she would be in the hands of a drunk?'

Strictly adhering to Paachu Yemaan's terms of employment, Joby didn't speak a word to the girl. He pushed the cycle and kept looking behind him uncomfortably, glancing every now and again at an old cracked watch that Sureshan had given him. He thought he heard the clank of metal on stone every once in a while. Whenever he looked at his watch he struggled to increase the pace of their progress. No sooner would he speed up than the turgid tyres of the cycle would act as a brake and slow them down again; Joby would silently remind himself for the umpteenth time to fill air in the tyres before the evening trip. Scathing expletives would rise in his throat but he would choke them down.

In sharp contrast to his silence was Priya's continuous chatter. She did not care for any of her uncle's conditions and was determined to enjoy her rides with the funny man. Moreover, whenever her school reopened after even the shortest of holidays, Priya always had butterflies in her stomach. She felt uneasy, as though she constantly wanted to go to the toilet or was coming down fast on a swing. Her stomach roiled and her hands shook. She would feel, for some reason, like she was going to school for the first time. She would try to deal with this uneasiness by talking continuously. As soon as her home was out of sight, she asked Joby if he would teach her to cycle. Met with stony silence, she moved on to her next question which was whether arrack tasted sweet or bitter. He gave her a wounded look and she laughed because she saw how red his nose was. Then she spoke a little to the bitch, who wagged her tail because there were no conditions against wagging tails. Then she told both of them about her classroom, about the butterflies in her stomach, about how she longed for the day she would be promoted to a class where she could use a pen instead of a pencil, about the one bully in her class who never bothered her because her uncle had been a policeman, how she sometimes fed her lunch to dogs like this one ('Is it a boy dog or a girl dog? What's its name?' She wasn't old enough yet to know boy dogs from girl dogs...) so that her aunt wouldn't be sorry that she hadn't eaten her lunch, about a teacher who had such rocking hiccups that everyone laughed at him, about how her uncle absurdly wished she would grow up to be a policewoman while she had quite another plan that involved a giant wheel. Her chatter went on and on. Then she stopped talking to take out her water bottle. All this talk was making her thirsty. Joby looked wounded as her movement made the bicycle wobble. She answered his look by suggesting he could talk now and she would never tell her uncle. She wasn't very loyal; that much was clear.

Joby looked at her sitting hunched over and clasping on his cycle carrier like a monkey on a branch. Her words continually fell on him like needles. He wasn't listening to most of what she was saying but the continuous drone irritated him. The pain behind his eyes was acute now and every once in a while he looked over his shoulder but then quickly looked ahead again as his stiff neck made such movements very painful. And all the while there was one thought that resonated in his mind—why had he taken up such a hateful job? Perhaps some part of him had responded positively to his friend Barber Sureshan's attempt at rehabilitating him. He almost smiled as he thought how it is true that even the most fallen of men will experience a rush of optimism at the slightest chance of getting another shot at a regular life.

But even as he thought this, he realized wistfully that what he should be feeling right now was the rush of arrack down his throat. The yearning passed and he continued examining the rush of optimism he had felt. There was no fallen man who would refuse the opportunity to engage in a job that was socially acceptable. The last time he had worked at a proper job was many years ago. He only had vague memories of falling asleep in Eeppachan Mothalali's rice mill when he should have been carrying sacks of rice heavier than him. He could not recall if that was his last attempt at a job. There had been numerous odd jobs with this boss and that, menial jobs like carrying loads, fixing tyre punctures, greasing up old scooters and more. Each of them had been terribly boring and physically taxing and he had been unable to stick to them for long. Like Sureshan had once said, 'Joby cannot stick to any of these small jobs. He is spending a lifetime waiting for that Big Job.'

That was just what he had done. Now, pushing the little girl on the cycle, Joby pictured himself in his youth when he had ferried the children of Karuthupuzha to this very school. Many of them were now working at various jobs in town, while some had migrated to cities. Even at that time, though he had a good thing going and was earning more than satisfactorily, Joby's heart had kept flirting with ideas of something bigger. He had sometimes dreamt of a big transport business for children (because he loved children), with branches across the state or perhaps even across the country. His business would own tens of thousands of autorickshaws and tempos that would take children to school and back. And on top of it all he would sit, never driving himself but reaping the rewards of his vision and enjoying being the owner of something big.

In spite of his hangover, Joby smiled. He had no big transport business to manage, no numerous autorickshaws or tempos to inspect, no line of drivers to pay off or account ledgers to inspect. All he had was this job of pushing a little girl up and down the pathways of the little town in which he had always lived and in which he would be buried. But at least this was something, and despite the thoughts that warred within him, the pull of arrack and the pain that wracked his head and muscles, Joby thought, no man, no matter how low he had fallen, would pass up an opportunity to play a useful role in society again.

'...Head Maash knows about the affair,' Priya was saying and Joby began to dimly register something of what was being said. 'And it's not like they wanted to keep it too much of a secret. We knew all along. They thought we were too small to know, but they were wrong. You know, when Kannan Maash and Ambili Teacher looked at each other, everyone knew. Head Maash was genuinely worried, them being the two best teachers and all that. He said they would give us the wrong idea, that a love affair on campus was acceptable.'

She chattered on and Joby tuned her out. He looked over his shoulder uneasily. Lilly growled at a young rabbit in a field they were passing but, not given to athletics, did not chase it. Moreover, she was tired already with the latest developments in her master's life.

Observers pointed out later that a couple of days before he had begun his new job, Joby had grown exceptionally anarchic. Apparently, on the day he had met Paachu Yemaan and received a lecture first from him and then from Barber Sureshan, he had made up his mind to drink himself silly. He had begun in the afternoon and by evening could be seen lying under the big, perennially fruit-bearing jackfruit tree near the market, bottle in hand, shouting obscenities the nature of which made the birds abandon their dinner midway. The tree smiled down at him and shook free a big, half-eaten fruit next to his feet. But Joby had already lost consciousness.

The next day—which was the day before he was to begin his new job—he had been spotted bright and early with a bottle in one hand and a stick in the other with which he seemed to be imparting training to Lilly. Townsfolk reported that the bitch played along until he began to hit her rather painfully, at which point she had left his side and maintained a safe distance. By noon he had reached Sureshan's barbershop, pitch drunk, and announced that he was taking up the job Paachu Yemaan had offered him. Barber Sureshan took one look at the man and wondered at the efficacy of the plan. Driver Velu, who was inside the shop at the time, made the sombre observation that perhaps his goodness of heart was actually driving Sureshan mad. Why else would he take it upon himself to cure this incurable drunk and use someone as temperamental as Paachu Yemaan as the central figure in his plan? Anyone could see that it wouldn't work. It was a bad plan, as simple as that. Abu, the newspaper recycler, craned his neck out of his shop and sang an ancient limerick about picking up trouble lying on the wayside and about how the most innocent people unknowingly wreaked the most damage.

Meanwhile, leaning on the doorstep of the barbershop, Joby was barely coherent, swearing sincerity and commitment to his new vocation. The solemnity of it was causing him to sob. 'I will protect Yemaan's little girl with my life,' he wailed. Barber Sureshan stepped out, took hold of the drunk's shoulders, and shook him violently. Then he asked him if he was serious about taking up the job. Joby cried his consent in the manner of someone taking a pledge in church. For better or for worse, that evening Barber Sureshan confirmed to Paachu and Sharada that Joby would come on time the next morning and take Priya to school.

Some people said that the reason Joby drank much more than

usual on those two days was simple. He was showing his defiance to Paachu Yemaan who had tried to 'police' him back to sobriety. According to this theory, like most people of Karuthupuzha, Joby was actually mocking the ex-Inspector for still trying to terrorize and discipline people when he should have been leading a quiet, retired life instead.

Others claimed that it wasn't as complicated as that. Joby knew he was drinking himself to destruction and he knew that he had just been given his last chance to return to normal life. These two days of exceptional debauchery were his final act of flagrantly irresponsible behaviour before submitting to Paachu's efforts to transform him into a healthy and responsible citizen.

In truth, Joby himself could not quite figure out why he had binged. He only knew that his binging was weighing on him particularly heavily now. It was making this frail little girl seem every bit as heavy as a sack of Eeppachan Mothalali's rice. He heaved and puffed. Abruptly, he put the cycle on its stand, walked up to the shrubs by the roadside and vomited profusely. He waited, then brought up some more. Then he wiped his lips and continued pushing the cycle.

'…I, for one, have decided,' Priya was saying, totally unperturbed by his vomiting, 'I am not going to have an arranged marriage. I have decided to run away even if Uncle and Aunty aren't against my affair…'

A little lightened after his upheaval, Joby thought of his wife. Maybe because he had just heard the word marriage. They were crossing a broken-down bridge over a creek just then. As the cycle rattled over it, he was struck by a vision of the saintly Rosykutty with not a spot to mar her anywhere, body or soul. He thought of their wedding night. A faint smile lifted one corner of his lips as he recalled, in a different life, all the weight of dreams and the almost painful excitement with which he had come to his nuptial bed that night. (Nuptial bed! it sounded so powerfully hilarious now.) Before the wedding, his friends at that time, two farmers and a clerk at the local bank, had not given him much time to himself. They had teased him about the marital ecstasies he was about to experience and the sanctions on the individual that would now be lifted for him. They told him he would now put on weight because his wife would cook for him and give him all kinds of joys. They had said they would now see very little of him since he would be spending so much time behind closed doors with his woman. Admittedly, they spoke so earnestly because they were drinking on his money. He could not even remember their names now, but he remembered how they had systematically raised his hopes about married life. So much so that he had approached his first night with a throbbing heart. There was anxiety, embarrassment, uncertainty and an overwhelming sense that his life was changing, all clothed in a beautiful mix of excitement and anticipation of the bliss that was to come.

Joby felt bile rise in his throat and he spat angrily. That deterred Priya only for a moment, and she resumed chattering about settling down with a husband somewhere in a modern city with a big fair and a giant wheel.

Maybe the problem was that his excitement and eagerness had painted marriage in colours that were too glittering to be true. Because it took only the first night to convince him nothing was quite the way his friends had painted it. Rosykutty was beautiful to look at. Oh, that was such an understatement! At the time she had thick black hair that fell all the way down to her lower back. Her smile was enchanting and it would not be an exaggeration to say her eyes shone. Quite simply she was ethereal, a magical being descended from the heavens.

What she lacked was life. Sometimes she made him think of a dead woman walking. What made it worse was that he had loved another woman not so long ago, and had assumed that marriage and its consummation would help him forget her. Not a chance; all Rosykutty did was bring back painful memories of the other woman day in and day out.

His wife was never excited about anything. Nothing seemed to ever touch her. In all his years with her, he had never once seen her emote. Yes, she smiled, even laughed sometimes, but it wasn't because she found something really funny but because at certain times laughter was the response required. Her reactions were automated, not too original, not at all spontaneous. It was as if nothing ever touched her deep enough to move her. Why, he could not even get her to fight with him. Try as he might, he could not irritate her, disappoint her, make her talk back to him, or even give him a strong opinion about anything. Rosykutty's life was one flat line, and whenever he looked at her he thirsted for a drink.

In fact, it was astounding but true that Rosykutty had never once rebuked him for his drinking! He wondered if she rationalized it as a phenomenon that men engaged in. Or maybe she never needed to rationalize anything. Odd or routine, things just existed and she existed alongside them. As he went from employment to unemployment, and from regular drinker to confirmed alcoholic, she was merely the mute witness, whose total, non-reactive silence made him drink the more.

Joby realized that the little girl had fallen silent. They were nearing school and she was overwhelmed by her customary nervousness on reopening day. But when he looked at her, sitting tight and full of life on his bicycle seat, a new and very uncomfortable thought popped into his head. With intense guilt he recognized that her very existence was irritating him! She was so young and blooming with life, chattering away non-stop, discovering love for the first time, while he laboriously pushed the bicycle along, bile in his throat and bitterness in his soul. He, the man who was always kind to children, felt his energy sapping when he observed Priya's liveliness. He was irritated by her weight on the bicycle that was making his old muscles ache and burn in the sun. It irked him to see how she was drawn into the moment, body and soul, fascinated by the littlest things, nervous about school because of a mere ten-day break, while he couldn't look beyond the darkness behind him. He was deeply regretful that her painfully thin limbs and pinched nose and watery eyes evoked not his usual tenderness towards children but a new causticity verging on raw anger.

His mind shuttled back to his wife who, he thought, was a ghost of a woman who didn't even realize she had ruined him in many ways. Meanwhile, there was the lady he had loved once upon a time, a lady who sang in the sweetest voice he had ever heard; she was still unmarried and still lived in this very town. That was his life—defeated, decaying and perpetually thirsty like a desert squinting up at the sky for a bit of rain.

With a sigh, Joby debated whether he could put the little girl down and ask her (or gesture to her) to walk the rest of the way. School was just around the corner. They could hear the sound of children shouting. The last bit of the road that led to the school gates entailed a rather steep climb. The pain behind his eyes had moved to his temples and he knew that he had to wash it away with his first refreshing, soothing, cold arrack of the day.

'I can hear school,' Priya said nervously. 'I can hear the noise.'

As he debated whether or not to send the little girl the rest of the way on her own, he began to slow down. But then he thought of Yemaan and all his conditions. He wondered if Paachu Yemaan still packed enough punch to make a serious enough dent in his life. He probably didn't and it struck him that the real reason he had agreed to do this was not to rehabilitate himself or because of the Yemaan's threats. He had taken the job because he believed that, sooner or later, Yemaan would have to start paying him, and that would mean money for more drink. How simple!

His entire life, as he recalled it, revolved around finding money to drink. Soul-killing jobs that he couldn't hold, failed dreams about making it big, an automation for a wife, an unrequited romance… these were what had turned him into a buffoon. A drunken buffoon, in fact. One whose life revolved around drink and the means to get it. He had bought his wife a sewing machine. Day and night she stitched without complaint. She was hardly different from the machine itself. But the money she brought in helped buy his arrack. Arrack was something he was never without. Indeed, even if there wasn't rice or sugar in the house he would buy his arrack because his wife wasn't the complaining type. Besides Rosykutty's efforts, if he put on a show or recited funny poetry to the drunken louts in the toddy shop, someone usually bought him a drink. That was the way he lived his life. And now he had undertaken this little bit of unpleasantness because the ex-Inspector of Karuthupuzha would pay him eventually, and that would help buy more liquor.

His grappling with all these thoughts had made him temporarily forget the pain of pushing the bicycle uphill to the gates of the school. The school comprised a few small buildings swarming with children. Some of the naughtiest boys had already dirtied their uniforms. A male teacher (whom the children called "Maash", while the female teacher was simply "Teacher"), was walking around busily, a long cane in hand. Everything was hot and dusty in there. Joby put the cycle on its stand and stood aside. He did not help the little girl dismount. She got off on her own, struggling a bit to keep her balance as the cycle swayed. When she had dismounted, he deliberately left without saying goodbye.

Little Priya looked on as the funny man, funny dog and funny bicycle disappeared. Her legs felt a bit wobbly because of her cramped posture on the bicycle. But that did not prevent her from calling out to Joby: 'Come to fetch me in the evening. Four o' clock. Sharp. And don't drink before you've dropped me home. Remember my Uncle Paachu's conditions!' Not that she herself had met her Uncle Paachu's conditions, given that she had kept up a constant chatter throughout the ride.

The little girl's exhortations didn't have much of an effect on Joby. He mounted the cycle and pedalled fast, making for the toddy shop. Yes, he knew that one of the conditions was to not drink before he dropped Priya back home in the evening. But he couldn't help himself. In fact, he felt a thrill at this show of defiance on his part. As the cycle hissed downhill on its almost flat tyres, he felt the bile rise up his stomach and knew he was going to throw up again.

6.

An Interrogation

'So you are saying, my little one, that my first condition has not been violated?' ex-Inspector Paachu asked, later that evening. 'That Joby was in fact not drunk at all—hadn't drunk a drop—when he came to pick you up after school today?'

'Absolutely, Uncle,' answered Priya quietly, but with a strong emphasis on both words. She stood in front of her uncle, quite unnecessarily like a fugitive, while he sat on the sofa in their front room, his brow furrowed, the day's newspaper beside him. Priya's eyelids drooped slightly—it was a sign that she was about to show stubborn resolve. Paachu knew that look.

'Are you sure?'

'Absolutely, Uncle.'

'But how can you be sure? How acquainted are you, my little one, with drunken men?'

'Well, Uncle,' Priya said, looking outside the window as if the answer to that one might be found there, 'I know, for sure, that if he had had a drink he would have smelt bad. I know that men with drink in their stomachs smell terrible. I know that from the workers in our orchard.'

'Hmm,' her uncle pondered. 'But just for the record...just to be sure, you understand; did he smell of that stuff—the stuff our labourers smell of—when he took you to school this morning?'

'A little, yes.'

'So how do you account for that? Did he drink right in the morning, early morning, before picking you up?'

'I think that was some of last night's smell still in his stomach, Uncle.'

'Ah!' said Paachu with deep satisfaction. He settled back into the sofa. 'Excellent inference. You will make a fine police inspector one day, my young mouse!'

Priya wondered what expression to put on for that. All she was sure of was that she was not letting go of the funny drunk called Joby. She had found him an infinitely better companion on her way to school and back than her uncle. Even with his silence, or maybe because of it, she found Joby very interesting and amusing. She knew that the man occasionally fell asleep pushing the bicycle and that made her rock with giggles. She had also fallen in love with the lanky dog (Joby hadn't yet told her if it was a boy dog or a girl dog, but she would get it out of him), and even the rusty cycle that vibrated when it moved. She wasn't letting go of all that by giving her uncle even one wrong answer. Yes, she had seen, sure as daylight, that Joby was swimming in liquor when he had come to pick her up in the evening. Why, the man could hardly walk, and at times he used his very bicycle to hold him up! But she loved to see him so drunk. And it was infinitely exciting to be pushed on a cycle by a man who was fast asleep. Joby was the one silver lining to this whole school business which she otherwise found cumbersome.

For her uncle Paachu, here was the classical police quandary. Earlier that evening he had waited eagerly, the newspaper in front of him for Sharada's benefit (although he was actually looking out of the window from inside the house—he would normally have been reading the paper while sitting on his easy chair on the outside porch), waiting for Joby and Priya to arrive. He had wanted to discreetly observe if Joby would be drunk. He was gathering evidence, if you will, so that he could prove to his wife that she had made a terrible mistake. He would crack maybe a few bones of Joby's too, and terminate his services on the first day itself. Ever since Priya and Joby had disappeared down the bend in front of their house that morning, he had been uneasy. So much so that he sensed a bout of constipation arriving and had asked Sharada to prepare boiled bananas for dinner.

His uneasiness hadn't been on account of concerns for Priya's safety at all. No, he was sure that Priya would be safe, or the experiment wouldn't even have gone this far. The journey would take place in broad daylight and the roads would be peopled with children and their guardians, shopkeepers and more. It wasn't that at all. It was, instead, the nagging feeling that he might have been wrong. That he was in all probability wrong. The policeman in him revolted against this notion. Would a seasoned alcoholic keep off his drink for an entire morning and part of the evening just because a retired policeman had told him to? Would Joby have observed all the conditions that had been imposed on him?

The real question in all this was, did Joby fear Paachu enough?

He spent all morning thinking about this. His contemplation was so deep that he'd had to re-read all the articles in the newspaper on the first pass. After lunch, when he should have been napping, he was pondering how to gather the undeniable evidence that Joby had broken his conditions. It would give the policeman in him immense satisfaction to prove the violation, plant a punch in the drunk's belly and terminate his services then and there.

Retired, not dead.

He didn't think for a moment about having to drop and pick up Priya again from the very next day onwards and to continue with it until something else could be arranged. He thought only of penalizing Joby for not fearing him enough. He wanted to hurt him physically for breaking the rules. And he wanted to make Sharada realize that people do not change overnight and things are not always what they seem. God, she was so naïve! All her years with a policeman hadn't sharpened her caution one bit.

Later, he had sat on the sofa and not on the porch so that he would remain hidden, giving Joby every opportunity to behave indiscreetly and carelessly when he dropped Priya off. When they arrived, sure enough, it seemed to him that Joby was swaying a little. Hearing the cycle bell Sharada came out of the backyard and was about to go to the door when her husband held her back. They observed through the window as the drunk waited until Priya dismounted (they were glad that she did it on her own and Joby did not help her and thus touch her). With no sign of a goodbye, though Priya waved, Joby turned the cycle and went out of their gates. Paachu observed that the man had begun to run slowly alongside the cycle, preparing to mount the vehicle, but then he had seemed to change his mind and reduced his trot back to a walk. He began walking beside the cycle instead of riding it. Which is what you did, Paachu thought, if you suddenly realized that you were too drunk to ride a cycle.

Paachu debated whether to call Joby to him so he could prove that he was drunk. But what if he wasn't, after all? Wouldn't he make Paachu Yemaan look silly in front of his wife and niece? Instead, he told himself, I will get it out of Priya. That will have greater effect.

Naïve Sharada denied that the man was quite drunk. Infinitely stupid, she even suggested that the bitch walking beside Joby had swayed a bit, too! So Paachu realized that the only way to prove the case was to get it out of little Priya. She had been escorted by the drunk. She should know.

Now the problem was that his little niece was denying it. That wasn't something Paachu had seen coming. Priya had not even fallen for the trap about Joby stinking in the morning. He was half convinced that he had perhaps got it wrong and that Joby hadn't really been drunk when he dropped her back, but he decided to prod her further.

'After dropping you off at the school did Joby seem in a hurry to leave?' Paachu questioned, picking his tooth with a matchstick like he used to in the police station while grilling the accused (who largely consisted of people not more crooked than miserable gamblers who played cards in the town's coconut groves). 'Did he wait at the gates till you went to your class, or did he fly away on his cycle as soon as you had got off?'

'He waited.'

'Hmm,' Paachu wasn't at all convinced. Had there been a second's delay before she processed the question? Joby wasn't quite the type to wait to see the girl enter her class, as far as Paachu knew. Why, just now, when he dropped her back home, the drunk had not even waved goodbye. 'You aren't lying to me, are you?'

'I'm not lying,' she lied.

'Hmm,' he said again, rolling the matchstick on his tongue, 'Okay. Let's see now. You understand why I'm asking you all this, right, little one? It's only for your safety. I need to be sure you're safe with that man.'

'Yes, Uncle.'

'And by the way, how is his riding? Does he balance the bicycle well with you on the carrier?'

'He did not ride it, Uncle,' said Priya, more ready for surprise questions than the card players at his police station had ever been. 'As you had instructed, he only walked alongside while I sat on the carrier.'

'Oh,' said Paachu. 'I mean, how on earth did you reach school on time then? I would have thought Joby might have ridden the cycle once in a while.'

'Not even once, Uncle,' she said, her eyes drooping, even though she wasn't lying this time.

'My, my! The man has taken my conditions very literally, then,' Paachu said, gloating with pleasure. 'So you are fine with him, then. You wish to continue having him ferry you to school and back, I take it?'

'Yes, Uncle.'

And then Paachu asked, 'If you're so convinced then the man must have been very interesting indeed. What stories did he tell you on the way?'

In the kitchen, Sharada was laughing in spite of herself.

'No stories, Uncle. You had told us not to speak a word to each other.'

'Praise the gods, little lady! Are you telling me that you were together for such a long while in the morning and then again in the evening, and not a word passed between you?'

Priya nodded and Paachu again felt light-headed, almost intoxicated, with the fact that his conditions had been met with such uncompromising obedience. Retired he may be, but that drunk still obeyed him and feared him. And yet he said, by way of conclusion, 'What a boring man that Joby is. Doesn't he know how to deal with little children? Not a single story, not one funny anecdote, no quips from mythology, no nothing. God!' But his face was suffused with pleasure.

Out of his sight, his wife almost burst out in laughter again. But her merriment hid a deeper worry. This was to do with Paachu's changing relationship with people around him, especially Priya. Even now, when he had questioned little Priya in typical police style, the scene was amusing, but there was an awkwardness about it that hadn't existed before.

She replayed the scene in her mind. A little while ago Paachu had come in from the orchard and had gone for his evening bath. Priya had been loitering near the outdoor bathroom, looking for birds' nests with eggs. Paachu had always been a violent bather, singing badly and loudly, splashing water about and clanking the mug against the bucket. Every once in a while he would clear his throat with an ear-shattering roar. When he emerged from the bathroom half-dressed, he would start to jump on one leg to clear the water from his ears. Watching from her kitchen window Sharada saw little Priya burst into peals of silent laughter. Paachu had glanced at Priya and it was difficult to divine if he was irritated at her mirth or simply indifferent to it. Whatever he had intended to convey with his look, Priya had stopped giggling immediately and had gone rather red in the face. There used to be a time when Priya would have openly laughed at him and he would have started to rock with laughter himself. It was sad, this change between them. A little later when Paachu sat down to 'question' Priya on the front sofa, it most probably might have looked to Priya like he was actually pulling her up for making fun of him. Sharada knew that he had been planning to question her about Joby, but that wouldn't be how it appeared to the little girl.

As it is, Sharada knew, Priya thought a lot of things her husband did these days were to punish her or shape her for the future he wished for her. Often this was true. But sometimes it was just Priya's own misinterpretation of her uncle's actions, who simply wasn't careful about these things. But this was in keeping with the pattern that had begun ever since Paachu retired—his behaviour was increasingly prone to being misunderstood by other people. His mannerisms, speech and gestures were turning more and more awkward as he aged. When his intention was only to appear serious and weighty, he actually came across as mean and selfish. When he was being thoughtful and analytical, it seemed like he wasn't listening at all. When he would have a rare go at humour it would simply fall flat. Even his attempts at affection were treated poorly, especially by Priya, at whom they were largely directed. Sharada felt she spent a lot of time every day running behind her husband and explaining to other people what he really meant and clarifying why they shouldn't be astounded by his behaviour. She wasn't very successful. Her own niece was fast alienating herself from Paachu. Sharada felt a nagging pity for her husband, whom only she seemed to fully understand.

'Hello, get me Inspector Janardanan, please,' she heard Paachu say in the other room.

He was telephoning the police station! What now, she thought.

After a short delay he spoke into the phone again, 'Good evening Inspector. Who have you put on my case? Ah…Bubru. Hmm. Is he any good? All these new chaps…do they know about policing? Particularly about trailing a suspect?'

Sharada cringed. What was this, dear God!

'Okay…hmm, Bubru. I'll do a little background check on him...'

Trailing a suspect? Had Paachu actually asked for someone from the police station to spy on Joby and Priya, or had she heard wrong? And what would have made the police oblige?

'How many years has he been on the force? Hmm…all right…'

As far as she knew, the men at the police station were actually ringleaders of the mob that found Paachu ridiculous and funny. What would have made them take Paachu seriously enough to assign someone to trail Joby and Priya? But she didn't have to wait for her answer, because Paachu was speaking it out for her.

'I'm paying this Constable Bubru the drunk's salary; please tell him to remember that. Yes, yes. Oh, very much. Hmm…please ask Mr Bubru to give me a full report after the first week…Yes, that's good.…Very kind of you to say that, Inspector Janardanan. Thank you.' He banged the phone down.

In the kitchen, Sharada stood listening to her own heart thump in her chest. If what she understood was correct—and she couldn't see how else it could be—her husband had taken this way too far. He had bribed the policemen to have some constable follow Joby around discreetly.

Sharada knew then that this whole business with Joby would come to a bad end. And it would invite fresh laughter from the town. The only reason the police had obliged Paachu—apart from the bribe money that should have been poor Joby's wages—was because it would give everyone another chance to laugh at the former inspector. What a colossal joke it would be. First, Paachu had hired Karuthupuzha's infamous drunk to ferry his niece and then hired the police to protect her from the very same drunk. What would photographer Varky do with it, she wondered. Paachu had given him the perfect subject on a platter. And that old ex-military man Pariera—he would cluck his tongue and 'perfectly understand' a fellow retiree's turmoil. That would embarrass her husband all the more. The maidservants would giggle away and whisper the ridiculous story to each other from behind wash stones at the riverside. Old women would say that Paachu had gone insane and was paying for his past sins (he had killed a man, remember?). Young men would gather under trees and add absurd details of their own invention to the already hilarious anecdote. Housewives would wait for their husbands to come home in the evenings, bursting to tell them this funny tale.

And to think that this whole thing was her idea!

At first, Sharada simply panicked. Then she prayed to her favourite god, Lord Murugan, cupping her hands before a small picture of the deity that she had placed on a shelf. As she continued to pray, her pain began to ebb away.

As she had done over and over again since Paachu had retired, she reminded herself that the attempt to rehabilitate Joby through the good offices of her husband had, in essence, to do with the larger project she had taken upon herself—to get her husband to do something noble and good that would raise him in the esteem of the townsfolk. She wanted the people of Karuthupuzha to see that while he had been a strict and powerful policeman all his life, he was now a kind-hearted and noble soul as he approached old age. She wished that the people's fear of Paachu Yemaan would be replaced not with ridicule and scepticism but with love and veneration. When Barber Sureshan had put things the way he did, she had seen a natural and easy opportunity. Just one day had passed since the plan had been put into motion and her husband had already succeeded in messing it up. Getting the police involved was something even she hadn't expected of him.

She felt gripped by a sense of helplessness—something that had occurred thousands of times in her life with him. Whenever she tried to change him just a tiny bit, in ways she couldn't predict he always seemed to return to the way he basically was. It seemed absolutely impossible to bring something softer into his heart, some noble emotion or desire to do good.

Yes, this whole Joby business would come to a bad end. A policeman to trail a girl going to school! The town would mock Paachu and he would spiral into a deep depression. And all she could do was stand by and watch.

Sharada's eyes welled up as she prayed to Lord Murugan. She prayed that her husband might graduate to being his age; that he might adapt to the fact that he was now retired from being a policeman; that he might be content with a peaceful life of loving and looking after his wife and his little niece. She prayed that the townsfolk wouldn't mock her husband; that they would see the anguish in her heart and forgive her husband for having been a terror. But most of all she prayed that by some miracle her horrible little idea would come undone and Joby would go back to his drinking and Paachu would continue to ferry Priya around.

Sharada knew that if she suggested to Paachu that he fire Joby, he would only get very angry. 'I'm not here to hire him and fire him according to your whims,' he would say. Maybe I'm blowing this all out of proportion, she thought. Maybe it will all work out. But she fervently wished that Paachu hadn't got Karuthupuzha's police involved. She instinctively felt a deep mistrust for Inspector Janardanan. She believed that the police were only waiting for an opportunity to humiliate and punish their former boss.

7.

Men in Khaki

These days there is plenty that has changed about the one place Sharada dreaded the most—the Karuthupuzha Police Station. The slither of time has introduced new things, starting with a fresh coat of whitewash on the otherwise decrepit building. Set against vast golden fields, the station can be seen from very far away—it reminds you of a matchbox that has caught fire in the burning sun. Rusty cycles are piled up next to the compound wall; they have been confiscated from numerous drunken riders over the decades. A police jeep is parked in front of the station. Up close, the police station abruptly resolves itself into what it actually is—a quintessential government building, its very walls and roof tiles announcing the fact that no one has ever really cared about it. This part hasn't changed, and it never will. When you enter this station you will be greeted by the smell of old and decaying files, dust and betel juice. You will also detect the strong, acidic smell of human urine. It is unlikely that the ancient steel almirahs and creaky shelves will ever be replaced or that you will be greeted by the sight of policemen briskly going about their duties.

But for now let us just stay with the changes that have taken place—the whitewash on the outside walls (sloppily applied but then you can't have everything). And although the files are the same, albeit with fine dust on them, the steel almirahs still grow out of the cement floor like ancient monoliths, the smell of urine still burns the eyes, and in the corners of the roof are the same team of spiders that have observed Paachu Yemaan retire and Inspector Janardanan take charge, many of the policemen in the station are new, or have new responsibilities. Although the new inspector sits, like the old one, in an inner room which is his own, he prefers to come to the front of his unnecessarily big table and lean against it. Having observed him at times when he thinks he is alone, the spiders on the ceiling know that Inspector Janardanan is plagued by haemorrhoids so that he cannot sit for too long. These haemorrhoids have the ability to irritate this man or make him morose. Apart from the times that he is thus irritated, Inspector Janardanan is quite the opposite of Paachu. He is composed, always rested, often poetic, famously romantic.

On the morning after Joby's first day of employment with Paachu, Inspector Janardanan was in a terrific mood. He had come out of his room and was leaning against a table in the constables' chamber. Mouth filled with betel juice that issued a fresh aroma and an occasional droplet here or there, the inspector was adding to the brightness of the day with the inherent happiness that he experienced on days when his behind wasn't hurting. It was clear that it was this man's personality that had brought about a great change in Karuthupuzha Police Station.

'Kimivahi madhuraanaam mandanam naakriteenaam?' he enquired, before translating: 'What, pray, is not ornamental upon a beautiful form? Anything, *anything,* will only add to the beauty of one whom nature has endowed with a magnificent form. You understand, men? On a poor woman who is beautiful, even a hole in her garb looks alluring! Even poverty moves us to a form of pity that is close to aching love, when it is a beautiful woman who is poor. It's a subtle point I am making here, men, but one that must have occurred to you at some point, if only you had taken care to make a note of it. If you are worshippers of beauty, you will see how the poet has magically conveyed a great truth of the universe.'

All the others in the room were leaning against their desks as it was indecorous to sit when their chief was standing. Kuttykrishnan, a young constable with a large rifle doubling up as a walking stick on which he leaned, spread his hands heavenwards to show deep agreement with what the chief was saying. This constable was forever inside the station when he was meant to be outside, guarding the entrance, because he was forever looking to agree with his chief. His eyes poured out great admiration for Inspector Janardanan and his brow was stretched to reflect his deep concentration.

'Nature conspires to bring together all the elements to add beauty to what is already beautiful,' Janardanan was saying and a droplet of betel juice made a spot on a paperweight at a nearby desk. He ceremoniously walked up to the window and spat noisily onto the ground outside.

Leaning against an almirah, gradually turning into the bottle-green colour of the almirah itself in his deep desire for camouflage, was Constable Sukumaran. He was the oldest man in the station and was due to retire soon. Everyone had a soft corner for this man, who was mild of manner and inconspicuous. A tiny hint of a wince almost surfaced on his wrinkled face at the noise the chief made while spitting but it immediately disappeared into the background like the rest of him.

A little away from him, shifting his weight more and more onto a desk so that he was almost sitting on it, was Constable Chandy. He stared with owl-like eyes at this new chief of his. One couldn't quite make out what was on his mind. It was generally suspected that Chandy still owed allegiance to the previous inspector upon whom he had fawned for most of his career. Though not a man of strong character or intelligence, Chandy could not switch his allegiance entirely to the new man so abruptly. He remembered the way he had served Yemaan, the way he had driven the police jeep for him with the sirens blaring though there was no need for them, the way he had whispered 'Yemaan is coming, make way for Yemaan' at the cinema when Paachu and family arrived to watch the evening show, the way he had sometimes negotiated Yemaan's bribes for him with truck drivers who wished to pass contraband items on and the way he had held his head respectfully low when Yemaan insulted him. He remembered the way his eyes had sometimes threatened to spill tears when Paachu Yemaan had granted that he had done a good job. These moments were rare, but even now he thought of them with deep gratitude and a lump in his throat. Perhaps right now, as he stared with his round eyes at Janardanan, he was thinking that this man would never take the place of the one true Yemaan in his heart. For all his poetry on beauty and the deep philosophizing, Janardanan would never win Chandy over to his side, it seemed.

'Talking of beauty, the form of woman is but one manifestation. Have you observed a cow? With her velvet skin and deeply complying eyes…oh! There is no better example of nature's beauty than the cow. Dhenunam asmi Kamadhuk, says the Lord Himself! Meaning,' Janaradanan held his arm up and touched his forefinger to his thumb, 'Among cows, I am the wish-fulfilling Kamadhenu. So Lord Krishna is looking out of her eyes in an expression of bounty.'

Also listening in respectful silence was Jaleel Ikka, the jailer who had replaced the previous jailer, Raveendran. From time to time this man looked into the prison, as was his duty. Behind the thick bars stood Karuthupuzha's most frequent prisoner—also listening appreciatively. This prisoner had been known as Neerkoli, or the grass snake, for such a long time that it was said that even he had forgotten his real name. He was a petty thief against whom nothing could ever be proved. But everyone knew that he stole chickens and sometimes young goats, because whenever these creatures disappeared from households, he disappeared too, for some time. When he reappeared, the police would instantly arrest him and put him behind bars for a little while in order to straighten him out. He was called Neerkoli because, like the grass snake, he wasn't really poisonous at all. And like the grass snake which disappears under water when startled, he too, vanished whenever guilty or spooked. So frequent a guest of the police was Neerkoli that, but for his lack of uniform and the bars in front of him, he might have been mistaken for a policeman.

'And everything about a cow is so serene,' said Constable

Kuttykrishnan as if these were things he and his boss had observed together. He knew that Janardanan liked short interruptions to assure him that his audience was listening and that his speech wasn't turning into a monologue. 'Can you think of milk in any colour other than white, the colour of serenity?'

'Milk in any colour other than white! Ha ha ha, what a ridiculous thought!' Janardanan guffawed, looking quizzically at the others; even though he had been slighted, Kuttykrishnan did not mind. 'By the way, all this talk of the cow reminds me that Velayudhan is looking to sell his cow. Beautiful piece of work she is, healthy and bounteous in yield. Her udder is the size of a small pillow, I tell you. And he is quoting a very good price, which I can bring down further. Any buyers?'

This was the trouble with listening to Inspector Janardanan for any length of time; apart from being a policeman he was also a broker, middleman and negotiator. This wasn't a skill he was born with. It was something that he had developed in a previous town where he had been Head Constable. In that town most of the cases that came to him were of the type which, in his opinion, could not be resolved using conventional policing methods or the law. In fact Janardanan quite disliked the law. He felt that laws did not solve problems but usually only compounded them. Laws did not make people understand and tolerate each other. They were imposed on people, firing their indignation and fuelling their stubbornness. Laws forced obedience, giving a person no option but to comply with a way of being that did not grow out of his own way of doing things and seeing the world. It was the law, in the first place, that made people resort to illegality, because whatever the law, the instinctive reaction of people was to figure out how to circumvent it. Instead of doing things according to the law, high-flown talk and empathetic negotiation (usually laced with uplifting Sanskrit verses) often brought about just settlements. So when a fishmonger came to him saying a neighbour had stolen his fish, Janardanan first spoke and listened until he began to feel that the man was in the right. (You can always *feel* when a man is right, and also when a man is lying, Janardanan often said.) He would use his police powers to make the neighbour pay back the complainant—not in cash, so it didn't hurt so much, but in kind, say, with an unused fishing net. When an employee complained that his mothalali, his boss, hadn't paid him last month's wages, Janardanan would have a word with the mothalali and find that, to be fair to him, the employee had been missing from work for most of the month. So he gently but surely would push the mothalali to part with just a few utensils from his wife's kitchen, which she wouldn't mind so much because their departure from the kitchen would only get her rich husband to buy her some new utensils. These utensils would be given as compensation to the employee, making *his* wife in turn very happy, so that there was peace. In this manner, Janardanan, the head constable, settled case after case peacefully, negotiating and making people see sense rather than enforcing the inflexible rule of law. He gradually turned into an accomplished negotiator. Over time he figured out that even when there was no complaint, no police case as such, he could still use his skills to help people buy and sell used goods. He was a master at negotiating prices and being a policeman his clients often complied with his suggestions just to be in his good books. He got a small commission out of every deal and that made him very happy. Not being a married man in spite of his age, Janardanan lived comfortably off his salary plus this supplementary income.

Much as he was appreciated among townsfolk for his brokerage skills, his subordinates at the station quite dreaded them. When he directly asked them to buy something, such as now, they could not refuse him. As Janardanan deliberately made his suggestions very ambiguous his staff did not know whether he was acting as a broker or a boss when he brought them a deal. As a result of all this, no sooner had Janardanan taken charge than new things began to show up in his subordinates' homes—a rusty old fridge in Chandy's house, a pair of slightly odd-sized boots at Jaleel Ikka's, a young goat and a black-and-white television set in Kuttykrishnan's, which joined a collection of battered encyclopaedia and some creaky chairs, all of which he hoped would one day earn him a promotion. Now he looked intently down at his own boots, hoping that the chief wouldn't turn to him for this cow deal. Though it would be a sound investment to buy the cow and please the chief, he simply hadn't the money just then. Constable Chandy shifted his weight on the desk, carefully moving a few papers as if they were incredibly important documents. Only Neerkoli looked directly at Inspector Janardanan, apparently wondering if he shouldn't just steal such an illustrious cow once he got out of here thereby solving all their problems.

Luckily for them, Janardanan moved on from looking to close the deal with his colleagues, 'I was asking our venerable ex-Inspector Paachu, you know, if he wanted the cow. I mean, it made sense to me. The old man is retired and has all the time in the world to bathe and milk the cow and keep himself engaged. What do you think?'

'A cow would be just what he needs, if you think about it,' Kuttykrishnan said with immense relief.

'But no! The venerable ex-Inspector was annoyed at the suggestion,' Janardanan continued. 'Not of very sound judgement anymore, our Paachu Yemaan, eh? I only tried to impress upon the man the goodness of a peacefully retired life milking his own cow and looking after his wife and niece.'

All laughed, except Chandy and Sukumaran.

'And that wife of his! Looking after her should be such a pleasure,' continued Janardanan who, embarrassingly enough for Chandy and Sukumaran, was known to have a soft corner for even old ladies. 'A true goddess, that lady. No, no, I really mean it. I'm not sneering. It's just that such a bull of a man truly doesn't deserve a partner as graceful as her. Why, if I had a wife like that I would have burned my khaki and sat at home.'

Kuttykrishnan began sniggering. With great agility he adjusted to the changing moods of his boss. He had been deeply moved by Janardanan's concepts of beauty seconds ago, and now he saw that it was time for light talk.

'But our hard-headed ex-Inspector, of course, does not see her beauty at all! He still prefers to play the policeman when he has the option of a fine retired life with a decent pension and an apsara, a real creature of the heavens, to spend it on. Absolutely hard-headed, that man! Do you know, when I took charge here, a few months into my new job, this Yemaan, as you all address him, came to my home one evening and had a drink with me. I imagined at first that it was the beginning of a great friendship. Half-way into the first drink he began lecturing me about policing in Karuthupuzha, like it was very different here, something they didn't train you for. To listen to him I thought this was one of those bandit-infested towns, you know, with at least one murder happening every night. I wondered why no one had warned me about this before. And then I realized, our man likes being bombastic. That's why he keeps that big moustache, like a dead lizard, above his mouth! Ha ha.

'Mr Paachu's point was that, though retired, he ought to be involved in all policing activities here as before. He should be allowed to help. "Only I know the law and order peculiarities of this town," he said to me. I couldn't believe it. I couldn't believe that someone would want to be associated with this job when he could simply sit at home with that wife and enjoy a pension. What a funny bird he is, that man! Naturally I told him that we had the manpower here to function on our own without having to rely on our retired policemen. I also told him that, in the little time I had spent here, Karuthupuzha did not seem to be a rogue town. Why, thank the good lord for our Neerkoli here or we wouldn't know what we were here for.'

He went over and patted the petty thief through the thick bars. Neerkoli beamed with pride. Chandy began browsing through a thick ledger to show that he was going to play no part in insulting Paachu Yemaan. Jaleel Ikka and Kuttykrishnan smirked. Inspector Janardanan spat noisily out of the window again and continued, 'You won't believe it but when I refused his suggestion that he might be allowed to interfere in station matters, the man just got up, put his glass down and went away. That was how rude he was. I was given to know that the very next day our Yemaan, the Yemaan of all of us, shot off a letter to headquarters complaining how the law and order situation in Karuthupuzha had deteriorated under the new "soft" inspector. And guess what he cited to back his observation? He spoke about one streetlight being stolen. Then he wrote about how that haunted well to the west of town is being allowed to terrorize the townspeople (as if it is the job of the police to arrest rumour-mongers and ghosts). He listed instances of drunks being permitted to fall unconscious at peoples' doorsteps. These were examples of the "severe law and order shortcomings" under the present "soft" inspector.'

'And did headquarters take prompt "action"?' Kuttykrishnan asked, in the same tone of mock seriousness as his chief, showing great interest in the story though he had heard it several times already.

'Yes, they acted very promptly,' said Janardanan. 'Headquarters replied within the same week, delicately suggesting that perhaps ex-Inspector Paachu might like to join the prestigious club of retired police officers that had a branch in the city. They didn't say so outright, but they obviously figured that might help him pass the time.'

Janardanan began to guffaw loudly, sending sprays of betel juice in all directions. Constable Sukumaran wondered if he should get inside the almirah and close the doors. Chandy wiped his left eye into which a drop had landed, then went inside to wash off the stain. Kuttykrishnan began guffawing, letting a dripping line of red betel juice on his forearm remain there for the time being. Jaleel Ikka laughed with genuine mirth. Neerkoli, still flushed from the Inspector's praise, contributed with a smile of admiration.

'And yet, my men, I did not bear any grudge. I still spoke decorously to him; in fact I still do. Because I believe life is too short for grudges. For all things un-beautiful. I acted like I hadn't known at all about his correspondence with the head office. When I met him on the street one evening I told him about a good writing desk that Ponnappan Aashari, the carpenter, wanted to sell. It was not about the deal, honest. I asked Mr Yemaan to buy it for his precious daughter....'

'That's his niece,' Kuttykrishnan interjected. 'He doesn't have children.'

'Oh, yes, yes, I know,' Janardanan continued, 'though I cannot imagine someone like that goddess wife of his not bearing children. I mean, it is said that women with wide hips, you know, curvaceous women, are very fertile....'

Constable Chandy, who had returned from the bathroom, cleared his throat. He looked tormented. 'Anyway. So I asked him if he wished to buy that writing desk, you know, as an investment for his niece. She could use it as a study table. It was pure teakwood, seasoned too. My intention was to get the man busy looking after his kin in his old age. I thought when he shifted his attention to his niece's education he would turn away from being a policeman at last. But then, as our masters have said: "Upadeshohi moorkhaana prakopaay na shantaye. Payaha paanam bhujangaanaam kevalam vishavardhanam". Anyone knows what this means?'

They all shook their heads. Kuttykrishnan wondered if he shouldn't learn a little Sanskrit in the evenings.

'It means,' Janardanan said in the tone of a great guru, 'advising fools will not calm them down. It will only make them angrier. Just like feeding a snake will only actually increase its venom. The man did not buy the desk at all! In fact he acted like *I* might have some vested interest in it. Then he went home and wrote another letter to headquarters. This time he suggested that retired police officers should be allowed the use of the police jeep. What a cracked nut. I suggested that he buy a writing desk for his niece and he thought he should be allowed to continue using the jeep!'

'I've heard he hates taking his niece to school on his scooter,' Jaleel Ikka said quietly. He held a pencil between his fingers in an unconscious craving for a cigarette. 'It goes against his tough policeman image.'

'Hmm. In any case, this time, the head office did not even bother sending a reply,' Janardanan said. He then turned and walked into his room, because it was time for him to sit down. They all followed him into the inner room. Jaleel Ikka wedged the swing doors, so that the prisoner Neerkoli could continue to listen.

'Yes, he hates taking his niece to school and back,' Janardanan said, sitting down after once again spitting loudly out of a window. 'He will only like it if he can use the police jeep for it. So he went and had his next grand idea. This one is a true masterpiece, men. You know what he did? He hired that drunk buffoon Joby to take his child to school!'

Someone, presumably Kuttykrishnan, gasped loudly in a show of surprise, though the fact of Joby's employment was quite widely known by now.

'Joby, that walking arrack shop, of all people!' the Inspector guffawed again. 'And it doesn't end there. After he had employed the most eligible person in town, he had this mild, distant doubt plaguing his sharp mind—would Joby do the job well enough? Was it remotely possible that he might bring that little girl to harm, since he had this negligible drinking issue? Ha ha!

'So then our Yemaan called me again. Well, you won't believe what he asked for this time. He wanted a constable to trail Joby and his little niece on their way to school in the mornings, and then back from school in the evenings! As an ex-inspector, this, according to him, was a minimum privilege.'

'Oh!' Kuttykrishnan exclaimed, pretending this was news. 'If I heard you right, Paachu asked for a constable from among us to spy on a stupid drunk?'

'That's right.'

'What nerve!' Kuttykrishnan said, looking around at the others. 'What does he think the police are for? I hope you gave him a piece of your mind at last.'

'Oh, I thought of doing that,' Inspector Janardanan said, 'But then I thought it would be more fun to comply with his request.

After all, what great work do we have here? It doesn't take all of us to arrest Neerkoli.'

They all laughed at that, even Chandy.

'You men ought to have heard the way he asked for a Constable,' Janardanan continued. 'Asked, not requested. Said it was the responsibility of the police to ensure the wellbeing of schoolchildren! Ha ha, how comical. It's difficult to get angry with such people. Whenever he comes up with ridiculous stuff like this, Paachu becomes all authoritative and uses big words, grand phrases, all lawyer-like. Hee hee! Then he pretends his listener is already convinced. Wellbeing of schoolchildren, it seems! I almost laughed into the phone, but then I decided, who am I to deny us all some good fun? I said okay. So men, I have put our Bubru on the case.'

'Ah, I was wondering where Bubru was yesterday and today,' Kuttykrishnan said.

'It's not just fun for Bubru, it's money, too,' Janardanan said with mock seriousness. 'You know, the Yemaan is paying Bubru for his services. And I figured that Bubru is the best among us for all this; he loves this discreet, shady stuff. Man of the dark, he is.'

Two of the oldest spiders on the ceiling exchanged knowing glances. They knew that Janardanan would get a share of the money Paachu would pay Bubru, of course. They knew that though you wouldn't think so to hear Janardanan speak thus behind his back, it was Constable Bubru with whom he was the closest at the station. For all the desperate and incessant efforts Kuttykrishnan made to please his boss, it was Bubru who was Janardanan's confidante. Bubru had in his nature the right degree of cruelty, ruthlessness and indifference towards police discipline and rules to endear himself to Inspector Janardanan.

'Bubru is supposed to keep watch on Joby and the child,' Janardanan was saying, 'and give the respected Yemaan a full report whenever asked.'

'I wonder why Bubru took it up,' Jaleel Ikka said and then immediately answered himself. 'For the money probably. But I think he will sleep away the day and claim his prize. Will he really follow that drunk around?'

'Oh yes, he will,' Janardanan said. 'That's our Bubru. I tell you, he likes this kind of thing. He will trail the child and the drunk all day, and if I know him, he will create trouble for them, as well as for the great Yemaan just for the fun of it. Don't ask me how or what kind of trouble; wait and watch. There will be some fun in Karuthupuzha at last!'

The chatter went on for some time, with Janardanan and Kuttykrishnan forming theories about how Bubru would mess things up for Paachu and Joby, because messing things up was Bubru's speciality. The man would take money from Paachu and create trouble for him, simply because such evil jokes were his idea of spice in life. While most of them laughed, Chandy and Sukumaran continued to look around embarrassed, torn between lingering loyalty to their ex-Chief and the new drift in the station. Chandy briefly wondered if he should go over and report to Paachu Yemaan all that he had heard today and impress upon him the dangers of first hiring a drunk to ferry his niece, and then hiring an absolutely insensitive and unscrupulous—even dangerous—man like Bubru to follow them around. But he knew that it wasn't his place to advise the ex-Inspector. He had never really been granted the familiarity to talk freely to Paachu Yemaan in spite of loyally serving the man for decades. Sukumaran, in his turn, was only deeply puzzled. He did not think all this would amount to any deep trouble for anyone. If he knew the people involved, this would all end very shortly. Joby would simply not turn up in the mornings and Paachu would fire him and then Bubru would not be needed either. That's how it would all end, probably within the first week itself. But what puzzled Sukumaran was the change that seemed to have come upon Paachu Yemaan. What had happened to the man? Why was he behaving in a way that made the whole town laugh at him? What on earth had happened to the once serious and by no means stupid man since his retirement?

'Okay now,' Janardanan said in a bored voice, settling back in his chair and cracking his fingers. This was the sign that the show was over and the men could go back to their places so that he could take his nap. 'That orphan hasn't brought in the tea yet…find out what is happening.' Kuttykrishnan went out of the room immediately to telephone the teashop. Janardanan yawned, dribbled red juice, did not realize it, and continued sleepily, 'And release that Neerkoli. If you hold him a little longer the ruffian will make the government buy him lunch. And by the way, men, think about that cow. Velayudhan has taken good care of her. Decide among yourselves who wants to buy her. Oh, you should see those udders….'

8.

A School Romance

Joby looked down at the sleeping form of his wife. The kind of powerful, almost violent, and heavily guilt-ridden hate he felt for her was not unlike what he had felt from time to time when he looked at the little girl on his bicycle. Rosykutty was still beautiful, after long years with a drunk, and that irked him all the more. She was like marble—white, smooth, cold and glorious in spite of what the seasons tried to do to damage it. The grey strands in her hair seemed to contribute to her perfection.

Joby washed his face several times to clear it of the effects of the previous night's drinking. Then he made himself some strong black coffee, which did him good. As he went through his morning ablutions, he thought about this whole business of trying to get back into the good books of the town. Barber Sureshan, out of the goodness of his heart, was trying to rehabilitate Joby. But he wondered if any of it was worth it when all he stood to get was a sound beating or an insult from Paachu Yemaan in place of a salary. It had now been quite a few days into this charade and each day he feared that the ex-Inspector would come down on him for one thing or the other. He had missed a couple of mornings when he simply could not get out of bed but, surprisingly, Paachu Yemaan had simply filled in for him without complaining. It looked ominously like the man was waiting for him to make a bigger mistake so that he could deal with him with finality.

He came back to his bedroom to change into his sweaty pants, and looked at his wife again. A memory surfaced of the first fight they'd had—if you could call it a fight because she had refused to fight back.

In the early years of their marriage, as Joby was trying to get used to his wife's lack of personality and her curiously emotionless state by filling himself with arrack, matters came to a head. It was inevitable because every day she shattered another dream of his about marriage; dreams he had created in the depths of his romantic heart and dreams his worthless friends had filled him with. When she came out of her bath, her hair sticking to her head and droplets of water clinging to her neck, something still stirred painfully in him. He thought of what life could have been. But then she moved like a doll, silent and automated, and he would be forced back into his present reality. He saw that he only desired her the way you might desire something in the heavens; in some sense she was never completely attainable. This was how things stood in the early stages of their marriage, and this was the setting for their first fight.

Rosykutty had a peculiar habit. She would place objects on the very edge of shelves and tables. For example, when she put containers on the dining table, they threatened to fall off and shatter on the floor. At night she would place the jug of water on the bedside table in such a way that about half of it stuck out into thin air. While dusting the shelf in their living room she would replace the timepiece so precariously that it looked like a little man staring down a cliff, contemplating suicide. Most things, from pots and bottles in the kitchen to powder tins, jugs and torches in the bedroom to old newspaper bundles, watches, combs, dictionaries, photo-albums and candle stands would totter on the very edge of shelves across the house. This habit of hers had mildly irritated Joby from the outset. Time and again he would push some of the things back so they wouldn't fall off. But now, as the stress within him mounted, his irritation was climbing. Whenever he saw something placed precariously, he would begin to feel increasingly angry. One night at dinner he spoke to her abruptly, almost gritting his teeth, 'Why do you always place things at the edge, so the slightest wind will make them crash to the floor? Are you…are you mad?'

Not one thing had crashed to the floor so far, was what her answer should have been. Everyone has his or her peculiarities, was what she ought to have added. His turning into an unmistakable alcoholic could have received mention. And then he might have countered these with the question as to why she wished to wait for the first thing to fall off, and why she did this in the first place, and what really was her problem, and whether she was a normal human being at all. He might have pointed out that perhaps she had something to do with turning a perfectly normal young man into an alcoholic. But all this had no chance to be discussed, for Rosykutty got up, and without a word pushed the pots of curry and rice on the table back away from the edge, sat down again and resumed her meal calmly. Joby felt his heart jerk about frantically like a tethered boat in a storm. Though he had already been quite drunk at dinner, he had more arrack that night after she had peacefully fallen asleep.

The next evening when he came home from the toddy shop, he saw that the timepiece was once again looking down from the edge of the neatly dusted shelf. He picked it up and smashed it on the floor. It turned into a million satisfying bits of springs, needles, glass shards and little wheels. He then walked to the kitchen and began sweeping all the tins and pots and pans that had been placed on the edge to the floor. By the time he had moved to their bedroom and was breaking the jug of water and other objects that lined the edges of the shelves, Rosykutty was looking at him with moderate alarm. After half the house was shattered, Joby went out, got on his bicycle and rode back to the toddy shop.

That was their first real fight but she had refused to reciprocate. After that things moved away from the edge and he felt a little euphoric, because he seemed to have made an impact on her. But it lasted only for a short while. Within a few days, on the shelf in the kitchen, the tins had moved to the edge. A month later, the new water jug protruded halfway into the air. Gradually everything was back to normal, and even the new timepiece stood looking gloomily down at the floor like its predecessor. Years later, Joby began narrating this as a funny anecdote to listeners in the toddy shop. Many people pointed out that if their wives had been half as pretty as Joby's Rosykutty, they would easily have forgiven this. Many allusions, often uncouth, were made of his wife's beauty but Joby refused to see the ugliness of drunken men discussing his wife because at the end of it they bought him free arrack for the entertainment that had been provided.

So now, this miserable morning, some days after he had first picked up little Priya from her home, he stood looking down at his sleeping wife. He saw that she was ageing, which was a relief. It would have been really frustrating if she had stayed young—not reacting even to the passage of time. As he gazed at her he wondered again what his motivation was in taking up this job, if Paachu Yemaan wasn't even going to pay him. Then he sighed, pulled his pants on and went to get his cycle after cynically blowing his sleeping Rosykutty a kiss.

◆

A little later he was once again pushing his bicycle with Priya perched on it. As was normal, the little girl was talking continuously. She was by now used to his absolute refusal to respond to anything she said. In order to compensate, she would often say something, imagine his response, respond to that and so on and on. As they passed an expansive paddy field she was saying: '…and today they will check on it. We were all betting on who will win but I think the teachers will stop it before it starts.'

Occasionally Lilly would stop sniffing at interesting things by the roadside and look back suspiciously. She growled when there was a sharp but faint clank of metal against stone. Joby, too, looked behind him because he was sure they were being followed. But his movement was slow, painful, almost creaky, so that the form that was behind them was always able to comfortably slip behind a tree.

In spite of his creakiness Joby had to admit to himself that he was feeling just a tiny bit better nowadays. This was because now, after years, he would have his first drink only in the evenings after dropping Priya back home. He didn't drink through the day simply because it was too much of an effort to get back to the school with his head swimming and then hide from Paachu Yemaan when he dropped Priya back. In the evenings, of course, he drank a lot more than usual to compensate. He would enter the toddy shop a thirsty spirit and begin guzzling much to the pleasure of the other drinkers who were immensely entertained by his desperation. They would make him repeat stories of how he'd been hired by Paachu Yemaan to ferry the bad-tempered ex-Inspector's precious niece to school and back. Jokes would do the rounds about Paachu Yemaan, his wife Sharada and even about Barber Sureshan who, it was now widely known, had brokered this monstrously funny deal.

'It was going to happen anyway,' Priya was saying. 'Everyone knew it. They were the only two young people in the whole school, so everyone knew—Head Maash, the other teachers, and even us students—that Kannan Maash and Ambili Teacher would fall in love. But still when they fell in love, everyone was surprised....'

With a burning forehead, his eyes squinting against the gradually brightening day, Joby listened to the girl talk about the budding love story between Kannan Maash and Ambili Teacher in her school. He had heard about it at the toddy shop in great detail. It was the topic on everyone's tongue nowadays, but it was amusing to see how it was even the topic on this little girl's tongue. Joby wondered how old Priya was. Eight? But her talk sometimes made her seem older.

'In the early days, when they looked at each other, everyone knew, though *they* thought no one knew. They thought it's like in the movies, when the hero sings for the heroine but all those watching still don't know they're in love. In the early days, I am saying. Later on it became well-known....'

The morning breeze, the pleasant smell of the standing crop, the sight of the many-coloured butterflies in the shrubs by the road—all these continued to make Joby feel better. It was in a relaxed state of mind that he listened to this new version of the love story of Kannan Maash and Ambili Teacher.

In the early days of his infatuation, Kannan Maash would just look at Ambili Teacher and smile. At first Ambili Teacher smiled back in the friendly manner of a colleague. But later when she realized his smile sprang from his growing love for her, she stopped returning his smile. It wasn't that she was shy; she was scared of what was going on. But why did she fear him?

Everyone in Karuthupuzha knew that of the two, Ambili Teacher was the smart, efficient one. She was full of youthful energy and moved about swiftly like one who couldn't be bothered with time-consuming processes like love and romance. Kannan Maash was a soft, almost child-like man, short and slightly stocky, with intense eyes. Most women, upon laying eyes on him, would try to mother him. Women felt comfortable in his presence.

'Then, slowly, Kannan Maash stopped smiling at her openly,' Joby heard Priya say. 'This was a long time after he began falling in love, you understand? He realized at last that when he smiled she was terrified. Ha ha!'

Joby again looked at Priya. She sat on the carrier, clutching the seat in front of her, stooping slightly to take the load of her bag, her legs tucked beneath her, and her thin hair often falling upon her face. Joby felt the rush of an emotion, vague but powerful, that quite stunned him with its suddenness. He wanted to reach out and hug this little girl who refused to be quiet and chattered on about love.

The moment passed and he drifted back into the spell of her narration.

'So he stopped smiling at her and even looking at her,' Priya went on. 'Poor Ambili Teacher! We could see that she was silently waiting to see if he would smile at her again. But he was now very careful not to terrify her, so he totally turned away from her!'

That should have been the end of the love story. But Kannan

Maash couldn't let go because he was truly in love. He did something very clever.

Whenever he was teaching in a classroom where Ambili Teacher had the very next class, he would write love poetry on the blackboard and ask the children not to rub it away! He told them to keep staring at the verses and repeating them in their heads until the next teacher came along and rubbed the board clean. And thus Kannan Maash told Ambili Teacher of his love, through pristine poetry scribbled on the blackboard. Being a teacher of literature, he had a storehouse of poetry to pick from. He chose verses according to the mood of his love—sometimes from our mythology, sometimes from contemporary verse, occasionally lines that were deeply philosophical, some beautiful, some tragic, some coy.

All the children knew that the poetry was for the benefit of Ambili Teacher. Everyone played along, everyone enjoyed the verses in their context and every child felt great joy at sharing the secret. As for Ambili Teacher, the children could see that she initially did not divine at all the meaning of the verses on the board when she entered the class. Gradually, as their meaning dawned on her, she would go to the board in a hurry (to hide her joy or her anger?) and rub the verses away. At the end of her own class she would scribble terribly dull mathematical concepts on the board to show that she had no part in all this.

Priya's tinkling laughter filled the air and Joby realized that he was actually listening to her every word. And he thought, amusedly, that life is like a jackfruit. Whichever way you cut it, whichever angle you slice it, you meet fresh flesh and seeds—whole sweet arrays of them. He had turned down this path and now he had discovered this little girl was more than an irritating piece of cargo that he ferried about. She was an observing, thinking and talking being—a new array of sweet flesh and seeds—whose opinions and insights were often that of someone far more mature and older than she actually was. Gradually, he was trying to engage with her in a way he couldn't have imagined.

'See, even he finds it funny,' she was saying to Lilly, 'Hey doggy! You find it funny, no?'

Joby gave Lilly a little shove with his foot, cleared his throat and addressed the bitch, 'Good girl, Lilly. Walk girl; walk fast, Lilly.' For the first time he had spoken out aloud, but he had only spoken to Lilly, so that Paachu's condition wasn't violated.

'Oh, he's a she?' Priya exclaimed, excited beyond words. 'Lilly? What a sweet name! Lilly, we're going to be friends as we're both girls. I was a little disappointed because I thought I was the only girl here. You know, I don't much enjoy talking to boys alone. Good, good!'

They went on in silence, but only for a bit. It seemed Priya was pondering about how much to divulge. She was thinking and examining in her head about how close she felt to Joby and to Lilly who she now realized was a girl like her. So they went on for a little bit and the only sound was that of the wind and Lilly panting.

The amazing part about the love story of Ambili Teacher and Kannan Maash was that when it truly became a two-way affair—when the teacher finally began to fully reciprocate the Maash's love—love seemed to have spread everywhere on the school campus. Boys and girls in the classrooms began shyly smiling at each other. Some of the boys in higher classes bought nose rings and silk ribbons for the girls. The peon and the cleaning woman began passing love notes disguised as paper planes to each other. It was noted that the peon began ringing the school bell in a peculiar, musical fashion.

'Even in our class...' Priya was saying and then she paused, suddenly a shade shy: '...in our class, too, it began, though I know that we are very young for it. Lilly, don't you go and mention this to my aunt Sharada. My aunt Sharada says that even if we fall in love now it will not be real love, as we are not old enough for it. But you know something? That Surej bought me an eraser as a gift. It was a fragrant eraser, the kind that smells of jasmine whenever you erase a mistake with it! But Surej sits with Jaggu—who's nothing better than a bully—in the library period. They look up bad words in fat dictionaries and giggle.'

There was an interesting addition to all this—something that even Priya did not know. Joby had heard that when love began to flower spontaneously everywhere in school, the Head Maash and a few of the moralistic older teachers went mad with worry. They began breaking up couples having lunch under trees and dispersing groups of boys and girls, which only added to the excitement.

Then the drunks in the toddy shop had added their own twist to the whole affair. It had to do with a seedy cinema called Jawahar which was located on the outskirts of Karuthupuzha, a little off the main road that led to the city. The theatre regularly featured films that deliberately blurred the line between delicate lovemaking and plain pornography. All sorts of men visited Jawahar—drunks seeking more stimulation, those addicted to sexual adventure, as well as those severely disillusioned with their marital condition. People walked to the cinema from Karuthupuzha or got off the bus at the previous stop and walked the rest of the way. Being seen at Jawahar or walking into Jawahar was taboo, so they resorted to all sorts of stratagems to remain unseen. Some would wrap a towel around their heads or use a hanky or palm to hide their faces as they turned off the main road to Jawahar. All the secrecy added to the excitement of watching sleaze on the big screen. Another unwritten rule was that if you met an acquaintance at this cinema you were not to acknowledge the person, nor were you to ever breathe a word to people in town about whom you spotted here. Once inside these rusted gates everyone was equally guilty and no one knew anyone.

So it was in violation of all existing norms that a few months ago it became known among the townsfolk that the Head Maash of Karuthupuzha's school had been witnessed urinating in Jawahar's rundown lavatory. No one knew who had spotted the Head Maash there and who had crudely decided to leak such sensitive information. Better sense eventually prevailed and, contrary to the small town's usual habit, the incident was quickly buried before it could erupt into a scandal.

Nonetheless, one bit of damage was done. Kanakam, the Head

Maash's wife, who wasn't so young anymore, heard about it from the maidservants. The woman cried heavily that night, and stopped talking to her husband from the next day onwards. The Head Maash went into total denial. He prohibited Kanakam from listening to such baseless rumours. He told her that he had absolutely no need to go to such theatres (what was its name?) and that people ought to know better than to create dirty stories about decent folk. He pleaded with her, went down on his knees, tried to hug her and kiss her, threatened her, and even shed a few tears himself. But Kanakam stuck to her silence. Weeks and months went by. She wouldn't relent. Every day she cooked a certain pumpkin dish which he hated and ate her meal separately in the kitchen.

As the months passed the Head Maash stopped trying to deal with his wife's silence. He grew morose himself and began spending more and more time with his colleagues. Then, when Kannan Maash and Ambili Teacher fell so much in love that the vapours of their love began to waft across the whole school, something happened to the Head Maash. Though on the surface he moralized and even discussed dismissing the two guilty teachers, deep inside he was affected much the same way as the children and the peon and the cleaning woman and the birds were affected. Love grew back in his barren heart! So one evening, just when he was about to wave his stick at a young boy and a girl sitting under a tree, he decided against it. Instead, he took his scooter and made for home before school ended for the day.

At home he parked his scooter, walked up to Kanakam who was cutting a pumpkin and fell at her feet with a cry.

'I am sorry, I am sorry,' he wailed and his tears washed her feet. 'I went to that theatre, Jawahar, only because I was curious. I just wanted to see what they were all going there for, it's nothing else. I-It's nothing else, I s-swear! I love only you, Kanakam. I love you and only you! You are my life....'

Moved to tears herself, Kanakam saw in her husband's eyes the kind of love she had only seen in their initial days together. It was magical. She forgave him with a kiss and they began spending the next few days—and nights—like they were newly married.

Some men at the toddy shop said that after he had made up with his wife the Head Maash was so pleased that he quit trying to moralize and gave his blessings to Kannan Maash and Ambili Teacher. Others claimed that it wasn't as sweet as all that. They said that, in fact, Kannan Maash once delicately suggested to the Head Maash that he was aware of the 'Jawahar incident' and that he might mention it by mistake somewhere if he and Ambili Teacher were ever pulled up for their affair; after that there was no question of the Head Maash punishing them.

All this was hidden from the children, Joby understood, when he heard Priya's version. All that they knew was that there was now so much love and song in the school that it had become a much more interesting place. As she chattered on, Joby's mind flew back decades.

He was thinking of the time long ago when young and serene mothers put their children into his rickshaw along with packed lunches in warm tiffin boxes. With what aching love they waved goodbye to their little ones as he drove them to school! He also remembered the rich, mellifluous voice of Saraswati Teacher, to whose music classes he took some of the children in the evenings. He heard it in his tired head now, and in the drift of that voice the leaves on branches by the roadside grew a more delicate green. '...But one thing is certain,' he heard Priya say, 'whenever I marry, I will run away from home. Uncle and Aunt are in for a shock—particularly Uncle, because he plans to make me a police inspector. I wouldn't really mind, but then I have decided to become a giant wheel operator, as you know. I have set my mind on it and not even Uncle Paachu can change that now.' She laughed suddenly, 'During the holidays Uncle Paachu continued with his training to make me fearless. He took me to Sundaran the mahout and made me walk under his elephant. I have always wondered what it would be like to walk under an elephant. I have heard of parents making their children walk under Sundaran's elephant so that they would lose their fear and stop waking up at night. But really, though at first

I was a little shivery, I found it quite all right. In fact, under the elephant it feels safe, can you believe it? Have you seen an elephant's face? It's forever smiling. Have you ever walked under an elephant? Uncle doesn't know it, but I don't fear elephants. It is lizards I fear. Ugh! They drop to the floor with such a plop! Uncle Paachu doesn't know that and if he wants me to be a fearless inspector he should really be making me get rid of my fear of lizards. I can walk under a hundred elephants. It's quite peaceful, really. The only concern is, if you care to think about it, how the elephant would feel. I mean, it would be rather strange to have a creature walk under your belly, wouldn't it...?'

No one else looks out of the window through which she sees the world, Joby was thinking. He wondered if the person trailing them could hear little Priya. He looked at Lilly. It was at the bitch that Priya was still directing her talk.

'The problem with Uncle is that he is retired,' Priya continued. 'It gives him a lot of free time and he grows irritated and angry. Aunty is so worried about him. She worries that when he gets angry, everyone laughs at him. Sometimes he is even angry with me. I used to sit on his lap when he was in the police station but now I don't. Of course, I am bigger now. And you know he buys me toys I don't want. That's funny but it is also sometimes so sad. He bought me a fire engine for my holidays. You should see my toy basket. It's now full of guns, tanks, soldiers, jeeps and stuff. I was thinking the other day, if I could hide some of them in my schoolbag, I could give them to Surej—you know the boy who gave me the jasmine eraser? It would be the perfect return gift. Boys would be delighted with Uncle Paachu's toys. Will you help me, Lilly? I could wrap two guns and several soldiers in an old newspaper and hide them in my bag, you know. I could even give some of the toys to that bully Jaggu. Maybe if he gets busy he won't look up bad words in the dictionary and spoil Surej also....'

Joby looked at the feisty little girl and thought that beneath all her bravado and good cheer there was something delicate about her.

Something so delicate it skimmed sadness. Look how skinny she was with her knobbly knees and pipe-stem legs. What was her Uncle Paachu thinking!

'I like dolls and kitchen sets. Dolls, especially. Uncle used to buy them for me when he was still working. But now it is all guns and soldiers, so that I become fearless like the boys. I only hope ... one day he doesn't....' she stopped suddenly, as though stunned. She looked at Joby directly and asked, 'You won't tell him ever, will you, that I said this?' She waited as Joby continued pushing the cycle in silence. Then she began again, 'Well, I hope Uncle Paachu will not one day buy me a van...a w-white van!'

Having said that she lapsed into silence. She looked uncomfortable and scared. Though he pitied her, he had to admit that he was relieved by her silence at last.

When they reached school, he wondered if he should help her get off the cycle. Instead, he turned to Lilly and asked, 'I could make little dolls out of coconut leaves, you know, if you like.'

9.

A Meeting at the Gate

That evening Sharada stood by the gate chewing on the tip of a tender blade of grass while she waited for Joby and Priya to arrive. Her husband was in the orchard with the workers. Sharada was relieved that her fears were unfounded and things seemed to be working out after all. Barber Sureshan had reported that Joby wasn't drinking during the day now. Priya seemed more than happy with the new arrangement; every evening the little girl would regale her with new stories about her journey on the bicycle. Sharada was especially relieved that on the couple of occasions that Joby hadn't turned up in the morning her husband had silently filled in without coming down on the man. It seemed to her that he was in fact quite happy with the work Joby was doing; she was hopeful that he would begin paying the man soon. She was very relieved that she hadn't tried to convince her husband to call it off after that first day. All that talk about Paachu bribing some constable to follow Joby and Priya appeared to have receded into the background. It only went to show that one must never act in haste. All things required time to come to fruition.

And soon there they were, rounding the bend in the road in front of the house. Joby seemed dog-tired and feverish, of course, but she fancied he looked a little healthier, a shade less yellow and waxy. At least he looked more sober than she had seen him in years, no, decades. He put the bicycle on its stand, nodded at Sharada and stood back so she could pick her niece off the carrier.

'How is the chore? Is she giving you a hard time?' she said to Joby, giving him a small packet of freshly fried banana chips. This was her first gift among many to follow. She had made a mental note to provide these to Joby on a regular basis, especially until her husband decided to begin paying him. Joby nodded, accepting the packet.

'You know, Aunty,' Priya began, 'this is not a boy dog, it's a girl dog! Aren't you happy to hear that? Her name is Lilly. *Lilly*! Isn't that a sweet name?'

Joby looked at Sharada guiltily, because this meant he had spoken, defying Paachu's orders. Sharada deliberately acted like this didn't occur to her and instead patted her niece lovingly and sent her away to bathe. As Joby was about to turn the cycle around so he could be on his way to the much-awaited first drink of the day, Sharada placed her hand on the seat of the vehicle.

'Joby, I thought I must tell you how thankful I am. Priya loves everything about this arrangement, and even my husband is pleased, though he doesn't show it.'

'Where is he?' Joby's voice was frail, needlessly guilty.

'He's in the orchard, out back, with the workers,' Sharada said. 'You needn't fear him. He is pleased with you.'

'Yes, Sharadechi. The Yemaan has every reason to be pleased,' Joby said in the tone of an obedient student. 'I stick to every one of his conditions. I never ride the cycle, never speak to the little lady at all, and I have even stopped drinking before dropping her back here.'

'I know,' Sharada continued, 'that's why I felt I must thank you and give you some of the chips. You must share them with your wife. They are freshly fried in pure coconut oil. You know, I admit that at first I was really apprehensive about the whole thing. Your friend, Sureshan Barber, convinced me. He was hoping that with this new arrangement you would drink less, because you would now have something to do during the day. He impressed upon me that you were very unhealthy because of your drinking. Apparently Purushan Vaidyan is really concerned about your health.'

Joby was vaguely surprised that there were so many people who seemed to care about what happened to him. 'Yes Sharadechi, thank you for this,' he said absently, but she wasn't letting him off yet. She tightened her grip on the bicycle seat.

'But let me admit now,' she said, a sparkle in her eyes. 'I also had a selfish motive.'

Joby raised his eyebrows a trifle. He continued to fidget, as his entire being craved a drink. He secured the packet of chips to the carrier of the bicycle, his way of suggesting that he ought to get moving.

'I wanted to reform my own husband, your Yemaan, with this,' she went on calmly, unaware of Joby's suffering. 'You see, my husband is not taking his retirement very well. He wants to continue being the hardened policeman he always was. Trying so hard isn't good for him.'

'Oh, you needn't worry, Sharadechi. Yemaan will come around slowly. He is good at heart.'

'I know,' Sharada said. 'But do you know something? This town mocks him. The more he tries, the more they laugh. They are delighted with every opportunity to laugh at him.'

'That's only a little here, a little there, Sharadechi,' Joby said, searching for the right words. 'Not everyone laughs at Yemaan. Why, most people still respect him. *I* still respect him.'

'It's good of you to say that, Joby,' Sharada said, surprised at her own rush of sentiment. 'But, really, I am a worried wife. You know, my husband ought to change, to transform. His police days are over and he must realize that. It's the time of his life when kindness, magnanimity, helpfulness and love for others should be what his heart is filled with. He should stop trying to cling to his past. That's what makes people laugh at him.'

For a long time, Joby had been unable to tolerate complicated thoughts and emotions, especially when he needed a drink. He felt miserable when someone spoke long sentences with big words and deep thoughts. Empty, superficial chatter was what he liked best; he didn't have to endure any mental strain to deal with that. Right now, he didn't know how to respond to what Sharada was saying. All he wanted to do was get on his bicycle and flee.

'I convinced him to hire you as part of my efforts to change him, you know?' Sharada continued, now talking to herself as much as to him. 'I wish to admit this. It wasn't only to rehabilitate you, Joby. I hope to…well…rehabilitate my husband, too, in a sense. You know, get him to play a role in saving you, and bring you back to life and health in the process.'

Much later on, when he had had his drink and the time to recall this conversation in peace, Joby could see what she meant.

'I hope you don't think I am being selfish,' Sharada said, looking directly into his stricken eyes, 'I would thank Lord Murugan if you came back to health with this job. If, through my husband's actions, a man is saved….'

Her eyes threatened to well up, and Joby was embarrassed. So, without thinking he said: 'That's fine, Sharadechi. Don't you worry. I will stick to all of Yemaan's conditions and he will have no reason to complain.'

'Don't worry too much about those conditions,' Sharada said, lowering her voice a little and looking towards the house. Then her lips curved in amusement, 'Do you know something? He has appointed someone to trail you.'

'I have known it, yes, I have known it every day. I could hear footsteps. Only, I don't know who it is.'

'Oh, it's that ugly man, Bubru—the constable,' Sharada said, again lowering her voice. 'My husband called up the police station and they were stupid enough—or amused enough, perhaps—to offer Constable Bubru's services.'

'Oh,' said Joby.

'Look, Joby, listen to me like you would your own sister. I know my husband is making this difficult for you. Please, for my sake, forgive him. Let some time pass with this new routine, and he will soften up, trust me. He is beginning to, I think. All I'm saying is don't leave it midway and go. And if you can hide it from Bubru, you can talk to Priya; I don't think that matters. She has taken a liking to you, and God knows, that child needs someone to—'

'WELL, IF IT ISN'T MY OWN WIFE CONSPIRING WITH A DRUNK!' thundered Paachu. He had come up unseen, approaching the gate from a different direction. Both of them cringed in fear at the sound of his voice.

'What were you telling him?' he shouted at Sharada. 'Were you asking him to throw my conditions to that dog there? I heard you. I was listening, ah! You were granting him permission to talk to Priya all he likes, with his stinking, drunken breath and petty, disgusting, vulgar, drunken talk, eh?'

'I—' Sharada began, but she thought that he might hit her and stopped.

'Yemaan,' Joby began, but he too ate his words because it seemed like Paachu might punch him.

'You drunk buffoon, be silent,' Paachu thundered at Joby. 'Why, you are no buffoon at all. You are a snake! A poisonous snake! I gave you a job. Who would have given you a job, you rotting filth? But I gave you a job and you want to break the few simple terms I had?'

'Yemaan, I...I didn't.'

'If you think I am going to fire you after this,' Paachu said, picking each word deliberately and with strong intent. 'You are mistaken. No, you are going to come back tomorrow and pick up my niece from here. And I will have you trailed by the entire police force of this town, mind you. If I hear that you broke any of my conditions, take it from me you rotten good-for-nothing drink-sodden garbage, I will break every bone in your miserable body. That should set you straight!'

With that he gave the rusty cycle a shove. It went flying and fell in a clanking heap. Lilly yelped as the packet on the carrier burst open and Sharada's banana chips scattered in the dust, each a small moon face grinning in evil mirth. Joby picked the cycle up and turned to go, giving Sharada a look that said it was all right, she needn't fret. Sharada's eyes pleaded with him not to react to Paachu's offensiveness.

Paachu turned to his wife and said, 'I think we should talk.' They went indoors.

Cycling down the road, his head in a whirl, Joby tried to get a grip on himself. That lady Sharadechi was such a kind-hearted, graceful soul and the Yemaan was just the opposite! He shook his head clear and pedalled hard, as Lilly trotted beside him to keep up. He needed arrack to cascade down his throat now. A tired smile almost broke the surface on his face at the prospect, but it didn't emerge for he saw a figure standing ominously right in the middle of the narrow lane. He applied the brakes and the bicycle emitted a rusty whine, setting his teeth on edge. The man blocking his way was huge, rock-solid and hairy. He had hair bushing out of his ears, behind each finger, even from inside his nose. Constable Bubru often went without a shave for days, because he liked thick hair to cover as much of his body as it could.

The bicycle stopped near the constable's feet. Bubru put out a hand and grabbed the handle-bars in an iron grip. Joby readied himself for a punch in the belly, because that's what policemen did to drunks.

But Constable Bubru only asked in his grating voice, 'Toddy shop?'

Without waiting for Joby to nod, the huge man climbed on to the bar in front of the seat. With a great effort, Joby got the cycle moving again.

The constable and the drunk made their unsteady way to the toddy shop, Joby panting and Bubru grinning cruelly. Lilly trotted alongside the bicycle, accepting the latest arrangement with the sort of equanimity only she was capable of.

10.

The Town That Laughed

Our small towns, especially Karuthupuzha, have this unmistakable and strange manner of behaving like an individual from time to time. The behaviour is that of a confused individual, not a resolute, peaceful or clear-headed one. The town's mind is riddled with the most intense conflicts, tides of opposing forces that no one can trace to their origins and painful uncertainties that prevent unanimous stands. These are similar to the conflicts arising within an individual mind. Each of the residents of Karuthupuzha was like an individual thought, swaying this way or that, but all part of an all-encompassing One Mind.

When a resident of this small town feebly and hesitantly takes a decision, a thousand countering doubts are immediately born to try and reverse that decision, and bring things back to the way they were before. Other residents would—with strange subservience to that omniscient One Mind—take it upon themselves to prevent the change brought about by that feeble and hesitant decision, with absolute disregard to correctness or propriety. Take Constable Bubru, for example. If you asked him why he had to appear every evening on the narrow lane to get on to Joby's bicycle and go with him to the toddy shop to make sure the man drank more than he could handle, he wouldn't be able to give you a clear, logical answer. He was just behaving that way because it was how the town did things.

Bubru forced Joby to begin drinking once again in the mornings. You might argue that Bubru did this because he got to drink too, but then Bubru himself hadn't been given to drinking in the mornings. He just made it his business—for reasons that seemed to spring from outside his own understanding—to make sure Joby did not drink any less owing to his new assignment with Paachu Yemaan.

Bubru was sweetly coaxing at first, but began to act tough if Joby resisted too much. One morning, when Joby feebly resisted coming to the toddy shop, saying he was ill, Bubru actually slapped him around a bit. Inside the shop the other drinkers took over, persuading Joby to drink more and more, many of them buying him arrack with a fever they could not have explained to themselves. It seemed as though Karuthupuzha wanted Joby to remain the chronic drunk he had always been. Sure enough, within a fortnight, Joby was drinking immediately after dropping Priya to school in the mornings, just like before.

Likewise, Karuthupuzha decided to laugh at Paachu Yemaan. She didn't want that poisonous laughter to stop. Ask any resident here why this was so and they wouldn't be able to give a logical explanation for their collective, mindless vindictiveness. Walk in to Madhavan Nair's tea shop any evening and interrupt his patrons' talk when they were laughing at the ex-Inspector's expense. Ask Rappai, the dwarf who served tea here, why the town couldn't just leave Paachu alone to lead a retired life in peace. The boy-man will look at you guiltily, accepting his share of blame but totally and mindlessly continuing with the town's agenda of mercilessly ridiculing the former police chief. There were, indeed, meek and mature voices—like that of Barber Sureshan—who pointed out how this was all very, very wrong, but these righteous arguments did not have much of an effect on the majority of the minds that comprised the mind and mindset of Karuthupuzha. Paachu would be laughed at and Joby would be made to remain a suicidal drunk, because that was the town's cruel intent, no matter that it was also home to kindly and reasonable souls like Sureshan. In this it was no different from other towns and smaller cities in the country. After all, aren't all our battles the direct result of that One Mind going on a rampage and not listening to the feeble voice of reason coming from individuals who are in the minority?

It was remarked among the chroniclers of Karuthupuzha's affairs that if God ever made His appearance among us and started to live in this town, after the first round of awe and worship people would begin to joke about Him. We would comment about the ludicrousness of His creation, and maybe talk behind His back about how all that mythology we had been fed as children was actually His propaganda. It was good, in a sense, that God stayed far up there in heaven and only touched our lives with His mystic, unseen and very distant fingers.

In a sense, the people of Karuthupuzha had never understood what to make of Inspector Paachu during his tenure. Like God, he was the unknown. They did not know if he was a cruel, bloodthirsty man out to gratuitously crunch bones and give out black eyes, or a dutiful policeman who had chosen this image as the one most suited to his job of maintaining law and order. The irony, of course, was that the law and order of Karuthupzha did not need maintaining. There was hardly any serious crime here, much to Paachu Yemaan's secret disappointment. Everyone knew that. Life was nothing but plain boring here, and any attempts at dreaming up nasty goons and underworld dons were simply the imaginings of a dull mind. Or, as in Paachu's case, his conjuring up was in order to bring the town totally under his control. But the townfolk weren't entirely sure of the nature behind his actions and so they feared him. The rumours that he had killed the petty thief Gopalan only increased their fearfulness. Paachu came to be seen as someone whom it would be dangerous to cross. And so, in spite of the town's penchant for cruelly mythologizing people, no one laughed at him while he was still in service.

But upon retirement, Paachu had abruptly turned into an ordinary mortal. He had become 'one of them'—the god who had come to live among them. Stripped of his official powers, Paachu was surely quite harmless now. So laughter erupted here and there. Though not too many people in Karuthupuzha were wholly venomous or hurtful (in fact, most were kind and sympathetic), when the One Mind took over, the laughter soon became almost universal. At first there had only been small jokes about how the town had turned into a den of goons, now that Inspector Paachu was out of office; how women now feared to walk on the streets and how gamblers in the grove would now be punished only with coconuts falling upon their heads. Then someone mentioned that the dead petty thief Gopalan had returned as a ghost, now that his nemesis had retired, so the womenfolk better keep a watch on their underwear once again. This one was a favourite and did the rounds the longest. Madhavan Nair's tea shop in the day and the toddy shop at night became the touchpoints for this joke. No one said it to Paachu's face, of course, but there were ways to ensure that it reached him.

The ridicule would, in all probability, have died down over time had ex-Inspector Paachu not kept it alive with his attempts at holding on to power, his fights for the police jeep, his continued outbursts and high-handedness. As a result people started to find everything about him funny—the tuft on his head, his loud discourses on his toilet habits, his advice to other policemen, his attempts to shape his little niece into a tough policewoman.... Someone created a rumour that Paachu had visited the town astrologer to find out if there was a star up there that was particularly concerned with the happenings in his bowels. Abu, the newspaper recycler, wrote his own poetry about Paachu's exploits as a policeman and sang them to the tunes of a certain old film song in the toddy shop. One of the labourers who picked mangoes in Paachu's orchard contributed the story that he had once seen the Yemaan make his little niece wear his old uniform (which was so loose on her that it made her look like a melting candle!) and salute him as a subordinate at the police station would.

But these were recent developments. It might be of interest to go back to the very beginnings of this laughter, to within a few days of Paachu Yemaan's retirement. For just a moment, at the time of his retirement, it was thought, especially by his subordinates in the station and his wife at home, that Paachu was in fact taking quite well to this new phase of his life. But that was not the case. Once he was firmly ensconced at home with no work to go to in the mornings and no official power to wield, bitterness and discontent began to take root in him. That was when the town began to laugh at him.

Perhaps the earliest triggers could be traced to an otherwise harmless old gentleman named Pariera. Pariera was a retired army man who, being the worst businessman known to modern times, had used most of his savings to open an antique shop in Karuthupuzha. Instead of settling down to a peaceful retirement Pariera felt restless and, one day, rubbing his hands together, said to himself, 'Pariera was not born to lead the sleepy life of a pensioner. Let me see if I can begin something these beautiful folk of the countryside have never seen.' And thus was born Pariera's Antique Shop in a place where most of the trees, stones and people were almost antiques anyway.

At first Pariera went about his new vocation with the intense, directionless energy of one who had set out on a new journey with too much spirit and too little thought. He enthusiastically invited people to check out his antique collection and even succeeded in making Moydeen Mappila, the wealthy brick kiln owner, buy a strange-looking urn that he claimed dated back to the Chola dynasty. Moydeen Mappila wondered what he would do with a vessel so old but he bought it out of graciousness and kept it in an inconspicuous corner of his massive house. Pariera had rubbed his hands together and exclaimed happily, 'Business is on!'

As it turned out, that urn of the Chola dynasty was the only item he ever sold. Initially some people looked in out of curiosity, but not finding any point to the wares Pariera was selling, he was soon left alone with his antiques.

At the time Paachu was still Inspector, but nearing the end of his rule. One particularly dull afternoon Paachu and his team of constables raided Pariera's Antique Shop. Paachu loudly proclaimed to his men,: 'It is highly suspicious how that Pariera sustains himself. What is going on in that dark shop of his, where not a fly wanders in? I wouldn't be surprised if we found some dead bodies hidden in there. Let's go find out. I spoke to Kunjumon's cousin who is a nurse in the army, and she hasn't even heard of a Pariera. Highly suspicious!'

So the police jeep came to a screeching halt outside Pariera's Antique Shop that afternoon. As a crowd gathered outside to watch, the constables, under Inspector Paachu's directions, turned everything inside out, looking into clay pots and tapping on hollow statues. They even broke a few antiques in careless aggression. It was as much excitement as Pariera had had in a long time and he was very pleased. He eagerly showed off his wares, opened up his empty accounts ledger and politely asked the policemen if they would have some sherbet to drink. On their way out Pariera offered Paachu Yemaan the gift of an intricately crafted antique knife that would never rust. The Inspector refused with some irritation.

With this raid, some interest had been regenerated in town about his shop and for that Pariera was grateful.

'Such things are good publicity,' Pariera told his antiques.

From then on Pariera incessantly pushed his friendship and goodwill upon Inspector Paachu. At the function to commemorate Paachu Yemaan's retirement Pariera clapped the loudest at the ex-Inspector's speech, and looked around at the others like he shared a secret with the great man. The very next day he visited Paachu at his home with some rum that he had obtained from the ex-serviceman's quota. Paachu thought that at least it wasn't a gift of some useless old knife this time. Pariera continued to visit Paachu from time to time, sometimes bringing him large cases of grapes and more military rum as a sign of his affection. On one occasion, he gifted him a beautifully carved walking stick. Paachu entertained the man's friendship though he could not understand it.

I raided the man's shop and now he's my friend, Paachu thought with amusement.

Parallel to Pariera's attempts to foster a bond with Paachu was his growing melancholy at the failure of his shop to attract customers. Sometimes he would feel sick of his stillborn business and would ponder about leaving town. At such times he would close his shop early and walk over to the western border of the town, in the direction that the petty thief Gopalan had fled to decades ago. This is where the small river, after which the town of Karuthupuzha is named, flows.

It's such a small river that it is really a stream for most of the year. This puzha separates the town from the hills and forests beyond. Its water is frothy white and it runs giggly and mischievous all day long. But towards evening, when the sun climbs down on the other side of those hills, their tall shadows fall upon the river, turning it black (or karuthu). On evenings when he was especially depressed, Pariera would sit by the banks of this puzha, watching it turn black in the shadow of the hills. In the belly of the river he could see smooth round stones that looked like dark heavenly bodies wrenched out of their orbits. Drinking deep from his melancholy he would later tell listeners in tea shops, 'Retired life is like the evening. You just wait for nightfall so you can go to sleep'.

Paachu realized, very late, that Pariera was pressing his friendship on him because they were both retired. Whenever Pariera turned towards him, it was with the intense relief of one who had found a companion at last. And Paachu couldn't shake him off as he had himself allowed the friendship to become rather rooted; there were a lot of things in Paachu's house, including some antiques, which Pariera had gifted. Besides, by now Pariera was well received in Paachu's household, with little Priya calling him uncle and Sharada serving him chips and goodies.

The trouble was that when Pariera saw Paachu dropping Priya off to school, he wouldn't let it go. He would stop the scooter and exclaim loudly, 'Ho-ho! The tough Inspector also has this soft side! Delivering his little niece to school. Such a beautiful sight, for which we had to wait till you retired. *That*, my friend, is the advantage of retirement and old age!' When he caught Paachu in the market buying vegetables with his wife, Pariera wouldn't just give them a quiet smile and move on. He would beam at them and say, 'Ho! He would measure up the thieves and goons of town, and now he picks up potatoes and cabbages in the market. Ask us retirees what it means, the fall of man! And yet there is a pleasure in this all, eh, my dear ex-Inspector?'

These innocent bursts of empathy from Pariera, when he would good-naturedly liken his situation in life with that of Paachu and crack a self-effacing joke, would invariably lead to sniggers from the vegetable vendors and shopkeepers by the roadside. In the tea stalls people slowly gathered around this batty old man because they found what he said funny. Even when he was being philosophical and profound, his listeners were amused. And even though he sensed that he was often the butt of their jokes, Pariera played along because he enjoyed being surrounded by people. Besides, he told himself, developing relationships is a must for business.

Now, there was an artist by the name of Hariharan in Karuthupuzha who had taken to holding exhibitions of his paintings in the town library from time to time. Though nobody understood his paintings, folks came to the exhibition out of the desire to be seen as appreciators of art. There was one such exhibition being held at about this time, to which Paachu went with Sharada and Priya. Like most of the others, Paachu, too, wished to convey to the town and to his wife that he had a connoisseur's streak in him. Appreciating art was one thing no one knew the Yemaan was capable of. When he met Pariera at the steps of the library he had a sense of impending doom, but he let the old man accompany him inside.

After going over the entire collection of paintings hung up on the walls, Paachu stopped beside one that consisted of a bright red spot with streaks of grey beneath it. He saw that the artist Hariharan was standing nearby, stroking his beard. He turned to the artist and said for all to hear, 'I suppose this is about the spiritual degradation of mankind? This here is the scorching sun that symbolizes an absolute lack of faith in modern times, causing this drought here, down below? Eh?'

Artist Hariharan, amazed by the insight, stood pondering over it. Pariera jumped in and said, 'Aged people like us, of course, see spiritual degradation everywhere.'

That caused a few giggles here and there, and the incident would have ended as such. But among the visitors was Chamel, who ran an old-age home in Karuthupuzha. Chamel was given to loud, slanderous jokes. He proclaimed loudly, 'One needs to look through the cataract of old age to understand your work, Hariharan.' This was greeted by peals of laughter and even loud guffaws. Everyone in the library burst out laughing, though it wasn't clear if the joke was on Hariharan or on ex-Inspector Paachu or on Pariera. Even Sharada smiled.

That, you could say, marked the true beginning of the town's laughter at ex-Inspector Paachu. Indeed, the quantum of laughter in the library far exceeded what was warranted by the joke. You will agree it wasn't quite one of those jokes that give you stomach cramps from laughing. And yet it seemed that there was the weight of a million unseen and unheard jokes behind this rather silly joke. The floodgates opened and the mirth came crashing down. The people in the library were now laughing, no, guffawing, right in the presence of the great Yemaan. It wasn't one man or one woman or one child laughing this time; it was the town with its One Mind.

Paachu left the place red-faced. Sharada immediately regretted her participation, but Pariera was oblivious. He was drawn into the mirth and took over from there, cracking jokes about poor eyesight in old age and mistakes of perception. Somebody introduced constipation; someone else threw in boiled bananas. The library was no longer a venue for Hariharan's strange paintings. It was now filled with folk who had come together to laugh about old age, the fall from grace of powerful men and particularly the hilarity of Paachu's situation.

A few days later, there was a crude incident. At nightfall some unidentified youth—perhaps just half a dozen of them—appeared on thundering motorcycles outside Paachu's home and burst crackers and sang songs. Their song mockingly dissuaded Paachu 'Yemaan' from punching them and kicking them because they had committed the grave offence of stealing mangoes from Avarachan's grove. The mangoes were only for Dakshayini the whore who had cravings for raw mangoes after she had become pregnant. The song further insinuated that as a duty-bound police officer Paachu 'Yemaan' would certainly be kind enough to understand and forgive a pregnant whore. It was a brief scene—they came on bikes, sang loudly and vulgarly, scribbled obscenities on Paachu's compound wall and fled before the ex-Inspector could react. The next morning Paachu complained at the police station, but it was obvious that the policemen were only amused. Thankfully, the youth had laid off after that one incident.

Soon, it was observed that the new inspector, Janardanan, was the chief humour-monger of the anti-Paachu movement. Though behind the scenes and never too direct or intense, Janardanan did regularly go around town subtly dropping details of Paachu's disgraceful past and present, adding stuff from his imagination, garnishing everything with verses from mythology and spinning his anecdotes in such a way that it seemed to be harmless humour. He told people how Paachu, for all his strict law-enforcement, had been nonetheless, on the payrolls of rich businessmen like Moydeen Mappilla and Eeppachan Mothalali. Janardanan revealed that Chacko, the lineman, who never had the courage to say this himself, had once unknowingly let slip over a drink that Paachu had terrorized the entire electricity office to not bill him for the power supply to his house. His fight to hold on to the police jeep was known anyway, but Janardanan disseminated specifics of the struggle.

In all this, Janardanan took care to keep his own image pristine and unsullied—he would never do anything as sordid as besmirching the image of his predecessor. He was simply a worshipper of beauty and a broker of small deals who believed not in law enforcement but in negotiation. He was only talking about the humour in the situation. Instead of openly slandering Paachu, he left the cruder part of the task to his pet and deputy, Constable Bubru.

Bubru was more insensitive than anyone else in the police station. He always got a strange high out of jeering at someone, never missed the chance to laugh when someone fell, and particularly hated men who had once been imposing bosses. In spite of the fact that he wasn't around when Paachu ruled, Bubru had, in his head, created scenes of Paachu's dictatorship out of all that he had heard. He had rapidly come to hate the man, as though he himself had been a victim. His hatred for Paachu was personal and total, fuelled by nothing more than the simple pleasure of hating, so to speak, that such men feel. So he took it upon himself to spread the stories he partly got from Janardanan and partly from his own muse. In the toddy shop he would say to whoever listened, 'Paachu once discovered something between Eeppachan Mothalali and his wife. Some intimate husband-wife trouble, you know, some quarrel and stuff. You know how the Mothalali is old while his wife is young and beautiful, and how everyone is so sensitive to this? Well, Paachu dug something up, and to this day he blackmails the poor Mothalali.'

Bubru found that discussing such stuff made him intensely popular. Indeed, Inspector Janardanan would sometimes point Bubru out to the other policemen as a role model for his ability to win the affection of the people in town.

The laughter which began with Pariera's unintentional bumbling was kept going by Paachu's enemies in the police station. Sometimes regular folks felt a sudden qualm about their role in all this, particularly when they could see that the good lady Sharada was suffering for it. And we already know that a small group of disunited voices protested the ridiculing of a retired man. But such people were regarded as spoilsports. Yet, despite all this the laugher might have died down in time, not out of any collective pangs of guilt, but because people had found something or someone fresh to laugh at.

The laughter might have died down had it not been for the photographer Varky.

◆

No one knew exactly when Varky came to Karuthupuzha, nor from where. Different people at quite different times noted that there was this new man, of average height, in Western clothes complete with cap and jacket, loitering around town with a giant camera slung from his shoulders. He was different from anyone the small town had ever had on her streets. He would wander around, often looking up at the sky, sometimes pointing his camera at the clouds and shooting as from a gun. Some people said that from time to time he would mutter to himself; others said that it wasn't to himself he was communing but to his camera.

Varky's wanderings seemed to slowly close in on a certain section of Karuthupuzha, a little away from the central marketplace. Over time, he was noted to be wandering around a certain hardware store. After some more days or weeks or months there appeared a new store with signage reading VARKY'S STUDIO opened in the space above the hardware store; giant dark windows ran almost the length and height of the store. Photographer Varky was open for business.

Gossip did form about Varky but it was vague, like everything else about him. Some said he was a truthful man of very few words, others that he was evil and silent. Thambi, the stunningly dirty orphan who distributed tea around the marketplace, seemed to be the only one who had gone up to Varky's Studio during that initial phase. Everyone accosted him to find out what he could tell them about Varky. Thambi beamed, displaying his rotting teeth, and said, 'He drinks a lot of strong tea. That is all he drinks.' Apparently, he was also a heavy smoker.

As time passed, a few people did go up to Varky's Studio to have themselves photographed, most notably Diwakaran the civil contractor, who had got an 'opportunity to go to the Gulf'. He climbed up the stairs for some passport-sized photographs. Later Diwakaran told curious folks in a loud, clear voice, 'Varky is not at all a strange man! Do you know, he is just an immensely shy person. Why, he even offered me cigarettes and we chatted for a long time. He is so used to looking through his camera that he feels very shy to look people directly in the eye. Oh, how we simpletons get all prejudiced about people! Varky hopes to do good business here, if only we would break the ice and avail of his services. I think he is a great photographer. He says the sky in Karuthupuzha is really great, and that is why he set up his studio here. He showed me some pictures of clouds. In the Gulf they would lap up photographers like him!'

Such was Gulf Diwakaran's standing in society that following his report many people went up to Varky's Studio to have their pictures taken. It was rumoured that Varky said even the ugly Thambi was immensely photogenic!

Then one day the chief members of one of the temple committees of Karuthupuzha decided to go to the studio, make Varky's acquaintance and even take the liberty of asking the photographer for a small donation for a temple festival. 'This is how you break the ice,' the committee chairman said. In the colourful darkness of his studio Varky received them, but when he learned that they had not come for photographs but instead to ask him for a donation, he literally drove them away, saying the town had not given him enough business to keep his tea supply going and yet it was already asking *him* for donations! The chairman and the rest of the committee members left the place in a hurry.

Later that day Varky sat alone in the studio for hours, smoking cigarette after cigarette, worrying that his temper had got the better of him. He should never have shown his anger to the temple committee people. He should have just given them a paltry donation and sent them away. Now they would go around town undoing the little goodwill he had managed to earn by talking and sharing his cigarettes with the likes of Gulf Diwakaran. He wondered how he could win back the favour of the people. Finally he had an idea.

Varky went to his dark room and began working feverishly. He worked for several hours, his camera watching him from its place on the best chair in the studio. Sweat broke from under his cap and flowed down his chin but he continued to work. When Thambi got him his tea, he found that the previous glass was untouched. Varky went on into the night, coming out of his dark room only to smoke. 'Varky is working,' Thambi reported to the townsfolk, his eyes wide. 'Not even drinking his tea. Working.'

By the next morning he had a surprise ready for Karuthupuzha. People gathered under his studio, at the road in front of the hardware store, and pointed to his huge window on the first floor. There, on display, was the most magnificent and terrible picture the townsfolk had ever seen. It was a hugely enlarged photograph of Thambi the orphan, complete with his crate of dirty glasses of tea, his hair flying about as he walked—no, glided—down the street. On Thambi's shoulder could distinctly be seen the little housefly that was his pet, its minute hands rubbing against each other and its translucent wings half-raised in preparation for flight. Thambi's eyes peered out of their dark, bony sockets, glinting with the magic intelligence of a wizard. The dirt caked to his wiry beard could be seen with vulgar clarity. The strength on his face was not of this world. Varky's photograph had turned the dirty orphan (who was actually a eunuch) into someone undeniably fearsome. Thambi the orphan, the most forgotten and ignored soul in all of Karuthupuzha, had turned overnight into something people couldn't take their eyes off.

Some smiled, some clucked their tongues in disgust and some shook their heads in confused admiration that morning as they looked up at the window of Varky's Studio. Everyone was awed. Many people passed by the hardware store repeatedly to check the picture out again and again. When Thambi saw the photograph, he was overjoyed.

The picture had the desired effect; Varky gained not a few admirers. Gulf Diwakaran said with satisfaction, 'I told you he was a genius. I realized that when I spoke to him. Those stupid temple committee folk simply annoyed him. Just look at that picture displayed on his window, folks, and you'll see the man has extraordinary genius.'

Thambi's picture earned Varky the sort of celebrity that lasted for quite some time. People came to him to have their pictures taken, to see how he would make them look, how he would transform them. Being nobody's fool, Varky saw that he had to give them variety to hold their interest. So after some time he pulled Thambi's picture down from his window and put up another—a harmless one of the sky at dawn. And soon that became a practice. Varky would change his display pictures, sometimes putting up elaborate canvases of nature, often mammoth close-ups of people, a few times pan shots of events or festivities and sometimes even of the rich dark interiors of his own studio. Everything he put up started to incite intense interest and speculation. People began to wait for what he would put up next. It became a matter of pride to have your portrait chosen by Varky to be enlarged and displayed; everyone secretly wished the genius photographer would choose him or her next. Many even began trying out new hairstyles and attire to catch Varky's eye. Some grew their nails long and wicked, some made their eyelashes pretty, but Varky's choices were unpredictable, following a logic that was apparent only to him.

His camera—a beautifully sophisticated contraption which itself was not from these parts—was quite central to his being. He spoke to it, listened to it, put it to bed at night, woke it up in the morning and wore it around his neck wherever he went. And the way in which he wielded it gave his subject a unique look. Once he put up a huge photograph of Eeppachan Mothalali's wife, Amminikutty. This was a close-up of her face as she dreamt at the window of their home. You could see one tooth missing. Eeppachan Mothalali had personally gone up to his studio to have the photograph removed. Some were sure that the Mothalali had paid handsomely to have the picture taken down.

◆

When Inspector Paachu retired, Varky's camera had turned towards the great man. It started off with pictures of his retirement function, of different poses of the legendary policeman's last uniformed moments, Paachu stepping down from his jeep holding his service revolver with the ease of one who had used it often, Paachu taking off his uniform cap and belt at home and more. In every shot, Paachu himself observed, Varky had captured the indescribable glory of a duty-bound officer who had spent a lifetime in the service of the law. First, a collage of smaller pictures of Paachu in different lights, angles and moods filled the window of Varky's Studio. Then bigger pictures came up, some with Paachu posing for them, although the best ones were candid shots. Paachu himself went up to the studio one evening to congratulate Varky on the excellent job the photographer was doing. 'These are not pictures of retired Inspector Paachu,' he said, speaking from his heart, 'they are relics of the victory of law over injustice. No one has ever captured my very being the way you have. Why, your pictures, my man, are almost as impactful, glorious and vital as my career in Karuthupuzha has been.' Paachu came down the steps of the studio that day in great emotion.

Ex-Inspector Paachu had expended so much emotional energy on Varky's first pictures of him that he had nothing left to say when the photograoger continued to put up pictures of him, not moving on to some other subject eventually as he always had before. The pictures had the same photographic genius even when they were only depicting Paachu taking his niece to school, buying vegetables at Poulose's grocery store, haggling with some vendor or the other, and generally going about the chores of a retired life. Sharada, who had been as pleased with her husband's initial pictures as Paachu, one day remarked to her husband that perhaps that Varky should now move on to displaying someone else's pictures. Paachu quarrelled with her, saying she did not appreciate true genius and that Varky was loathe to let go of a subject that really moved him. A little while later, though, he himself began to grow rather ashamed of some of the pictures of him that Varky began to display. There was one, in particular, that showed him addressing a small gathering of people at the town hall. There was nothing offensive about the picture itself but if you knew the context in which it had been taken—in it Paachu was actually giving a lecture on law and order to a sniggering group of people who had come only to be amused—then the picture took on satirical overtures.

Over time Varky's pictures of Paachu, though everyone saw that they were pure art, were in fact joining the vast category of things that showed Paachu in a funny light. No one actually said it out loud, but perhaps Varky realized that pictures of Paachu Yemaan were popular with the townsfolk. People actually gathered in front of his shop window, waiting for him to put up the next picture of Paachu. It was great publicity and perhaps that was the only reason Varky did not stop shooting this man. As for Paachu, he had so patronized the photographer initially that now he couldn't bring himself to say anything, even when he saw that the townsfolk openly laughed at some of the photographs. Besides, for a long time Paachu's hurt at being laughed at was perhaps overridden by his gratification at seeing pictures of himself (whatever it was that he was doing in them), blown up thus and showcased for the town to see.

Gradually, Paachu's retired life stood naked, in a sense, on Varky's display windows. The people of Karuthupuzha roared with laughter. The ex-Inspector, shorn of his glory and his uniform, was a thing of ridicule, though he was only doing things that any ordinary person would do in the course of a normal day. People guffawed until their sides ached as they looked at pictures of Paachu 'Yemaan' checking to see if some mangoes in his orchard were ripe. They walked far just to see the man shot in close-up as he exercised bare-bodied in the morning. They sat on a parapet on the roadside to overcome bouts of laughter at a photo of him shooing a cow away before she ate his plantain. And thus Varky's photographs fuelled the laughter directed at Paachu Yemaan from the One Mind of Karuthupuzha.

On lonely afternoons Sharada wondered if the treatment her husband had meted out to the townsfolk while in service had ever warranted such sustained vengeance upon him during his retirement. As far as she could tell he had really been quite harmless, beating up only the odd crook and magnifying rumours of the incident himself later. Her husband had never really been the kind of cold-blooded terror he had made himself out to be. True, he had sought all kinds of privileges from his position, but he hadn't been cruel or even overly oppressive, she thought.

Or had he been? That would remain the question of her life. The one she would never dare approach him with.

At times she felt that she did not really know all of his past. There might, just might, have been bloodcurdling goings-on behind the walls of that police station that she did not know about. Why else would a whole town gang up on a retired man? If this wasn't collective vengeance, what was?

At such moments of intense doubt, Sharada would stand before her Lord Murugan and pray that the past, if it was cruel, be undone. The Lord had the power, she knew, to change things across all time. He could undo the evils of the past and restore in her husband the kind of innocence she saw in his heart, or thought she did. He could make it be that Paachu had never hurt anyone, really, and all that was said about him was either meaningless or spiteful rumour. Lord Murugan could do that if he was moved to do so.

Another person, too, wondered about this laughter, though with a far lesser degree of hurt and desperation. This was Barber Sureshan. He sympathized with Sharadechi. But he did not know what to feel for Yemaan who, he knew, had once made it his business to be hated and feared across town. Yet, Sureshan could not understand how the small town could come together as one to laugh at this man.

At times when Paachu Yemaan came over to his shop to have his head shaved and his moustache shaped, Sureshan would roll the man's head around in his palms. At such times he would think there was indeed something comical about this man. Or was it something infinitely more pathetic? He couldn't say. Paachu always made Sureshan hang up the CLOSED sign outside his shop window because he wished for no ordinary mortal to walk in when he, the Yemaan, was here availing himself of the barber's services. Yes, Paachu was responsible for doing things that invited laughter. But the One Mind of the town just made it infinitely worse.

And as we know, ex-Inspector Paachu was not the only victim

of this collective mindset that was pitiless when it wanted to be. The One Mind of the town had actually forced Joby back into perpetual drunkenness, Barber Sureshan thought sadly, presumably so that it could continue to laugh at him. Sureshan had seen the positivity with which Joby had taken to his new job, but it had gradually been eroded. Sureshan wondered sometimes if he, or anyone else, had the power to go against the One Mind and set things right for a suffering friend.

11.

Joby's Greatest Love

The rain came pattering down, out of season and out of the blue. It hit Joby and Priya's umbrellas in heavy drops as they waded their way to school, and they had to shout to be heard. But, of course, it was not to each other that they shouted, for that would be a violation of Paachu's condition. 'Was Uncle Paachu always like this?' said Joby to the bitch Lilly who was totally drenched and loving it. 'I mean, was there a time he used to buy you dolls and talk gently to you?'

Joby had been transporting Priya to school and back for a few weeks now. In all that time, he had missed only two mornings. Not condescending to directly declare he was pleased, Paachu Yemaan had however blessed the arrangement by finally offering to pay Joby a modest monthly fee, warning right away that he wouldn't entertain any negotiations on the amount.

'Yes, of course,' Priya yelled back at Lilly over the sound of the rain. 'I still have the last doll he bought me, though she is all dirty and torn by now. He used to love me then.'

'Oh, he still loves you, I'm sure.' Lilly looked at her master, puzzled at what he was telling her. She detected the presence of some strange emotion in his voice. 'It's only that since his retirement he is a bit disappointed with the world.'

'He would have loved me more if I were a boy. If I could become an inspector, like he was, quickly.'

'And you would like to be a giant wheel operator?'

'Yes.'

It had taken Joby a little while to get over his initial dislike for the girl. As we have seen, this irritation had less to do with Priya's personality and more to do with Joby's fear of her uncle, the discipline and hard work that had been imposed on him and, most importantly, the withdrawal symptoms that had accompanied his cutting back on his drinking. When his intake of arrack had gone up, thanks to Bubru's efforts, he'd had to cope with working while under the influence of alcohol. Despite all this he had grown fond of Priya, all her little quirks and peculiarities. Looking at her cringing under the umbrella, he wondered if she was the kind of child that caught a cold from unseasonal rains. He hoped she wouldn't fall ill and his concern underlined how much he had started to enjoy her company.

'Say,' he looked suddenly down again at Lilly. 'I told you we are being followed by that stupid Constable Bubru, right?'

Priya nodded to Lilly.

'How about giving him the slip?'

She nodded to Lilly again, this time more vigorously. Priya was always ready for a game. He knew that Bubru would already have made at least one of his reports to Paachu Yemaan, and the fact that they were communicating by addressing Lilly instead of each other might by now be known to the Yemaan. Since Paachu had begun paying Joby wages, it meant Yemaan was prepared to overlook this; so maybe it was time to push the envelope.

They were coming to the end of the endless field. Just past it, the road would take a bend, Joby knew. He knew that Bubru was following them in spite of the rain, for he had seen bits of a plastic raincoat sticking out from behind a tree trunk a little way back.

As they rounded the bend Joby yelled for Priya to hold her umbrella tight, and pushed the cycle right through the hedge by the side of the road. He was confident that the rain would drown the sounds they were making. Once they were through the hedge the ground dropped steeply towards a hidden path in the grass.

The cycle rolled down this slope rapidly, heavily, Joby holding the handlebar with both hands and clenching his umbrella between his chin and shoulder. He prayed for two things: that Priya would not scream in her excitement and that Lilly wouldn't start to yelp out of fear. Neither made a sound. He beamed through his exertion at the thought of Bubru standing by the main road wondering where they had disappeared to. The hedge was a perfect screen.

By the time they reached level ground and the bicycle stopped hurtling forward, Joby was almost out of breath and on the point of blacking out. He heard Priya ask if he was all right, turning her head religiously towards Lilly. He nodded happily, put the cycle on its stand, walked up to a shrub and vomited.

I am given to these surprising bouts of adventure, Joby thought in wonderment. Despite his infirmities he would suddenly do things like climb up electric poles to rescue linemen or slide down slopes with a little girl on a cycle. He smiled happily, thanking God that they had not slipped on the wet grass.

They moved on again, down a narrow path and reached a coconut grove. There was no way Bubru would find them here. Joby planted the cycle and helped Priya get off, not touching her but holding on to her umbrella while she dismounted. Paachu's conditions had turned into a game between them and the first to break a rule would be the loser.

Priya sat down in the grass, adjusting her little skirt under her with ladylike smoothness. Lilly was trying desperately to tell her two friends that this stop was not in their routine and that they had made a mistake. But when Joby sat down, she settled next to him with a shrug that implied 'You're the boss'. She smelt of damp fur.

Soon the rain slowed to a trickle and then stopped. Only the leaves of the coconut tree shed droplets for a while longer. They both wondered about their show of defiance, then laughed with glee. Joby knew he probably would get beaten up by Bubru or perhaps Bubru would report this to Paachu Yemaan and the punches would come from there. But he didn't care. It was worth it, this little adventure—

it was something they shared and it made them laugh.

'Remember, I told you I could make you some dolls out of coconut tree parts? Well, how about now?'

Joby got up, looked around and began gathering the materials he needed. Out of coconut leaves and a small fruit he made her a little doll. The three spots on the tiny fruit were the two eyes and a mouth. Priya liked it very much. There was husk for hair and even a rudimentary skirt made of a single strand of leaf. 'I can do better with a few pins and some glue,' he told Lilly, as Priya settled down to examine her new toy. It was a long time since she had had a doll. Then Joby asked, 'So how is the love affair in your school taking shape?'

'Oh, it's taking shape all right,' Priya said absently, now talking to the doll. She seemed preoccupied and Joby left her to herself. But then she suddenly returned to Joby's question and began, still keeping her eyes on the coconut doll, 'Now Kannan Maash and Ambili Teacher are in a world of their own. They think nobody is watching.'

Joby quickly made her another coconut doll, this time a man with shorter hair and trousers. In Priya's imagination the girl doll immediately became Ambili Teacher and the man doll became Kannan Maash. She told Joby, looking at Lilly who was now fast asleep, how Head Maash had discovered that Kannan Maash was leaving messages on the blackboard for Ambili Teacher. Although his initial resistance to their affair seemed to have vanished suddenly, he did rearrange the timetable so that Kannan Maash's classes would never come after Ambili Teacher's. 'Why does the love between two people interest the others so much? Do they not have any other work?' Priya asked Lilly.

'Oh, I don't know,' Joby replied, looking accidentally at Priya and then turning away in a hurry. He prodded Lilly with his foot because he found it odd to be talking to a sleeping dog. 'Many people decide to turn against lovers for no reason. Jealousy, I suppose. But it need not always be *others* who are against love. There is something that is always going against love, I think; either the world or something else. That's why for love to come to fruition it's always a challenge. God has designed it in such a way that only the deserving get to see their love fulfilled. But think of it this way: isn't that what makes love so great? That very often it can lead not to life's greatest happiness but the very greatest sorrow? I found this in my love.'

'Hmm,' Priya said maturely. She had come to put on this expression now whenever Joby talked of things she didn't understand much.

'I think almost everybody falls in love in their youth,' Joby said, beginning on another doll, this one with a big moustache made of husk. 'I did, too. With Saraswati Teacher. We were both young then. So young!'

'Saraswati Teacher, the music teacher!'

'Yes. She teaches classical music to little children. Still does, I think.' He prodded Lilly again, and the bitch put her head up sleepily. 'I used to ferry children to her place in my autorickshaw; a lot of children, like grapes on a bunch. I used to ferry them to her pretty little house, in the south of town. She was all alone, like I was then. At the time I had already started drinking heavily, probably out of frustration that I was doing nothing more important with my life than ferrying little children around. I used to blame the world for not giving me a more important role.'

Priya's eyes widened as she stopped looking at Lilly and looked directly at Joby. It seemed like Joby was about to start talking about himself at last, with a kind of openness that was new to him.

'At first when I heard Saraswati Teacher singing it was nothing special. She sang classical stuff and the children sang badly after her. I leaned against the window evening after evening, sometimes with a bottle of arrack in my hand, sometimes already drunk, and sometimes eagerly waiting to take the children back home so I could go have my drink. To me her singing was nothing special, er...as I said, just another ordered, structured component of this hypocritical world with its hollow beauty and self-made rules. I mean, she sang in a certain way and if you sang any other way that would be incorrect, from the "classical" point of view. And yet, God hadn't come down and told us that these were the rules of singing, right? We had given ourselves those rules and then we stuck to them like they were the rules of God. So I was sceptical of this whole classical music business, and found nothing special in her voice.'

Joby wasn't attempting to use words that Priya could understand. He was just going on, talking more to himself than to her. She was intrigued that he could speak so well; he didn't sound at all like a man who sometimes fell asleep in drains.

'And yet I unfailingly stood by the window every evening, listening intently. I suppose I was beguiled by the contrast between her practised, mastered and controlled voice and the unpractised, un-mastered voices of the little children. I invariably compared the two. Whoever had made those rules of classical singing, God or man, I started to like the way she stuck to them; her absolute control over her own voice that made her stick to difficult pitches and sudden dips and climbs. I liked the fact that she never ever broke the rules of music, never felt like she might like to break them, even once, just for the sake of it. You understand, there was no anarchy at all about her. On the contrary, she seemed to have sacrificed so much, meditated even, to gain absolute mastery over herself so that she might perfectly comply. *That*, I found immensely attractive.'

'Hmm,' Priya said as though she understood him. She felt she had to play the role of the listener. It seemed to help Joby in some way.

'Well,' he said, waking Lilly again, this time absently. 'Very soon I was riding on her voice, standing there at the window, the way I rode on alcohol. Very soon I thought I could hear her swaraas in the sound of the wind in the night. Her singing put me at peace with the world. Apart from arrack, it was only Saraswati Teacher's voice that helped me make any sense out of my dull life. It filled my emptiness as I noticed how nuanced it really was. I could see that most of her students would never sing like her. And yet it was with such hope and clarity that she taught them!'

'You were in love,' Priya decided. 'Even Kannan Maash was very awkward at first.'

They were now talking to each other and letting Lilly sleep.

'Yes,' said Joby, and shut his eyes, sitting against the coconut tree behind him, so that he seemed to be talking in his sleep. 'I was in love or rapidly falling in love. But I did not know what she felt or if she felt anything at all about me. I mean, what could she feel about me, a drunk who only drove children about?

'Yet it was obvious to me that she had noticed me standing at the window. That she didn't object to me standing there meant the world to me. My stupid heart had perhaps concluded that that in itself meant she liked me. She was letting me listen to her sing, wasn't she? She was also letting me look at her when she sang. I don't know, I don't remember exactly what I was thinking at the time. A part of my mind should have asked itself what a young lady might find attractive in an autorickshaw driver who stood at a window with a bottle in hand every evening. But then when I heard her singing, I *felt* her love and thought it was love for me. To this day I don't know the truth of it. I don't know whether she ever, *ever*, felt anything for me at all.

'Then one day it happened! She asked the children to repeat the same raga over and over again until she came back. Then she got up and came out the door towards me. I saw that in a moment my fate would be decided. She was going to open her heart to me and the slight smile on her lips foretold eternal happiness for me. She was walking towards me and I realized that it was the first time that I had seen her standing, walking. Oh, she moved like a goddess! I felt weak in my knees and clutched my bottle tightly.

'She came right up to me and stood near enough to melt me! With a smile hanging to her lips like bits of song, she pronounced softly: "No drinking here. Toddy is not permitted."'

'I felt such a rush that she had addressed me directly for the first time. That was when I actually understood how far I had fallen into this. I was weak like a feverish boy. Through my dry lips I said the most absurd thing in the world: "It's arrack, not toddy." Her smile widened at that. Then she walked back to her class, gliding again like a thing of the heavens.

'After that I never brought a bottle to her window. My heart went into raptures to think I was sticking by *her* rules. I was complying. After that day I would deliberately show her that my hands were empty. Sometimes she smiled at me through her singing, in silent acknowledgement. And from that point onwards, so far as I was concerned, she was singing for me. Her singing was the conversation between us. It spoke for both of us, emptying out treasures of love towards each other. No, of course I could still not say she loved me, or even liked me, but I knew that she acknowledged my existence. To be fair to myself, it was more than that. She smiled at me often; as often as every evening, in fact.

'Now then, what's youth if you aren't going to be a little stupid? She had only told me not to drink on her premises, but I started to think that she had asked me to cut down on my drinking. So I cut down. I drank only in the evenings, never before, and the quantity was decreasing, too. The tough rebel was softening for love. And sure enough, I was quite certain that she felt something for me as well. I was sure of it! She blushed sometimes when she looked in my direction. I decided to experiment and stood at another window and observed that she seemed puzzled; her eyes searched everywhere for me. My presence seemed to add mellifluousness to her voice.'

Joby couldn't be sure of this, but he did feel that Saraswati Teacher and he were sometimes lost in each other; she would sing on and on, he felt, sometimes even forgetting the children who had come to learn. And it was an established fact that sometimes the classes would continue beyond their allotted time—the children's mothers had expressed their concern to him when he dropped them back.

Of course he did think about proposing or marrying. She was of a different community and in those times it might have been a revolutionary alliance. The rebelliousness of it was an added attraction to Joby. Why, they might be forced to run away from Karuthupuzha in order to get married!

Priya said, 'But then why on earth didn't you marry her? Why didn't you two run away?'

Joby sighed deeply. He turned to Lilly, because when practical matters struck him he also automatically remembered Yemaan's conditions, 'What can I say? The fact is, I never even proposed to her. It was almost as if all the exchange between us had been in her singing, and nothing else. Nothing real, nothing of this world. One moment I would think she loved me passionately, the next I felt I was nothing to her. I couldn't be sure she even knew my name. Absolutely no confirmation, you know...no solid confirmation that I could even suggest things like love or marriage to her. Maybe I thought that if I proposed I would kill it—I might do something crass, and that would bring something heavenly crashing down to the filth of the earth. It was all so silly! We just spent a lifetime together in a sense, she singing and me listening at the window.'

He was lost again for some minutes and Priya let him be. Then he suddenly said with a start: 'What about school! Get up, get up, we are very, very late!'

He handed her the last doll, a bald one with a heavy moustache made of husk. Priya made a face as if to suggest she might bunk school today, so they could continue with Joby's love story. She said, as he made her mount the bicycle, 'Even Kannan Maash thought at first that Ambili Teacher wasn't interested in him.'

But Joby was already thinking about what he would tell Head Maash, because little Priya had probably missed the first class. Punctured tyre, possibly. They could sell that story even to Paachu Yemaan if Bubru complained to him.

When they reached school a little later, he saw Kannan Maash and Ambili Teacher (he knew them by sight, of course, so famous was their love), teaching in adjacent classes in spite of Head Maash's half-hearted attempts to separate them. Joby smiled and with warmth in his soul he prayed that their love might come to fruition.

◆

On the morning when Joby was telling the tale of his love to the sleeping bitch Lilly and Priya was intently listening, her fingers fiddling with the coconut dolls he had made for her, Photographer Varky was up in his studio working. His head was cocked to one side so that the smoke from his cigarette could rise up and not be trapped by the bill of his cloth cap, so his eyes wouldn't smart.

All of a sudden he began muttering almost continuously, pushing his cigarette to a corner of his lips so it wouldn't fall as he mumbled. If you heard him you wouldn't understand a word, for this was a language Varky and his camera had developed between them. Although it resembled Malayalam it was no more comprehensible than the vaguely patterned clack of a typewriter. Only the camera and the photographer understood each other. Varky also adopted a certain nasal tone when he spoke it. Here's a translation of what he was saying then:

'So Karuthupuzha says we can turn invisible and float through the air to take our pictures, eh? Hmm. Good! Good for business. Always keep them awed, as my terrible father used to say, may he rest in peace. And have you seen the pictures we have taken together. Yes, we have flown with the bees to see the common flowers in a way that no man has ever seen them before. We have looked out of cobwebs and burrows in the ground. Good, good for us. Keep them awed. But yet, more than the skies, more than views out of snake holes and anthills and rabbit burrows, it is at each other's faces that people like to gaze. They like to see people—suffering folk, laughing folk, fighting folk, lonely folk, drunk folk, rising folk, falling folk….'

Varky sifted through numerous pictures of clouds, stars, cows and trees, discarding them all. The people of Karuthupuzha had been treated to these for almost two months now, and to keep the interest alive, it was time for a special shot. Again.

He fiddled in his developing tray with his tweezers for the picture he had been working on. He had told the camera how the people of Karuthupuzha liked to see forbidden expressions, sly smirks, guilty shrugs, greedy stares and other such secrets that were normally hidden from view. It was one such picture that he was tweaking in the tray right now.

Varky smiled through the cigarette smoke as a sharp image of Paachu Yemaan was slowly born on his canvas. In the photograph Paachu was all oiled and drawing water from his well. He drew water once a day for his bath because the exercise was good for his biceps. The gleam of oil on his naked chest contrasted with the white of his body-hair. The muscles of his arms conflicted with the tiredness in his eyes. But most interesting of all was the little tuft on his head that was standing up once again, this time for the sole purpose of posing for the invisible photographer and his invisible camera.

This would be the picture to go up next in his display window. He knew that people would gather under this one, pass comments and cluck their tongues, marvelling at where exactly Varky had been, to capture this so secretively, so momentously, almost surreally. He smiled his dark smile then and, if you were there to see it, you would find it hard to accept that the only reason he took and displayed his photographs was in order to keep his business going in the town of Karuthupuzha.

◆

The morning sun had climbed just a little higher by the time Joby had turned his bicycle from the school gates and mounted it. The sky was fresh, as if the rain had washed all that empty air and hung it up to dry. Joby felt a distinct pleasure at the thought that he had given Bubru the slip, which meant he might go this morning without drinking. This was a new sensation for him, where drinking wasn't the only thing he looked forward to. He thought he would perhaps spend the rest of the morning cleaning around the house a bit and later take a nap before lunch. He knew that by the time he had dropped Priya back home in the evening he would be thirsting madly for his first drink, but it still suited him to try to remain sober in the mornings.

As he rounded the bend he saw Constable Bubru standing like a dark mountain in the middle of the road, silhouetted against the sun. He did not fear this man, who would probably plant a punch on his belly for running away with the little girl. But he felt displeasure bordering on hatred at the thought that Bubru would now sit heavily down on the cycle bar and make him heave towards the toddy shop, to drink at his expense and to make him drink too, so that he would never get out of this stupor through the day.

He came to a halt next to the man-mountain and Bubru clutched the handlebar the way you clutch the throat of a chicken. 'Ah! You really gave old Bubru the slip, didn't you? Where did you disappear to?'

'I-we just took a break from the road. We came a different way, t-to...we had a puncture,' Joby said, bracing himself to be hit.

'Shoooo! Puncture. What were you two doing together?' Bubru said. But without waiting for an answer he jumped onto the cycle. The punch would come later, perhaps. They moved in silence for a while, with Bubru whistling and Joby heaving at the pedals. The man's immense weight was a harsh punishment.

'As you know, the great Yemaan of this town has assigned me the task of spying on you,' Bubru said after a while. 'To make sure that you perform your duty very well, without getting drunk and falling into some pit with his precious little girl. But me, ah! I know a man needs his drink now, don't I? I understand.'

Joby looked at the sun gleaming off the balding spot on Bubru's pate. It struck him that Bubru was laughing at both Paachu and Joby by drinking at Joby's expense every day in return for giving Paachu a clean report.

'I understand that you like to play your little games,' Bubru was saying. 'But if you give me the slip again.... You want to be my friend, right? It's not like I am forcing myself on you, right?'

Joby gritted his teeth and concentrated on working the pedals.

For a moment he actually considered vomiting all over the balding pate in front of him and then getting himself killed for it.

'I have always thought that men who drink together remain friends for life. So don't give me the slip, my friend.'

Joby wasn't really listening. Instead he was thinking of how Bubru and Inspector Janardanan went around town leaking malicious anecdotes about Paachu. He thought that Bubru had no need, really, to blackmail him with a negative report to Paachu. He could simply pick Joby up, throw him into jail and beat him to his death just for fun, no questions asked. But he preferred to kill him this way. By making him drink and drink and drink, more than his body, his mind and his pocket could take.

As they pedalled to the toddy shop, looking for all the world like genuine friends, Bubru whispered sweetly to Joby that if he ever gave him the slip again he would beat him to a pulp.

12.

Confessions to a Canine

'Have you ever been to a workshop?' Joby asked Lilly. 'Have you seen mechanics bent over the insides of autorickshaws and cars? Looking deeply into grease-covered wires and pipes and chambers that make no sense to you or me. Well, that's how I then began looking into my own heart, bending low over it like a mechanic, moving dark wires aside to go deeper, tapping on strange pipes, opening up weird chambers. Ha ha! I could not simply accept the love in my heart, convey it to the object of my affection and maybe hope it would flower into a proper relationship. Oh, no, that's for ordinary folks. For Joby, the drunk philosopher of Karuthupuzha, the attraction I felt for Saraswati Teacher called for immense analysis, hair-splitting arguments with myself, tortured conflicts and even pangs of guilt. I took the bolts and nuts of my mind apart. I dismantled whatever relationship it was that I was having with her. To see if this thing was *really* love. I was going mad, nothing less, while she continued to sing to me in her mellifluous voice.'

As Joby rambled on, Lilly lurked by his side, very pleased. She liked being constantly addressed by the two favourite people in her life. It was evening and they were returning to Priya's home, and Joby's pretty much uninterrupted monologue had only started when the little girl had asked him to continue with the story of his great love.

'I used to brood a lot,' Joby continued, panting as he pushed the bicycle. 'My heart fluctuated between extremes. I listened carefully to her voice every evening. There were elements in her voice that clearly did not belong to classical music. There was emotion, excitement, fondness, longing, frustration, satisfaction, passion, sacrifice and a million other things in it if you looked closely and with enough love. These were elements of her own; the translations of her heart. She wasn't adding these ingredients from the set laws of music, nor were they for the benefit of the children sitting in front of her. They were for me! I fancied that her voice hadn't been quite so full of meaning and emotion when I had first started bringing the children. These were later developments; oh yes! To be precise, she had only started to sing quite so sweetly, so fully, after our conversation.

'I played that little conversation over and over in my mind. The way she had walked up to me like a divine apsara and, rather than immediately declare her love, whispered to me in a gentle yet firm voice, "No drinking here. Toddy is not permitted." I went over that moment again and again, sometimes lying on my back by the puzha and listening to its constant giggles, and at other times looking deeply into a bottle at the toddy shop. I replayed my own stupid answer—that this was arrack and not toddy. I replayed the way she smiled at that and, deigning not to reply, simply walked back to her class. Why, her very act of stopping the conversation there seemed immensely attractive to me! The finality with which she walked back, trusting I wouldn't drink there ever again, knowing I wouldn't, was something I found deeply significant. It seemed to me that she knew me; knew things about me, personally, almost intimately. Why, there had been something intimate about that little conversation, hadn't there? I wondered if she knew my name; if she would ever ask me my name.

'The funniest part was I dreamed that the way she had gently chided me for drinking so much was the way in which a loving wife would chide her husband. And then in the real world I would actually respond to her by stopping the arrack for a day or two. Then

I would realize I was just dreaming and go back to drinking myself silly, growing unreasonably angry with her for not actually playing the part of a loving wife as in my dream. Hee hee! In my mind we would have little fights, with little storms of emotion and outside my dreams I would take revenge by actually getting very drunk. I told myself that my self-destruction was how I was affecting her, making life painful for her. I would harm myself, hurt myself and thus get even with her for my suffering. All the while she just sang, but I heard love in her voice.

'But did it just go on like that? Oh no, not at all. Sometimes, or maybe it was often, the rationalist in me would take over. I would cruelly ask myself to come off it. I would say, "Wake up you idiot, you pitiable little boy, wake up and grow up! She is a reputed musician, and her voice *has* to be full of emotion. That's why people pay to listen to her and to have their children learn from her. The sweetness and meaning in her voice are not from love for you but from her own talent. Some people are born with a thing called talent. Everybody is not a wretch who finds nothing more important to do than drive children around."

'It was nothing less than madness, I tell you! When the rationalist took over, I felt totally worthless, I sometimes hoped the Wound in the Earth would swallow me alive. I made a critical distinction between how a respected—no, admired—music teacher and a common driver are valued. I firmly believed (perhaps I still do) that only people who did "big" things, like owning factories or giant businesses, had the right to be loved or respected. I mean, in an ideal world, things aren't supposed to be like that, but sadly that is only the stuff of movies. In the real world there are these differences, aren't there? There is, indeed, nothing in an autorickshaw driver that can be admired by a teacher of heavenly music. The rationalist in my head told me that I wasn't good enough for her.'

Joby paused, put the cycle on its stand, and went over to the side of the road to cough and then vomit. As he was returning he glanced at Priya. She had a strange, unreadable expression on her face. Perhaps she was moved beyond words. Being the town buffoon, it had been years since Joby had had a serious conversation with another human being, far less the kind of heartfelt, passionate conversations he had been having with this little girl of late, especially on the subject of the great lost love of his life. And even though Priya could not understand a lot of what he said (for he had long forgotten to make concessions for her age when he spoke) she listened with feeling. Just listening to him open up to her seemed to fill a deep emptiness inside her. It made her little heart overflow with warmth. It made her his friend. And it made her feel for him when he was sad and filled with longing for unattainable things.

'You wonder why I drink so much,' he told Lilly, wiping his mouth and taking the bicycle off its stand. 'Oh yes, I drank this morning, too. That wretch Bubru makes sure I drink in the mornings. Well, maybe it's good. It's good to be in a stupor, you know? See, my problem is with reality. Reality never lives up to my expectations. So I put arrack between me and reality.

'Aah, so I had these nagging convictions of my own worthlessness when the rationalist came into my head. But that's nothing. No, it doesn't hold a candle to the other doubt I had. Ha ha, listen to this one. Forget the question of whether *she* loved me. Many a time I wondered if *I* was indeed in love with her! A part of me observed that the lover in me was a schoolboy; a cheap, fragile, emotional wreck who didn't know what to feel. When I sometimes heard the wind through the branches in the evenings and the temple music wafting in the breeze, I thought longingly of her voice. God knows, that is so to this day. But at the same time this part of me wondered if I was in love with *her*, her being the lady herself, or, indeed only with her voice. I don't know if you understand—I don't know if it's the same among dogs and bitches…hee hee hee! I mean, I could go without seeing her for a while, but I had to hear her sing. I had this aching on holidays when I didn't have to take the children to her. I longed to hear her voice but I wasn't craving to actually see her...her physical form. So was I in love with her or only with her voice? That was one of this great philosopher's major doubts.

'Then I undertook an experiment. In the darkness of my room I imagined her singing. And then, I tried to visualize her. You won't believe me if I told you, but while her music filled my head, I could not picture her face! I could see her form, her grace as she walked, but I couldn't exactly see her face in my mind. Why? I asked myself. Had the mechanic dismantled the vehicle so thoroughly that he no longer knew which part went where? For a while, I thought my experiment showed that I did not love her but only her voice. Occasionally, in moments of clarity I could see her fully. I could see the little gold jewellery that she wore that seemed to merge with the near-gold skin of her arms and neck. I could see her full lips and deep, kind eyes with their fresh, almost childish eyelashes. But these moments were rare, whereas at all times I could summon her voice. I could hear her songs in the birds in the air, everywhere. I told myself that it was her voice that lived in my heart. As for the rest of her being, that was something I was only infatuated with. It was the voice that I was truly in love with and I couldn't propose to a voice, could I? I couldn't marry a song.

'I took my experiment further in a dream one night, during one of my bouts of heavy drinking. (You see, I have the rare ability to *induce* a dream; I just need to repeat something intensely while I'm going to sleep and the moment I fall asleep it appears as a dream!) I dreamt that she had lost her voice. It was a nightmare. I was frightened by the deafening silence of her classroom, where she sat searching for her voice. When I awoke I found that I only felt pity for her! Surely, that voiceless woman, however beautiful and innocent, wasn't someone I loved or even knew.

'So you could say that this was another reason why I did not open my heart to her. Whichever way I looked at it, I wasn't clear on what existed between us. I didn't even know if she saw that there *was* anything between us at all. So I waited. I stood by the window without my bottle, swooning to her song day after day, waiting for an angel to come and solve my problems for me.

'Now—almost a lifetime later—one thing is clear to me: I could never have proposed to a lady like Saraswati Teacher. Never. I remember once when I had told my friend, Barber Sureshan, about the state of my mind, he smiled his serene smile. He then declared, in his usual mystical way: "My dear friend, tell me this: who knows a rose better—the scientist who takes each petal apart to study it, or the poet who looks at the whole thing with passion and sings about it?"'

They stopped by a roadside shop so that Joby could have a soda. His mouth was drying up from all the talking. A couple of passersby teased him, asking if he wasn't mistaking the soda for arrack. Joby made a drunken face at them because that's what buffoons did. They went away laughing.

'Well,' he continued when they were on their way again, 'I did what all great philosophers do when they come up against a wall. I packed my bag and left. I took the bus out of Karuthupuzha one morning. I told no one where I was going, for I did not quite know myself. I just wished to go away and stay away as a means to get out of my impractical fixation (yes, that's how I thought of it at the time) with Saraswati Teacher's voice. As the breeze from the open window caressed my face, I smiled to think of what the mothers of Karuthupuzha would do that evening when I did not turn up to pick up their children for their music class. What rumours would fly when I did not appear at the toddy shop. People would probably say a panther had eaten me alive. I wondered how Saraswati Teacher would react to these rumours.

'I reached the city, and after staying a while, went to other towns and cities. I did not stay at any one place long enough to put down roots. I roamed far and wide, half the time in a drunken state, drinking myself to sleep every night, doing odd jobs while dreaming about big jobs, hating my menial existence. Indeed, I was so miserable I wouldn't have minded dying. Strange as it might seem, I did not think much of Saraswati Teacher, nor her voice. I just roamed the streets looking for work, formed the darkest of friendships, frequented some…loose women, even got into brawls in some places. It wasn't a great journey of self-discovery. It wasn't a search for the meaning of life, or the great Truth. It was the making of a buffoon and a confirmed alcoholic.'

At this point Joby stopped. His stomach felt queasy, the bile rose in his throat and he wondered if he needed to vomit again. The memory of those dark days, dark nights, dark streets and dark people was roiling his gut. He waited for the uneasiness to pass, burped and then continued with his peroration.

'I was sick often. I had to stop drinking arrack. That didn't really cut down my alcohol consumption because foreign liquor was more readily available in the cities. Availability aside, I'd keep changing the kind of liquor I drank—of all things, out of considerations for health. An idiotic friend of mine would tell me that beer wasn't as harmful to the liver as rum. In a flash, my cramped little room would fill up with beer bottles. Then some other idiot would pronounce that beer caused kidney problems; it was wine that was actually good for health. A little of it every day would in fact protect the heart. That would make me switch again. I would drink an unimaginable amount of wine, and my tongue would be sweet all day long. Next would come along a very scientific friend who would quote a newspaper article that said too much wine could cause diabetes. It would be back to rum. And so it went. Various stupid friends, prolonged bouts of drinking with all sorts of alcohol, and all the while my alcohol consumption kept going up.

'I'd drink every evening with these lowlifes, who would eventually go home to their families, while I would go to my lonely room and keep drinking. Joby the alcoholic had come to stay!

'Out of fear of mothalalis at my different places at work (managers in cities are far more strict than ours here in Karuthupuzha), I would pick myself up in the mornings and be at work on time. Sometimes my very skin would be flaming with sickness. Most often my head would throb like there was a piston inside it moving up and down, up and down. You know, mornings in cities are terrible for a drunk.

The honks of vehicles, peoples' feet thudding as they jog (all terribly fresh and healthy), loud music from hotels…Oh! It's terrible. In addition to the blaring noise, all the positivity of a day beginning, all that energy is so sickening.

'By now I had long forgotten our Saraswati Teacher and her singing. Oh no, the tragic hero wasn't even thinking of the root cause of his sorrow. No lover would have forgotten his injured romance sooner. So perhaps, indeed, the rationalist had been right after all. Perhaps I had never really been in love with her. Perhaps, after all, there was no root cause for my misery. Perhaps the reason I took the rose apart petal by petal was simply so that I could turn into this dark, melancholic drunk. This was my calling.

'I kept travelling, going a little further away from Karuthupuzha each time. I ate little or nothing at all and in the nights I could actually feel and even hear the liquor moving about inside me. I never ate dinner. It would have been physically impossible as there was no room in my tummy after all the alcohol. Strangely, and I find this truly remarkable, the deeper I sank into the darkness, the more I began to develop a strange fascination for what you might call "normal" human beings! I contrasted their light with the darkness, dinginess and stink of my room and my world, and longed to be like them. I remember, one day I saw a young man taking his wallet out of his pocket. His arms were muscular and tattooed. His behind was so well developed, so toned and supple, that the pocket of his jeans clung to the contours of his body and he had to actually wrench the wallet out. Everything about him was so bright and healthy and fabulous! I felt a peculiar metallic taste in my mouth just to watch him. I actually cringed under the desire to be normal and bright and…and strong, healthy. For days afterwards I kept my wallet in my back pocket and fished it out like that man had done, each time feeling that metallic taste in my mouth. I imitated the "normal" and yet I always went back to the abnormal, unhealthy and withered life of the alcoholic.

'I felt that same curious admiration for some of the people who drank with me. Not all, but some of them. You see, there were those who drank regularly, drank heavily and yet were not alcoholics! How was that possible? It was beyond my understanding how suddenly one day one of them would say, "I'm not drinking today. I feel a bit funny in the stomach. A soda will do for me." I mean, what mastery, what absolute control! He would just sit there, this man with the soda, while the rest of us drank. I admired such people because they let alcohol into their lives to almost the same extent as I did and yet were not controlled by it. Normal humans! I admired them, for they could go without a drop, drink less one day, eat well every time they drank, and generally look after themselves while I rapidly killed myself.

'From time to time I would be seized by sudden fits of resolve, especially on the rare good days I had. When I bought a new shirt or a pair of good leather sandals, I would immediately decide not to drink anymore. With this new purchase I would tell myself that I was greeting a new life. Here was a changed man, one who was like the others, leading a life where there were other joys than alcohol. I would sport that new shirt or sandal and step out into the brightness, feeling the air on me and connecting with the world. Once I bought a new Luna, that small bike Chacko the electrician goes around on, you know? Well, that evening I did not drink! I drove around on the Luna like normal people did, content, without the metallic taste in my mouth (which I cannot categorize as pleasant or unpleasant). I remember I bathed twice that day and had a very satisfying dinner. And actually went to sleep without a drink. Because this was the new Joby, the one who pulled his wallet out of his back pocket and rode a Luna like a man of the world.

'But by the next afternoon I had relapsed. Of course.

'Here's where I should tell you more about alcohol, the only steady companion I have had for much of my life. The thing about drink is it enables you to lie to yourself and nurture false beliefs for an unnaturally long time. It makes you forget about too much honesty, principles and such things. Whatever the kind of person you originally were, the Great School of Alcoholics trains all its disciples to fit one description—that of a liar, a hypocrite, even a cruel one. Cruel to yourself, I'm saying. You wouldn't believe the number of drunks I know who have grown old believing there's still hope and still time!

'Alcoholics are weakly optimistic. Imagine a fly caught in a web, having its life sucked out of it and still looking up fondly into the eyes of the spider, hoping to win its friendship. That's the alcoholic for you—hopeful till the very end. Every alcoholic tells himself for decades, *One of these days I will stop all this and become a new man. And then, with my hard and unbelievable experience of life, I will be better off than the others. I will be a great poet or a great artist or a great something....*

'So I kept trying to connect with other people, but always remained an outsider. I kept doing menial jobs and aspiring for greater roles. I kept trying to find ideal love and found only raw, crass, unreal forms of it. I made newer and newer generations of drink friends as the previous groups grew out of it and found better things to do. I fluctuated between the pleasure of totally wrecking my body and health, and suddenly taking to brightness and morning walks. I must have looked a spectacle, with my long hair, shrunken body and hard, round stomach. Hee hee, in one town (I do not remember which), I remember standing on my balcony every day, shortly after waking up in the mornings. I would get up and without a shirt on, look out at the day through the vapours of the previous night's drink, my head throbbing and my stomach trying to push everything up. There was a balcony opposite mine, on which an old woman would be trying to feed a baby she carried around on her hip. Every time the baby refused to eat, the woman would point at me to divert its attention! Because when the baby looked at me curiously, it forgot itself and she would deftly shove more food into its little mouth. That's the kind of exhibit I had become—a better option to distract infants than crows, cows and dogs.

'Well, I could go on and on about my life as a drunk, but I

suspect you are falling asleep. So let me cut it short and tell you how things finally panned out.

'The last town I was in was a damp place where the sea winds blew. It was maybe a little bigger than Karuthupuzha. Here I stayed in a sunny two-storied house. I lived on the first floor and the owner, an old widow, lived on the ground floor. She was a strange one! Well past middle age yet not stooping old, she had the chin of a man and the long fingers of a ghost. I noticed that people kept away from her. But one night she knocked on my door and from that night onwards we started drinking together. I found that she wasn't a bad sort at all; she was a loner and a bit weird, but in a harmless way. For example, she had made friends with a lot of crows who she thought were her dead relatives who had come back in their next lives. She put rice out for these crows on her window sill and they came and pecked at it as she watched fondly, talking to them and laughing with them. One rather handsome crow, with a grey head and a sleek black body, she claimed to be her husband. In his life with her he had loved it when she rolled rice into balls with ghee, and, truth be told, when she now rolled rice balls in ghee and kept it out, it was only this crow that came to eat it. The others left the rice balls for him.

'So we began drinking together, the landlady and I. I opened up to her about everything in my life, past and present. One night she said to me: "Mister Joby (she always added the 'Mister' to indicate we weren't too intimate—she did sense the impropriety in us being alone together in a room at night, in spite of her age). I don't know what your problem is, but I do know that you are wasting your life. I sense at times that you are depressed. Terribly depressed. Why don't you do something kind? You will feel better."

'I don't know if that woman, whose dead relatives were crows, meant anything when she said that, but it struck a chord. Maybe I could make my life count by doing something good and kind.

'I lay awake that night and thought about it.

'The next morning I called up my mothalali at the beedi factory I used to work in at the time and pretended to be sick. Instead of going to work I went over to the local orphanage. I wished to donate all the money I had saved for six months. It wasn't much, but then the fact that after giving it away I would not have a penny on me felt immensely good and grand. So I walked to the orphanage.'

At this point in his tale Joby fell silent. They were walking along a narrow road with shrubs festooned with inedible berries on either side of the road. There was total silence all around. Joby didn't realize that he had stopped talking and that the narrative was only carrying on in his mind. He pushed the bicycle silently onwards. Lilly looked enquiringly at her master. Having been with him most of her life, she could almost hear him think; she had heard him think this particular thought several times before. She knew that Joby couldn't find words for it. She whimpered in sympathy.

What had happened that day at the orphanage was this. When he reached the place with his pockets bulging with cash, he saw the most beautiful girl he had ever seen. She was barely in her twenties. That morning, as she watered the flowers inside the orphanage grounds, she looked so beautiful that Joby quickly checked to see if her bare feet were touching the ground.

How could he explain to his two friends today—one a canine and the other a little girl—what he himself had barely been able to understand that morning, ages ago? That girl in the garden didn't seem real to him. She was so painfully beautiful that he started to look for a blemish on her. He started to look for something to mar her perfection, because he felt that the tiniest mistake in her beauty would immensely reduce his suffering as he looked at her.

He found out shortly afterwards that she was Rosy. Everyone at the orphanage called her Rosykutty out of fondness, because they all treasured her beauty like it belonged to them. You wondered who in their right minds would leave a girl like that to be an orphan. What parents would let such a treasure go!

When he returned with all his cash still in his pockets and told his tale, his landlady cackled and they drank for the rest of the day and late into the night. Over the next few weeks the landlady turned into his mother and discussed an alliance with the head of the orphanage. Joby and Rosykutty became husband and wife with him still feeling it was all a long dream.

They had stopped under a banyan tree and Joby suddenly realized he wasn't speaking aloud to his audience. 'Well, did I tell you that it was at that orphanage that I met Rosykutty and I got married to her, rather hastily?' he said, picking up his story again. 'She was as beautiful as butterflies in a garden and that was enough for me to realize that I was finally in love. I married her immediately.

'Now that I think of it, it was as though a jigsaw puzzle had fallen into place. I had gone there to be kind—to help the orphans with all my earnings—and then the most beautiful girl I'd ever seen appeared before me like an angel. And the fact that she was an orphan meant I would actually be doing her a great favour by marrying her. I was quite convinced that there was a God. It was all so unreal, it just couldn't be.

'Ha ha! To this day, I don't know if my Rosykutty is for real. I sometimes check her side of the bed when I wake up at night to see if she has evaporated. Ha ha ha! She is an angel all right! She was not meant to live among the likes of us. I still look for a blemish that will make her real. I know that you cannot understand.'

They were rounding the bend in the road; past it was Priya's home. But once again he stopped the bicycle. Lilly walked some way ahead and then stopped to turn back.

'That's my story, and I don't know if I bored you,' he said, finally turning towards Priya and talking directly to her. 'When I came back to Karuthupuzha, some years after I left it, now a married man, I heard from people that the music teacher Saraswati was still unmarried. I didn't feel anything at all.'

He looked into Priya's surprisingly tiny face, feeling a pang of guilt. His soliloquy would have gone way above her head. He could not understand what had made him go on thus, not even caring to see if she was listening. But her face was sad. Slowly, still sitting on the carrier of the bicycle, she moved her head until it touched his shirt sleeve. She breathed in fumes of arrack and just when he feared she might sob, he heard her voice, 'You know, the scientist who takes a flower apart? He's a botanist. The one who studies animals has a funnier name but I can't remember it.'

13.

Retirement

Karuthupuzha sat, like everything else, on the endless arm of cosmic time. Things died, were reborn, life went on. The older pigeons, too tired to fly, fought losing battles against the cats that came to eat them. Their remains joined fallen leaves, dead insects and lizards that dissolved into the rainwater and became part of the soil. Yet when the rain sent up an aroma from the freshly wet soil, it wasn't one of death but of life.

Paachu Yemaan, who stood clutching the bars of the window of his first floor bedroom, did not like this smell. The moist, warm smell seemed to make him lethargic. Of all the smells of nature, Paachu liked the burning smell of lightning the best. He had smelt something similar in his youth, during his days at the police training camp whenever a gun was fired. That smell charged him up. This wet soil smell, on the other hand, was what put old men to sleep in the mornings, he thought with some dread.

This morning, the unthinkable had happened: Paachu had failed to ramp up his temper in front of his mirror. He had stood for quite a while looking at his own reflection, employing the usual techniques to break into fiery anger. He thought of petty crooks in the police station's jail. He thought of lawbreakers, gamblers under coconut trees. When these failed to turn the colour of his eyes to a fearsome red, he conjured up images of heroes on film posters with their fists clenched. As a last, desperate resort, he invoked pictures of the angry gods and goddesses who sometimes clutched the severed heads of demons in their hands. He looked on dismally as his eyes remained a sickly white and his giant moustache did not tremble on its own.

All that was rising inside him was an impotent irritation at his own failure. Perhaps the problem was that he was only staring at himself in the mirror. Perhaps he needed someone to direct his wrath at. His gaze landed on his black coffee, which had long gone cold. He played with the idea of thundering at Sharada for always bringing him his coffee cold, but he was terrified that she would see that he wasn't really angry and was only pretending. She might even stifle a giggle, which would be humiliating. He continued looking around the room. His eyes rested on a tiny spider hanging precariously from its invisible web from the ceiling. Outside the window he saw a lizard perched on a branch, unmistakably observing his every move. He noticed a line of ants that had slowed down in their march to glance at him and nod to each other. It was scary. People said that the photographer Varky could turn into some creature and take pictures from up walls and down branches. He knew all this was nonsense, but for a moment he couldn't help imagining his next picture at Varky's shop window—the ex-Inspector yelling at his poor, hapless wife!

'Tut tut!' he spat, 'you're as stupid as the rest of them!'

But he moved away from the window nonetheless. He felt naked in his own room; he was exposed on his porch when he oiled himself for a bath, when he gently pressed the mangoes in his orchard to see if they were ripe, when he sat down to a meal of boiled bananas, when he did almost anything. Photographer Varky! Paachu wondered for the umpteenth time what he could do about the man whom he had once praised so fulsomely.

Of late Paachu had stopped oiling himself out in the sunlight of his backyard before his morning bath. Up until a few months ago he used to proudly let the sun fall on his body as he exercised near the well behind the kitchen. But now he exercised only in his own bedroom, with the curtains drawn. When he sometimes glanced at his reflection in the mirror, he was overcome with disgust at how ridiculous he was beginning to look when he was oiled and stripped to the waist. His chest was flabby, its droop feminine against its vulgar hairiness. His belly protruded unhealthily in spite of all that exercise. His biceps hung loose. Sometimes he couldn't help wondering if he had always looked this absurd. After all, there must have been something inherently ludicrous in him for the photographer to have chosen him for such a long drawn-out campaign.

Paachu recalled the last picture of him that Varky had put up: he was oiled for his bath and was exercising his biceps by drawing water from the well. The tuft on his head had been standing up like someone eager to not be left out of the photo. The white of his chest hair looked decidedly pathetic. The only way that picture could have been shot without Paachu knowing was by Varky turning into a lizard or a spider on the wall opposite. The photo had been an instant hit in Karuthupuzha and held the record for remaining the longest in the shop window of Varky's Studio. It was rumoured that the footfall in Varky's Studio had increased spectacularly since that picture. Even Eeppachan Mothalali, who had once had to bribe Varky to pull down his wife's picture from the window, had come over to the studio with said wife to have a picture taken. Some people even suggested slyly that if Paachu charged for the picture, Varky might have paid.

Paachu sighed. Everything goes wrong on mornings such as these, he thought. He looked woefully at the neatly ironed uniform Sharada had laid out on the corner of the bed where the mosquito net had been loosened. He knew that his bowels wouldn't move today even if he slipped into the whole uniform—cap and baton and all—and strutted briskly around the room. He visualized the contents of his intestines hardened, stuck against the walls of his innards, refusing to come out. Boiled bananas, three times a day. No salt. Nothing fried, nothing with eggs. The only way things could get worse was if Varky put up a picture of him eating boiled bananas.

'Damn,' cursed Paachu Yemaan, listening morosely to the hum of the fan as its slight breeze listlessly swayed a corner of the mosquito net. He wished it was siesta time already.

Things were not going his way at all, and for some time now. Why, just yesterday, he had had something of a quarrel with little Priya and the girl wasn't talking to him now. He knew that she would stay away from him today, probably for the whole day. The fight had begun when he suggested that they could perhaps disengage now from that drunk Joby. After all, Uncle Paachu was doing nothing in particular throughout the day (and it was painful to him to admit that), so he could perhaps resume ferrying her to and from school. They could stop on the way for some roadside ice-cream soda, which she loved. They might even do this every day. What's more, they would only need to start much later from home because they would go by scooter, and that would mean she could sleep a little longer in the mornings. Paachu went so far as to suggest, though she wasn't to raise her hopes yet, that if the lump sum following his retirement finally came from headquarters, they might perhaps buy a jeep just like the official one.

So it was only natural that he would get a little irritated when Priya seemed completely unmoved by all this. She brought her eyelids halfway down and simply shook her head to everything, without even waiting for him to finish.

'Damn,' Paachu cursed again. 'What has that drunk done to her to replace her own uncle? Why, he can't even stand for a while without falling asleep!'

The memory of how she used to climb on to his lap in the police station and how all the constables would fuss around her rose within him, and it hurt him in that obscure place in his heart.

It had been a terrible mistake hiring the drunk and then bribing Constable Bubru to spy on the two. Now Bubru was turning into the bigger problem. The man was having a lot of fun—dark, loathsome fun—at Paachu's expense. Paachu had learned from the men who worked for him in the orchard that Bubru was drinking with Joby right from morning. Every once in about two weeks Bubru came in to report to Paachu Yemaan. He'd adopt a tone of mock seriousness, narrating with relish how Joby and Priya had given him the slip and turned up late to school after doing God knew what. Bubru enjoyed seeing Paachu's helplessness when he had reported how Joby and Priya spoke to each other every day by directing their conversation at the dog, effectively laughing at Paachu's conditions.

Paachu found it unbearable to endure Bubru's torment, and had told Bubru to put an end to the spying. But the labourers in his orchard told him that Bubru continued to tail Joby and Priya. When the compensation from Paachu had stopped, Bubru had simply bullied Joby into parting with a share of the wages Paachu paid him. Only the other day he had come to Paachu and, with a terrible pretence of loyalty, had revealed to him, 'That drunk is now teaching your niece to cycle. God help you, sir! I wouldn't be surprised if the child comes home drunk one of these evenings.'

Paachu now looked into the mirror again and imagined striking Bubru on the face. His heart started to beat harder at the prospect, but he still wasn't getting angry. With dismay he realized that it wasn't anger but fear that he saw in his bloodless eyes. Was he growing to be afraid of Bubru? For all the slander, he did not seriously believe that Joby would bring Priya to any harm. He quite trusted Priya's childish trust for the drunk. It was Bubru who was beginning to seem ugly and dangerous.

Paachu saw that despite his bitter struggles to remain tough and his daily practice at building up his anger, he was actually turning soft. A very uncomfortable development had occurred recently. Paachu, Sharada and Priya went at least once a month to Varghese's Cinema. Like in the past, Constable Chandy still bought them tickets in advance. (Paachu now forced Chandy to accept a small commission for booking his tickets; he would never have dreamed of standing in line for tickets himself because the very idea of going to the cinema would have to be abandoned if Paachu had to queue up with commoners for the tickets.) The films were always the same: they were under new banners with different actors, but the stories were always the same—some intense melodrama, some angry heroes and melting heroines, at least one rape sequence, one or two moralizing speeches that never seemed to end, and some stiff fighting with barrels toppling, pots breaking and men flying. Nothing had changed in this regard. The change was in Paachu. Now, during sentimental scenes, Paachu actually felt tears threatening to spill out! When lost siblings were reunited, when ladies discovered the hidden but innate worth of their heroes, when the hero's best friend died in his arms, Paachu felt like crying. He had to struggle to hold back his tears. At such embarrassing moments, he swallowed hard, burped, sneezed and made all sorts of loud noises lest a sniffle escape. He knew that the sentiments in the films were all the same, that they were predictable, clichéd, boring and excessive. Yet, involuntarily, he was moved to tears each time. He suspected that Sharada knew, and was tortured by the thought that little Priya knew as well. Once or twice he felt that in the darkness her small face had turned towards him.

Another awkward development was that he now increasingly seemed to have nothing to do. His daily routine seemed hollow and pointless. When he went over the same motions again and again, even to him it seemed that he was merely pretending to be busy. He walked up to inspect his orchard in the morning and then again in the evening. He suddenly seemed to have discovered an inexplicable concern for his fruit trees. He seemed to have developed an empty, embarrassing passion for them. He also frequently roamed in and out of the kitchen under the pretext of asking Sharada something and then realizing that it was pointless to ask her that. Seeing him this restless made her worry about his health. Sometimes she touched his forehead to check if he was running a temperature. Most days he would lie down on his chair on the porch to read the papers and then get up again, go inside and switch on the radio. Numerous times during the day he would visit the lavatory to see if he could empty his bowels. This was what worried Sharada the most—so much so that she telephoned Purushan Vaidyan, the doctor and sought his advice.

Paachu had trained himself never to do things that were pointless. This was an invaluable skill during his days as inspector, but now it only left him with more time to do nothing. For example, until a while ago, Paachu was used to pointing his radio carefully to the west, like everyone in Karuthupuzha who believed that west-facing radios gave accurate weather forecasts. He would completely trust the weather forecast that was given when the radio faced the right direction and would plan his day accordingly. When it predicted it would rain he would carry his umbrella when he went out to the orchard in the evening. If there was going to be a lot of thunder and lightning he would prepare to spend the whole evening on his porch, watching the rain. If it was going to be dry and sunny, he asked for boiled bananas in advance because such weather invariably brought on the constipation.

But of late he had stopped listening to the forecasts. Sharada noticed and was worried. In truth, Paachu had simply realized that he had no task to undertake that called for such meticulous planning. His orchard wasn't a huge expanse—he could simply rush indoors in case it started to drizzle. If he wished to enjoy thunder and lightning he could go and lie down on his porch when it began; there was no great need for him to know beforehand.

Similarly, he figured that there was no particular need to keep checking if the mangoes were ripe—the workers would do that for him. The vendor who bought coconuts from him would pay even if Paachu didn't keep calling him; he had never once defaulted on payment in all these years, probably thanks to Paachu's police background. He stopped cutting out articles from newspapers as there wasn't a single article he had ever reread later from his scrapbook. There was no point pestering Priya about her homework, Sharada about what was for lunch or his workers about their union and politics. They always had the same, mindless things to say.

He seemed to be sleeping for longer intervals during the day and having trouble falling asleep at night. The other night he had kept Sharada awake, complaining about how Joby and Priya were speaking to each other through that dog and laughing at him. Of course, Sharada was only amused. She said sleepily that maybe it was just these kinds of antics that endeared the drunk to Priya, and then promptly dozed off. Paachu stayed awake, thinking uncomfortably that perhaps she was right.

Of late, Paachu seemed to look forward to falling ill. It was almost as if he was eager to come down with a fever. Every time he sneezed he would place a palm on his forehead, hoping it was a fever so that Sharada would fuss over him. Whenever he came down with a fever, Sharada placed wet towels on his forehead, checked very frequently to see if his temperature was shooting up, prepared steaming black coffee with pepper and jaggery, coaxed him to drink it in spite of its pungency, sent someone to the local English medicine shop for cold balms and even some pills that Doctor Ambookkan had prescribed ages ago, rubbed balm right through the hair on his chest, held her balm-smeared fingers up to his nose to breathe in, made him inhale steam with a thick blanket over him to prevent the vapour from escaping, and generally sat by his side through the day. She even woke up at regular intervals at night to check on him. It was almost as if Sharada prayed that the fever would get her and leave her husband or her little niece.

At such moments, again, Paachu felt like crying. While he tried to hide his emotions by being fussy and cranky, Paachu was increasingly beginning to enjoy these sudden surges of emotion. Though he liked to believe that his sorrow seemed so sweet as it was a response to Sharada's love and dedication, it cannot be ignored that he primarily felt immense self-pity on such occasions, and possibly that was what he enjoyed so much.

This morning, standing before the mirror, he wondered if his inability to work up a temper was because he was coming down with something. Sure enough, there was a rumble deep in his tummy (like thunder on a faraway hill), and he pushed the spot above his bellybutton to check if it hurt. 'Oh, all I need now is a stomach problem!' he groaned under his breath but with concealed longing.

He sat down heavily on the bed, almost tearing the delicate mosquito net, and absently wondered what he must do about his little niece and the little fight they'd had. He couldn't resist thinking that if he now came down with a terrible stomach illness, Priya would be moved to forgive him. What if, in a fit of sympathy, she even gave up her friendship with Joby? A drunk couldn't take the place of an ailing uncle who had carried her around as an infant, could he?

Paachu Yemaan imagined he was dead and being laid to rest by the townsfolk. In his vision, it was raining and people were gathered under an endless stretch of black umbrellas. 'Paachu Yemaan, the former inspector of police, is no more,' they kept whispering, as if finding it impossible to believe that such a man could die. Priya was clutching Sharada's saree and crying her heart out. Sharada rested her head on her husband's dead feet, too numb to even shed a tear. Joby stood in a corner, abandoned and sad. Even Constable Bubru was sorry that the joke had gone too far.

He shook himself free of the stupid vision though it had immediately lifted his spirits.

The problem was, this coldness from little Priya was driving him to melancholy. What was more, that drunk Joby was trying to teach her to cycle. On a bicycle that was two or three times her size! And how could he teach her without lending a dirty hand? Had he touched her? What if she fell down and hurt herself?

He could not pull up Joby and sink his fist into him. Priya would hate him! The girl seemed to have forgotten that Paachu was her uncle, her blood, her kin—her parent, in fact. Joby was a drunk who had marched into their lives only the other day thanks to their collective stupidity. He cursed himself for feeling awkward about dropping Priya on his scooter. This whole damn problem was because of his bloated ego, nothing else.

He gave up trying to practise building up anger that morning and was thoughtful for the rest of the day. Sharada saw that the newspaper was untouched the whole morning. And she noticed that

that was the day her husband sacrificed another routine of his: he stopped reading the paper four times. 'What do I have to do with it all anyway?' she heard him mumbling one day. 'The same things keep happening in the world, in spite of me.'

She again strategically placed the Mahabharata, the Ramayana and the Gita in his path, but he still did not pick them up.

As the days seemed to stretch on and on, visions of fatal illnesses, death and other such tragic occasions on which the people of Karuthupuzha would recognise his worth were becoming more and more frequent. Nothing else changed in his life. Each day seemed more unbearable than the previous one. He continued to be irritated with Priya's new friendship. He found it unbearable that sometimes she was openly bored with him. She cherished the coconut-leaf dolls from Joby more than the plastic guns and Patton tanks he bought her. She laughed with Joby, cried with him, and told Sharada word-for-word the stories he had told her, often mimicking his drunkenness so comically that Sharada laughed and laughed. Paachu eavesdropped on these conversations sometimes and his heart ached as Priya seemed to drift further from him with every passing day.

He had tried and failed to shrug Constable Bubru off. Inspector Janardanan called once or twice to enquire about Bubru's service, and Paachu could hear the laughter in his voice. Photographer Varky continued to display his work on Paachu for all to see and savour.

Pariera's regular visits and his unassuming friendship now began to provide Paachu with some much needed respite. Another source of comfort was his visits to Barber Sureshan's shop, where the barber gently held the Yemaan's head in his palms before cutting his ridiculous tuft off. Through all of this, Paachu continued to stand at his window, trying to shake off the feeling that the aroma that the rain evoked was not one of lethargy after all, but of warmth and home.

14.

A Haircut and a Shave

Barber Sureshan could smell the abundance of the jackfruit tree through the window of his shop. He thought about the years when the tree used to be completely barren and its current perennial fertility seemed almost magical. There was so much of joy under the shade, the barber thanked God whenever he saw it. He would sometimes imagine that even if a terrible drought ravaged Karuthupuzha and nothing else grew, this tree would still feed everyone.

As he looked out at it now, there was a smile on his face. The smell of wet soil merged with the scent of ripe fruit and animal fur. The aroma of his incense sticks only added to this intoxicating mix. He saw two little birds bathing playfully in a puddle between the tree's roots. A buffalo was inspecting a fallen fruit while a beautiful bird trotted up and down its back. A little higher up Sureshan could see a yellow snake, almost hidden among the newborn leaves. It was so sweetly asleep, it wasn't aware that day had dawned and the market was slowly beginning to buzz with activity.

A little distance away, a battered-looking truck was emptying sacks into the basement of a shop. Abu the recycler was singing obscenities to an old tune for the benefit of the people waiting at the bus stand. Some of the men laughed at his singing while the women looked away. Perched on a faraway electric post was Chacko the electrician. He had resumed climbing poles only two weeks ago after the sudden panic attack that had hit him on the day of the storm. Barber Sureshan noticed Paachu Yemaan walking towards his shop from the far end of the market, umbrella held up even though it had stopped raining. He had a cloth tied over his pate, which told Sureshan that he was hiding the tuft that had grown right back up. Sureshan hurriedly dusted his already clean but ancient salon chair. He needlessly rearranged the comb, scissors and tin of talcum. He slid a fresh blade into his razor. He got the scented massaging oil down from the shelf. He was just adjusting the wick in his lamp when Paachu Yemaan walked in and sat down heavily upon the chair.

'Put up the CLOSED sign,' he commanded with the air of a superior officer demanding a closed-door meeting with his subordinate.

'Right away, Yemaan,' Sureshan complied. He left the window ajar so that the magical aroma from the jackfruit tree could still find its way in. He took Paachu's umbrella, removed the cloth on his head, folded the latter neatly and placed both on the wooden bench behind them.

The barber would have uttered his usual phrases of greeting, asked after Sharadechi's health and little Priya's wellbeing, but something stopped him. He sensed that the Yemaan was bursting to talk and was only arranging and rearranging some things in his mind before he began. So he quietly started to stick the tuft up with some water from a bowl, making it stand to its maximum height.

'You people have really worked me into a corner,' Paachu said finally, glaring at Sureshan in the mirror.

'Yemaan?'

'Where do you people get your ideas from?' Paachu continued. 'You and that wife of mine. You are so clever, you can manage to make a corpse feel restless in its grave.'

'W-what happened sir? Has Joby caused any problems?'

'Oh! The Wound in the Earth swallow him, like the idiots in this town say! I cannot even fire him now without my niece turning against me. The drunk has really taken her into his custody.'

When Paachu said this, Sureshan could sense despondency, and not anger, behind his words. As he massaged the Yemaan's round head the barber saw something he had never seen before. The man was sad, infinitely sad; and when you observed it, it was like descending down a dark shaft that kept getting darker as one went deeper. There was no trace of the soft breeze that was blowing through Karuthupuzha in Paachu Yemaan's heart; the smell of the damp earth and ripe fruit had not touched the recesses of his soul. There was a certain cold, dark barrenness that made Sureshan shudder. Because of this, when the Yemaan began to ramble on in his whiny, impotent voice, eyes shut and head held loose under Sureshan's hands, the latter heard him out without a word.

Paachu Yemaan's thoughts slowly began drifting as he surrendered his head to Barber Sureshan's skilled hands. As Sureshan's fingers deftly moved, massaging his head and neck, Paachu's complaints slowly began to reveal the reasons for his sorrow. He spoke about Constable Bubru who refused to stop his torturous reports. He insisted he knew what the sly Inspector Janardanan was about; after all, who better than him to understand the truth about policemen. He knew who the the few straight ones were and he was aware that the majority were corrupt and against him. He clearly saw how that rotten drunk was himself their victim. They were killing Joby, yes, he saw that. Bubru had forced Joby back to his drink even when the drunk, with a great effort, was trying to wean himself away from it. He even knew an inside fact—Bubru systematically rubbed into Joby his worthlessness, convincing him that he would never be anything more than a miserable alcoholic. Bubru used the tone of a friend when he said these things—a friend who would speak the truth even when it was so bitter that no one else spoke it. Day after day, Bubru gradually destroyed what remained of Joby's self-esteem with his talk and with forced arrack, coaxing him now like a friend and threatening him now like a policeman. In return, Bubru had a lot of dark fun and free arrack.

Sureshan was astonished that Paachu Yemaan possessed such

insight and regarded Joby with such sympathy. A lot of the stories reached him, Sureshan knew, through the labourers in his orchard.

Sureshan needn't worry, Paachu said, switching from complaining to comforting him. It was not all his fault. Paachu knew that the barber had only tried to help. As had his wife Sharada. They had thought they were doing a great good by bringing Joby under Paachu Yemaan's care and solving the problem of Priya's transportation with it, all in one clever move. He was aware of all that. He himself was not one to be taken in by their deft talk, was he? If he had agreed to the idea it was only because he saw merit in it. That was why he had permitted it all to happen in the first place.

But now the problem was that he couldn't even put an end to this mess without breaking Priya's heart and making her hate him. The arrangement had gone sour long ago, as far as he was concerned, when he saw clearly that it wasn't doing Joby any good. What he could not understand, Paachu suddenly burst out, was how the drunk had won the little girl over to his side with such finality. What had he done, apart from staying drunk and breaking Paachu's very sensible conditions? Little girls are so unpredictable. He thought he knew her. Why, Joby was her new uncle now!

Therein was the heart of Paachu's misery, Sureshan saw as he snipped away at Yemaan's tuft. Paachu wished to end the arrangement not because of Bubru or Janardanan or anything else. Joby had taken his place in Priya's heart, and he knew of no way to reverse that.

'I cannot figure it out,' Paachu was saying, his words slurring, like he was a little drunk himself. His eyes were still shut. 'Priya talks so much about Joby, even imitates his drunken accent and walk. Sharada enjoys watching her do this. Of course, she loves her aunt the same as before, so Sharada has no cause for complaint....'

When he watched Sharada bathe little Priya in their backyard, he often felt he was like the lonely characters who drank in the woe of solitude and sang songs in those silly melodramatic movies at the theatre. Of course, those characters were always far younger, and they invariably had a happy ending.

Priya had never quite loved him the same way since he had retired, he was sure of that. Perhaps, like the whole of Karuthupuzha, she had only adored him in his resplendent uniform and everything it stood for. Shorn off it he was just a tiresome old man to her too, one who stuck onto the world like mud to a wheel, reading newspapers and listening to weather forecasts as though they mattered to him and he mattered to them.

Barber Sureshan, in his limitless compassion, understood all this as he massaged the Yemaan's head. He saw that the man's folly lay in his reading of the little girl. Paachu Yemaan was seeing a change in the girl when it was actually he, and not she, who had changed so pitifully since his retirement. Earlier he had felt a delicate, protective, sympathetic and aching love for his little niece. The fact that she was so tiny—and that her parents had died suddenly and left her in his care—had brought that love out of him and she had felt it too. But now, it seemed that self-pity had overtaken his feelings of love.

For a moment Sureshan was terrified that the man would start to cry with his eyes closed.

'Should I tell Joby to gently ease off?' Sureshan asked him. 'Perhaps Yemaan can tell little Priya that it makes Joby unwell to push her on the bicycle.'

Paachu gave a heavy sigh, opened his eyes and shook his head. 'I guess Joby is the only entertainment she has nowadays. It's all right. Let's see how far this goes.' And then he sighed and added, 'Perhaps Joby is the one good thing that has happened to my little girl. Perhaps this is the only right thing I have done in a long while, eh? What do you know?'

They sat in silence for some time. Sureshan went up to the window and looked out. He was waiting for the concoction on Paachu Yemaan's head to dry. This was a special Ayurvedic mix of medicinal oils from Purushan Vaidyan that Sureshan reserved for his most esteemed customers. It had a pungent aroma that nonetheless suggested healing and goodness, like a grandmother's bitter advice. The good doctor claimed that it helped relieve stress. Sure enough, in no time Paachu Yemaan was snoring away.

Outside, a slow drizzle had begun. With Barber Sureshan watching, the size of the droplets grew until each drop became a voluminous seed from the heavens. Sureshan took a deep breath and closed the window. He remembered that the rain meant he had lost a bet with Thambi the orphan, who had said the day before that it would rain today as per the forecast in the tea shop radio. (Thambi thought that forecasts varied from one radio to another.) Sureshan had said that the forecast would be wrong as usual and it wouldn't rain. Sureshan would now have to give Thambi a free haircut and a shave. He would again need to put up the CLOSED sign outside when he was doing that, but for a very different reason—no one in Karuthupuzha would enter his shop again if they saw the terribly dirty Thambi getting a shave on the same chair, with the same knife and scissors that were used on everyone else.

He turned around when he heard Paachu Yemaan stirring. Paachu lifted his head up lethargically and then, noticing the pattering of rain, looked urgently into the mirror at the wooden bench behind him to make sure he hadn't forgotten his umbrella. Then he said, his voice still drowsy, 'There's another reason why my niece does not find me as interesting anymore. You see, I have subtly changed my parenting technique. As I think I should, because she is growing up. Children grow up so fast, you know. My wife does not see that, obviously; she bathes her still, and rolls rice up into balls and feeds her with her hands. But I say you cannot treat children the same throughout their childhood. You need to recognize that they aren't babies anymore, or they themselves will fail to recognize that and will want to remain babies throughout their lives.

'You know, I have always wished that Priya will not be left wanting because of the absence of her mother and father. I have thought of everything.'

Sureshan nodded his agreement into the mirror as he gently mopped off excess oil from the Yemaan's pate.

'Last year I decided not to buy her those little-girl toys anymore,'

Paachu Yemaan went on. 'You know, those fat, stuffed dolls, yellow and green cups and spoons, silly little doctor's kits with plastic stethoscopes and all. It's time she grew out of those.'

'Why, Yemaan? Priya is still very little, isn't she?'

'Yes, but I do not wish her to grow up to be girly and weak. That is why she has lost interest in me. Let me tell you a great secret. Keep it to yourself; I am not ready yet to reveal this to the townsfolk.'

Sureshan knew what was coming, half the town knew already. But he kept a straight face and took his hands off the yemaan's head, as if in anticipation of a major announcement.

'I would like Priya to be the Police Inspector of Karuthupuzha when she grows up.'

Paachu waited for his words to sink in. Sureshan feigned an expression of surprise and reverence.

'This town needs a law enforcer from the family,' Paachu went on with great severity. 'Yes, Priya is a girl, but nowadays there are plenty of bold young ladies in the police force. What should stop her from taking charge here? In spite of everything that Janardanan and Bubru and the others can do, I am sure I still have enough pull at head office to get her placed in Karuthupuzha.'

Paachu Yemaan looked rather comical when he spoke so gravely, Sureshan was thinking. But he quickly dismissed the thought.

'And you tell me this. Is it becoming of the future Police Inspector to be playing with little-girl toys? Yes, I know she is very young. So let her continue to play with toys, But they must be the right sort of toys—that's why I buy toy guns, soldiers and little jeeps for her. What children play with affects their character. Parenting must take all this into account. Sharada does not know that. I do not wish her to grow up too ladylike and delicate.'

'But Yemaan,' Sureshan ventured. 'Isn't it too early? I mean, Priya is still a small girl, don't you think? She has a lot of time before she is going to be inspector....'

He then began to trim and shape Paachu's immense moustache, forcing the man to be quiet and recline his proud head. But Sureshan saw that the momentary silence was like the flame running down the fuse of an explosive.

'Police work,' Paachu resumed the moment Sureshan lifted his hand, 'is not like cutting hair. It takes character, courage, a certain quality of the mind. These qualities do not develop overnight.'

He looks so comical, Sureshan thought again, almost like a cartoon character suddenly acting and talking like the hero in a movie. But in spite of the fact that he was delivering the bombastic dialogue of a hero and using grand gestures, no one could, even for a moment, mistake him for a hero. It did not make him anything other than the buffoon of the film.

Watching the rain rattle against his window Sureshan mused, it is just that right now Paachu Yemaan's turn has come. We are all the same. When we become too weak to play the hero we all turn into laughable imitations of our best selves—buffoons. And if we are doubly unfortunate, the One Mind simply picks us out from among the other buffoons, those who have lost their mojo, and mocks us to death.

'…in making her more of a tough nut to crack,' the Yemaan was saying, gesticulating into the mirror with his head turned towards the ceiling as Sureshan worked under his chin. 'In making her less, you know, sissy. Why, right now she will catch a cold if the wind fans her hair! Oh, no, sir, I want all that to change. I will toughen her up, even if she hates me for it! In fact, that's the chief reason I permitted Joby the drunk to ferry her to school and back.'

He fell silent and moved his head to the side. Sureshan wiped the lather off his chin. The shave was over, but Paachu Yemaan sat on in deep contemplation. Then he said gruffly, a strange expression in his eyes, 'Twice a day, in the company of a stinking, miserable drunk. To toughen her up. Isn't that just what a future inspector needs? But instead. Instead.…'

Sureshan stood back. Something was happening to the ex-Inspector. The salon chair creaked in agony. Sureshan wondered what he should do if Paachu Yemaan began to cry. He was glad he had put up that CLOSED sign. He looked on as the Yemaan hid his big, cannonball face in his large hairy hands. The veins on his freshly cleared pate stood out thickly, almost threateningly. He shuddered once, then began to shake violently. Even the rain outside seemed to ease a little, in the tension of the moment.

But just as Sureshan was about to gently touch his shoulder, Paachu Yemaan began to shudder greatly, like the earth quaking. He lifted his face from his hands, and the shop filled with the sound of his loud guffaws. He laughed uncontrollably, looking at his reflection in the mirror, and at Sureshan occasionally, repeating 'Instead... instead....' After the initial surprise Sureshan too began to snigger, joining in Paachu Yemaan's pure, unchecked mirth. They looked at each other in the mirror and exploded into renewed bursts of laughter.

Suddenly the door flew open and the rain poured in. Caught by surprise, the laughter stopped for a moment. It was Thambi. (Of course, it had to be someone who couldn't read the CLOSED sign).

The orphan proclaimed jubilantly: 'I won, I won!'

And that set off their sniggering again, building up to guffaws louder than before. Thambi began to laugh, too, without comprehending what they were laughing about, sending spittle flying. Paachu Yemaan observed that there was a housefly squashed against the orphan's hair, just above his ear. It seemed dead, but when he began to shake with laughter it stirred and flew about the room.

Absolutely disgusted, Paachu quickly paid Sureshan and went out into the rain, still rocking with laughter.

15.

'Yemaan Needs a Decent Burial'

The ants at the far end of the courtyard led a particularly peaceful existence. Being the courtyard of a bachelor, there wasn't much human activity around here. No one swept the ground too often or sprayed those terrifying poisons that some ants from other regions spoke about. These little black ants lived in perpetual harmony and satisfaction with their environment, gathering food, storing it for harsh weather, never desiring more than their share. Now they were walking steadily back to their nest in the tree in a neat line, chanting a uniform prayer of gratitude to the gods. It was late in the evening and the sun had already set outside the compound wall, its final rays lighting the way for the ants to scurry back to their home.

There was a metallic clank from somewhere far away in the courtyard and one of the older ants—a wise ancestor whom everyone revered—was suddenly gripped by a sense of dread. He turned around and discussed something with the younger ants behind him. The message passed down the line and it seemed that the peace of the clan was under threat. Sure enough, there seemed to be a dark, eclipse-like cloud suddenly descending from the heavens above them. There was another metallic clank, much nearer now. The ants added vigour to their prayers; it seemed like the gods were yet to be pleased. The smell of danger was unmistakable. They moved faster, the neat line disturbed in their panic.

Thunder descended from the heavens with such speed that no one knew what had happened. A tremendous explosion shook the world, and more than forty of them lay squashed against the tree. The ancestor ant was among those dead, his frail body squished into the wood. In extreme panic, their line all disturbed, the ants ran all over the trunk. Some of them fell away into oblivion. Others scurried over each other, muttering fervent prayers. Most of them let go of the food they had been carrying. The ones nearest home were again gathering into a line (there were diehard disciplinarians in the clan) when a second clap of thunder, far louder than the first, seemed to shake the very foundations of the universe. It was loud enough to seem like the end of the world. In the midst of the stunned survivors lay more than two hundred dead ants, some of them deeply embedded into the bark of the tree.

Constable Bubru smiled at their desperation and panic. He loomed over them, readying himself for a third blow with the branch in his hand. He waited. He wanted them to think that it was over. They would go back to forming a line and walking past their dead kin, accepting their fate and continuing their prayers, and then he would strike again.

He was their fate, their wrathful god this evening.

This was Bubru's favourite pastime. He moved and the metal studs on his police boots clanked against a stone. The ants panicked again. He chose a slightly bigger one to kill next. Its behind was pointed upwards as if in defiance and Bubru decided that it was its time to die. Its hubris needed to be trimmed. He brought down the branch again, but couldn't be sure if that particular ant was squashed. He brought down the branch again and again, chanting 'Rak-tak-tak-tak-tak-' under his breath like machine gunfire. He watched the ants fall dead and the tree shake in disgust. He loved the smell of squashed ants. He had heard that in some strange place far away, it was the practice of sadistic teenagers to gather quantities of a certain species of ants and burn them in tins. The fumes apparently gave them a high.

Bubru was in Inspector Janardanan's courtyard, waiting for him. Janardanan loved to make people wait. He had called Bubru over for a drink that evening and, just when it was time for Bubru to come in, had shut himself in his bathroom. It gave the man a sense of satisfaction to keep someone waiting. Bubru didn't mind. He could always kill ants to pass the time.

The smell of squashed ants invariably reminded him of his father, he did not quite know why. His father used to run a provision store in his hometown and Bubru had often wondered (but could never be sure) if he had first discovered the smell of squashed ants in that little store, among its damp sacks and old papers. No, his father never killed ants. The man was too unadventurous for such things.

Bubru revered his father. He had died six years ago, but that had made no impression on him. He still worshipped him like he was alive. He had never loved his father, for the man had never asked to be loved, only to be respected. He was sure even his mother had never loved his father. The man ruled over his family like a severe monarch, and Bubru's admiration for him was similar to what a subject might feel for his king. His brother and he would stand up when their father walked into the room, until the end of the man's life. They never had their meals together. Father ate first, then the two boys and then their mother. Father bought and sold properties, started and closed businesses, bought an old car and dumped it later, all on his own, consulting neither Mother nor the children. He went on a trip to the Himalayas once when he had the urge, and came back about a month later to continue his life as before. Every evening he drank alone in their dining room, and on nights when he used to drink a lot, the whole family's dinner was delayed; sometimes the mother and the two brothers went to sleep on empty stomachs. Father was Bubru's ultimate example of authority and power.

Every year when it was time to file his tax returns, Father would tell his two sons without fail, 'You should always pay your taxes. Never get on the wrong side of the government. The government is bigger than the individual. You can't fight it. It's far stronger than you.' And then he would pay his taxes and the boys wouldn't know if he was hassled or pleased about it.

One of Bubru's earliest memories was of a summer noon when his mother was carrying him on her waist. He was no longer an infant, but she still carried him about as if reassuring herself that he wasn't growing up too fast. Father came in through the door clutching in his palm some tobacco wrapped in old paper. With a twinkle in her eye, she teasingly enquired why he hadn't shaved. Father asked her to put Bubru down. Then he planted a tight slap on her cheek—with no anger or malice—and told her that in the family women did not command men to shave, and what she ought to do was bring him a glass of cold buttermilk when he came home.

Whenever Mother crossed the line, Father asked her to put down whichever boy she was carrying so he could slap her. But as the boys grew up Father stopped beating her, because it wasn't right to beat a mother in front of her sons, and besides, their mother had started to make fewer and fewer 'mistakes'.

The old man's message to his sons was clear, 'It's a hostile world. If you want something, you need to snatch it.' Bubru learned from him that there is no point inculcating in one's life such things as noble sentiments, refinement, even education. All the finer things that went into the making of one's personality and character were of no account as they would not help one reach one's goal. People with so-called 'loving natures' counted on elusive little things like fate and the stars to bring them what they needed. On the other hand, if you were forceful and relentless in your pursuit of your objectives, then it wasn't fate but you who was in control. Be cruel if you have to be; be unscrupulous. But whatever you do, don't be meek and pious and wait for the heavens to be kind.

'The heavens only gave you hands and feet and nails so you can fight for what your heart desires.'

Bubru brought the branch down again and killed a few hundred more ants. He felt infinitely strong and powerful. He enjoyed being that way. Smiling into the rapidly spreading darkness, he thought that perhaps his father might have been given to squashing a few ants himself in that little provision store of his.

He turned when he heard Inspector Janardanan's soft, almost feminine, footsteps approaching. The inspector was carrying a bottle of rum and a steel jug of water. Bubru knew that there would also be countless little packets of pickle in his pockets.

'What are you doing by that tree?' Janardanan said in his hollow singsong voice. 'I hope you are not pissing on my roses?'

'Oh, no, chief, never,' said Bubru, coming over to a flimsy stool and two chairs that were always left out in Janardanan's courtyard. He watched his boss arrange the bottle, the jug and then the seemingly endless packets of mango and lime pickles precariously on the stool.

'Ah!' Janardanan exclaimed with immense satisfaction as he poured out the drinks. They clinked glasses. Janardanan dipped his finger into his drink and splattered three drops on the ground in careful prayer to the wine gods. Bubru watched respectfully. And only after his boss had taken his first sip did Bubru start on his drink. Janardanan watched with pleasure and then remarked, 'Hmm, you are doing very well, Bubru. Only the other day I was holding you up as a role model for the others at the station.'

'Thank you chief, thank you. It's all because of your blessings,' said Bubru. He decided that he would fawn as much as he could now, because he found it a lot more difficult to do once some of the rum was inside him.

'Particularly those two,' Janardanan winced, glaring at his glass like it had pinched him. 'Sukumaran and Chandy. Sukumaran is older than I am and, ha ha, everyone knows he is going to retire a constable. He is like a saint, you know, and we don't need saints in a police station.'

'Well, he is too level-headed, chief,' Bubru said, pulling open a packet of salted lime with his teeth. 'Too calm to be a good policeman.'

'Yes, and that Chandy! He is still Paachu's boy. Let's see how far that gets him.' And then he began, 'Yemaam, iva kara—'

'Leave it, boss,' interrupted Bubru, who couldn't stand poetry, 'Tell me about the promotion. You said it's coming.'

'Ha! Worry not my boy, worry not,' Janardanan said. 'Inspector Janardanan sees everything, senses everything. I hold a lot of sway in how things turn out for all of you. I have already submitted my files on every one of you. And while I can confirm nothing at this point, let me tell you that you will soon have reason to celebrate. Here, drink up now.'

Janardanan launched into a long and rambling speech on Bubru's exemplary qualities. In truth, Bubru hated drinking with his boss, because Inspector Janardanan would get drunk the moment he took his first sip. But it was something he had to endure if he wanted that promotion.

'It's time you changed your lifestyle a little, my boy,' the inspector was saying, 'Maybe you can stop following that drunk—we'll see what to do with him. Meanwhile, you need to raise your standards a little. The town is going to look up to you soon, trust me,' he winked at Bubru. 'You're a young, powerful policeman; set to be police chief one day. Ha ha! I never disappoint people who stand by me, Bubru boy!'

'I know, chief.' Bubru was on his third drink, while Janardanan was still nursing his first. Rapidly, the subordinate was getting too drunk to fawn over the boss.

'This should reflect in the way you dress, the way you talk...start paying for your cigarettes—stop bullying tea shop vendors. People like a benevolent policeman, you know? And I am not just shooting through my behind...you will get a better salary soon, too, so you can afford to do these things. Trust me.'

Bubru maintained a stony expression but his ears pricked up at the mention of a better salary.

'And stop walking everywhere! People don't respect the clanking sound of your boots. That only suits constables, trotting around like horses. Ha ha! But you're still hush-hush when you follow that drunk around, I know that. How do you keep your boots from clanking when you're spying? Bubru, boy, you are a star! But you've got to change your style. Get yourself a vehicle. Oh, that reminds me—'

Bubru looked up at the sky in deep pain.

'Bubru, my son, you needn't even wait for a better salary,' Janardanan told him. 'I've got an unbelievable deal for you. You know our Ponnappan Aashari, the carpenter? Honest fellow and very sweet natured, too. Well, his old Lambretta is up for sale, can you believe the timing? *Just* when you need it. You need to rush though, before someone steals it from you. He knows how we stand, you and me. So he'll give you a very special price, I'm sure....'

'Chief, don't we have any banana chips? The rum is very harsh,' Bubru was desperate to change the subject.

'Do you think this is a bloody toddy shop?' Janardanan flared up, gulping down his drink and sucking on a lime. 'Look at the nerve! I don't keep a menu here for you to start ordering food. Ha!'

And so they spoke of this and that. Janardanan tried to push the sale again, sang a little Sanskrit ditty on love despite Bubru's protests, and spoke delicately about a certain rather pretty maidservant who, for some inexplicable reason, was too young to be a maidservant. By the time the liquor had run out Janardanan seemed very drunk though it was Bubru who had finished most of the bottle. Bubru got up with a burp, fumbled over to the edge of the courtyard and urinated heavily upon Janardanan's roses. He came back and lit two cigarettes, handing one over to his chief. Janardanan always smoked one cigarette while drinking.

Taking a puff, Janardanan said, 'It's time to give our Yemaan a decent burial.' He told Bubru how, some time ago, Paachu had telephoned Janardanan and commanded him to talk to that photographer Varky about the scandalous pictures he was putting up in his shop window. Paachu made it sound, predictably, like a law and order issue, and one that concerned all the good citizens of Karuthupuzha. Apparently Varky was clearly transgressing the law by displaying 'innocent citizens' in funny postures. It was libellous and clearly not permissible in 'good society'. 'The great Yemaan considers it beneath him to talk directly to Varky, of course. Especially since he had himself praised Varky and bequeathed his favours and blessings upon him years ago. Ha! What a remarkable son of a mutt.'

In spite of the whole town laughing at him, Paachu had yet not learned his lesson, Janardanan said. He still thought the new inspector was his assistant. It was becoming unbearable and it was time to settle this once and for all. 'A decent burial, yes. That's what the man needs.'

'Don't you worry, chief,' Bubru told him, his speech finally beginning to slur some. 'There's still some fun to be wrung out of this one. Trust me. You know what I'm up to, right? I catch the drunk and make sure he drinks. I make him drink right from the morning. This will show everyone how miserably Mr Yemaan is failing to "reform" the buffoon. People are already laughing about how ever since Paachu took over as his godfather, the drunk is more drunk than ever. Ha ha. This will also show Mr Yemaan how easily the drunk is throwing his conditions to the wind. Under his care and supervision our dear Joby must drink himself to death! I'll make sure of that. That'll be the biggest joke. Ever since the brave Yemaan began his good work the drunk is vomiting blood. Ha ha!'

Janardanan, on his part, had indeed paid the photographer Varky a visit like Paachu had asked him to. But instead of sticking to Paachu's request, he had gotten his own picture taken. A smart photograph of Inspector Janardanan in khaki. Next, Varky would be trying to capture Paachu—perhaps buying fish or picking up mangoes—so that the two pictures could be displayed side-by-side. The past and the present of power! That would really titillate the town and Varky would have brisk business.

The laughter and the rum had gone into Bubru's head. He stubbed out a cigarette and said: 'Chief, trust me, there's more fun in this Paachu business yet. Leave it to me while you see to that promotion. I have a plan. How about arranging a small accident? Let Paachu's niece have an accident while she's in Joby's care. That would really break Paachu's heart. He'll beat Joby to a pulp, hopefully even kill him. Ha ha ha!'

Janardanan stared at Bubru, unable to shake the feeling that Bubru's presence made it feel as though there was a vicious snake in his courtyard. The inspector gulped down the last of the liquor in his glass. He wasn't the man to condone hurting little girls or women. Why, he didn't even like enforcing the law too much. He believed strictly in negotiations, whispers, winks. He would have to get this brute to comply with that.

Comply with that so that they could give ex-Inspector Paachu a burial. A decent burial.

◆

On the same evening that changed forever the little black ants' opinion of their god in Janardanan's courtyard, another soul was thinking about his father, though not with a lot of reverence. Photographer Varky sat in darkness, the only source of light emanating from the pulsating glow of his cigarette.

Varky was talking in his garbled language, telling his camera for the umpteenth time the story of his life.

He had already told it about how he was city-bred, and therefore far more refined than most of these rustics around here. His father was rich—a dealer in electrical goods—and a businessman to the core. Which is why he was of rather mixed feelings when, as a child, Varky told him that he wished be a pilot in the Indian Air Force.

Varky had always dreamed of the skies. He fancied disappearing among the clouds someday. As a child he had watched airplanes disappear behind clouds and had thought that they actually briefly turned invisible among the wisps up there. He thought of all the passengers inside, so lucky to be able to momentarily turn invisible, their reality milky white. One day he saw a fighter plane, its sound separated from its body because of its amazing speed, like a clap of thunder that followed lightning (his father explained this in some detail), its awesome power unlike anything little Varky had ever known. He saw it appear and disappear until it vanished altogether beyond the horizon while its sound still hung in the sky. And then, with the all-encompassing resolve of a child, he decided that he would become a fighter pilot.

The disappointment came years later when they declared that he did not have perfect eyesight. He could never be a pilot in his life.

To come out of his depression, young Varky picked up a small camera that his father had abandoned and began photographing the skies. It turned into a hobby and then a passion. He roamed the city outskirts, went far down lonely highways and shot all types of skies—sunny ones and raincloud-ridden ones, starry skies, clear skies, skies with birds and without them, stormy skies, calm skies, black skies and white skies. It fascinated him that the sky was always changing: it transformed itself throughout the day and as the seasons changed. It was different on nights when the stars were sprinkled differently. It was different when you were happy from when you were sad. He imagined dissolving in the sky, spreading himself thin like a spirit, dead and alive at the same time. He stored a bit of these skies in his father's camera, to bring it down to his world on a piece of paper. And so the camera became his third eye; with it he could not just see but capture as well.

Meanwhile his father took one look at his photographs of the sky and gave him enough money to set up his own studio, along with the suggestion that he must turn his camera more towards the earth.

That was how Varky became a professional photographer, with his small studio in the big city. He was thankful to his father. But the problem was that the old man did not let him be. He continued lecturing his son about marketing his skills better; that he should focus on dull ceremonies like weddings and childbirths to win public sentiment and rake in money. Even more irritating was when his father paid him surprise visits in his studio, detected the smell of cigarette smoke and lectured him about his health. Seeing that his son was less and less impressed with these lectures, the father played another card finally. He told Varky that there better be a return on his investment. 'At least make sure that Varky's Studio can pay back

Varky Electricals the principal amount, if not the interest,' the man said.

This was good, in a way, because it prompted Varky to pack a small bag, taking his father's camera and a few gold ornaments, and leave the city without a forwarding address. He wandered far and wide, judging lands by looking at the skies above them, never settling down anywhere for long. He wandered his youth away, alone and different from the crowd, experimenting with his photographic skills, doing business when he was hungry and feeding his passion when he was full, until finally he had reached Karuthupuzha some years ago, very far away from his father's sphere of influence.

He told his camera about a curious development that came to his notice at this time. Now that he was away from his father, Varky found that he was an exact replica of the man. Once there was no father nearby to advise him, he followed several of his father's instructions anyway. He was now marketing himself quite aggressively, having come up with the unique idea of the window displays. He was as good a businessman as his father, if not better. Without his father's support, his head was no longer up in the clouds. After some time in Karuthupuzha, he had begun to focus all his skills on becoming a successful photographer in quite the material sense. He had collected all the photographs of the skies and burned them in the little kitchen sink of the studio. Shooting skies was nice but too idealistic; it wouldn't help him survive. Following the burning he had taken another major step: he had bought the most magnificent, expensive, intricate and technologically advanced camera that he could find. '*You*,' he told it fondly now, admiring its shoulder strap sprawled luxuriously on the armrest. It was a beauty, and it had, indeed, made him return to the skies again, occasionally. He had often put on display pictures of the sky and been commended for them by the folk of Karuthupuzha. In this way his passion had met his business instincts finally.

But for this precious camera he had had to sell every bit of gold he had, scrape up all his reserve money and even sell some of his more expensive clothing and utensils to scrape together the down payment. The rest was on loan and he was still repaying it. *They* were still repaying it—his camera and he.

In spite of the camera having drained so much of his resources—or perhaps because of it—he loved it so much that it had, over time, become a part of him. His third eye, once again. A part of his soul was in it. With it he looked at the world more often that he did with his own imperfect eyes. When he liked what he saw, he sliced it off the face of reality and made it permanent in a picture that was arguably finer, cleaner and deeper than all the pictures he had ever taken using any other camera.

He went up to it and touched it, his heart beating faster and his cigarette-tip glowing brighter.

Excitedly, they discussed the next picture for the window display. Before this town had finally spent all its laughter on ex-Inspector Paachu, they had to milk the opportunity dry. Varky's mind was working around that new inspector's visit. The man was obviously looking to settle some account with ex-Inspector Paachu, 'but that's none of our worry,' he had said. But there was an exciting idea there—amid mythological verses and discussions about scooters for sale—there was an exciting idea in that discussion. The past and the present of officialdom, Inspector Janardanan had said. That was an idea!

Varky looked at the picture of Inspector Janardanan that he had taken. He held it up for his camera to see. The picture slyly captured Janardanan's face in all its incongruity—making it look funny and downright obnoxious, with its thick, pockmarked nose and narrow, stupid eyes. It was amazing how you could strip a person naked even though you had only photographed his face. What lent the picture more value was the fact that in it you could see how proud Janardanan was about his own face! The new face of officialdom: naked, proud, stupid.

Now, it remained for them—for Varky and his camera—to get the other half of the project going. They had to get a picture of the old face of officialdom. They had to capture Paachu Yemaan equally naked. It was an exciting challenge, and Varky lit another cigarette with the stub of his old one.

Janardanan had meant, in his malice, to bring out the contrast of old and new—stupid old Paachu being replaced by the infinitely smart new inspector. But Varky and his camera knew that the pictures they had shot would bring out the much more dramatic fact that officialdom was always the same—idiotic, trivial and unchanging. There would be the nakedness of truth in the juxtaposition. And the joke would be as much on Janardanan as on Paachu!

Suddenly his camera reminded him about Paachu's toilet obsession. Did the ex-Inspector wear a lungi and smoke a beedi to build pressure in his tummy? Did he himself carry a small bucket of water, or did he make his obedient, demure wife do that for him when he was off to the toilet? Did he perhaps carry a newspaper under his arm to read while he went about his business? And what about his bath? Did he come out with his hair sticking to his pate? It would indeed be a sensation to have Janardanan's pockmarked face next to Paachu's tired one, all blown up and spread across Varky's window.

This was his life's calling, Varky knew. He stubbed out the cigarette on the carpet and sat down beside the big chair on which his camera rested. It gave him a high just thinking that soon they would invade Paachu's privacy like never before. And they would give Karuthupuzha an unforgettable picture.

◆

Paachu Yemaan was sprawled on his easy chair on the porch, snoring through the sunset. It was for the first time that her husband had fallen asleep in the evening and it worried Sharada. Everyone in Karuthupuzha knew that to sleep during twilight hours—the sacred time meant for offering prayers to the gods—was to ask for trouble. A curse from the heavens could easily result in you being reborn as a lethargic snake in your next life if you slept during evenings in this one. Besides, if that photographer saw this, the next picture would be of Paachu Yemaan sleeping like a lazy python at twilight.

Sharada was sitting on the cement floor chopping up some cabbages and potatoes for dinner. From inside she could hear the steady drone of Priya's voice singing a hundred and one repeated expressions of gratitude to Lord Shiva. Priya had been appealing to the gods all evening—without understanding a word—to bring peace upon this earth, remove pain and suffering for her and for all creation. In all likelihood her steady voice had turned into a lullaby for her uncle on the porch.

That afternoon Barber Sureshan had met Sharada in the backyard and spoken to her morosely. She had never seen Sureshan this concerned about her husband. After he had come in to have his tuft cut, Sureshan shared, Yemaan had opened up to him and it was clear that this terrible and merciless town was actually killing him! Everyone, from that antique dealer to Photographer Varky to Inspector Janardanan and Constable Bubru, were contributing to Paachu Yemaan's fall. And his deteriorating relationship with his little niece was further depressing him. Priya hadn't now, for ages, played on his lap or twirled his moustache or even laughed at him. His strategic parenting had estranged her. In fact, now it seemed that the little girl was the only one who did *not* laugh at him!

This town is killing him! Barber Sureshan repeated and Sharada fretted. Sureshan was not given to speaking so forcefully and his vehemence scared her. Joby was drinking more than ever and Paachu Yemaan was no closer to a peaceful retirement. Their plan had clearly backfired. 'Maybe it isn't so easy to set things right and to change people,' he said sadly.

But the real reason, he told her, for his coming over to meet her now was not just to tell her that their plan had failed. He felt that she could do something about it, but it had to be soon. He felt that Paachu Yemaan was reaching a tipping point. Barber Sureshan sensed doom.

Another thing he wished to tell her was about Constable Bubru. That man was pure evil. Joby may be a drunk and a clown but Bubru, on the other hand, was malicious and capable of causing physical harm to those he touched.

'Yes,' said Sharada, adding, 'then there is that photographer. He keeps putting those ridiculous pictures up for the whole town to laugh at.'

She told Sureshan about how Paachu had approached Inspector Janardanan with the request to stop Varky. But her husband had no friends left, no one on his side, she had said with tears in her eyes.

And now, as she sat on the floor and heard his gentle snoring, she wondered if Varky was lurking out there in the darkness. The thought scared her at first, but then it lit a fire in her. Her mind filled with images of their youth, when they were newly married and she was terrified of her husband. He had protected her from the world as husbands must, and yet she had often felt that it was from his hammer-like hands that she needed protection. She knew he loved her, but he often reacted very angrily at her slightest mistakes. He would yell, his moustache shuddering violently, if the back of his khaki shirt, or even the part that went inside his trouser, was not well ironed. He would curtly tell her not to interfere when she showed concern about his dealings with crooks who smuggled contraband goods. She had spent nights awake, wondering if he had really killed that thief Gopalan with his hands. His hands, she had been terrified of his hands. They were like steel covered in hair.

And yet, when her father had died and they had come back home after the funeral, he had been kind to her, speaking to her for some days as if to a child and even coming home early so that she wouldn't be lonely. When it was clear that she wouldn't be able to bear a child, how gently he had dealt with the news! Later, with infinite tenderness, he had suggested that they could bring Priya home and she could be her mother.

She had been terrified of him, and yet she loved him. It hurt her to see his pain. She prayed with a bursting heart. Her eyes fell on her husband's sleeping form—he slept like a man who was dead tired after a lost war.

The fire grew inside her. She did not know what she would do, but she knew that she would do something.

16.

A Little Pair of Eyes

Each of her textbooks required a different approach. When she sat in front of her Hindi book she pretended to be her uncle's radio, mimicking the static, bad signal and background music. When she grew tired of this, she'd drone on in a lost state, only so that her aunt could hear. In front of her English book she turned into a foreigner, practising different accents as she read the chapters. When she read out of her science book she skipped entire paragraphs, read sentences in reverse, used one scientific word in place of another and giggled to herself because she knew that her aunt would understand nothing. Her aunt had told her to read out loud so that she knew the girl was studying. So Priya's favourite subject was arithmetic, because the textbook couldn't be read out loud, and it left her free to daydream.

This evening was for arithmetic and the textbook had been open in front of her on the same page for the last hour.

Despite Aunt Sharada's strenuous efforts, Priya ranked among the last few in her class. She was not particularly worried about this as none of her textbooks really taught her anything about becoming a giant wheel operator. She hated her classmates who regularly raised their hands when the teacher asked questions. She smiled as she remembered the story Joby had told her when she told him this. He recalled that when he was as little as her he had actually beaten up a boy who continuously gave the correct answers in class. He threatened the boy with further violence if he continued making lesser mortals look stupid. The poor boy had stopped raising his hands and the teacher had thought that he had suddenly stopped studying. Ha ha! Joby was so funny.

Sometimes Joby said things that made her laugh at that moment, but made her hair stand on end when she thought about them later. At other times she shivered as she listened and laughed later. But she listened to every word he uttered. He, too, paid serious attention to whatever she said, unlike most adults. By now they had begun to talk directly to each other most of the time. Only when they were nearing home did they automatically switch to talking through Lilly.

Now, her eyes glazing over the senseless and boring figures in her arithmetic text, she remembered his last story. He had told her the story of the Wound in the Earth which she had found curiously interesting and even funny in places at the time, but which now made her shudder.

Some forgotten number of centuries ago (a century is a hundred years, Joby had told her), the elders of Karuthupuzha came together to solve the problem of water shortage every summer, when all the wells dried up and the women needed to go all the way to the puzha to fetch water. The river, however, was very far away and the path to it was riddled with danger—some of the women were eaten up by a panther from the hills while some others, mainly the pregnant ones, fell down exhausted and died on their way back with their pots of water.

The finest astrologers were called from distant lands and a prasnam was conducted. A prasnam is the astrological equivalent of a query—a human question posed to the gods. The astrologers who came—pure of mind and transcendent of spirit—sat down with some seashells, betel leaves, a wooden board, the sun, the moon and the stars among other things, and posed to the powers of the universe the question of what was to be done to save Karuthupuzha of her thirst in the long summers. The answer that emerged was deceptively simple—dig another well.

But, the astrologers warned, the gods had revealed that this well would need to be as deep as twelve ordinary wells. It would be dug by an insane but thoroughly competent well-digger who would arrive from up north for the express purpose of saving Karuthupuzha. The well-digger would choose the site of the well on a full moon night, and it would turn out to be near a Yakshippala, or a devil tree—a sweet-smelling tree with plenty of white flowers. As the well-digger began his work, he would encounter evil spirits under the earth who were primarily responsible for Karuthupuzha's woes. These he would send into captivity upon this tree and, finally, with no evil influence to hinder it, the well would perennially offer them water. The only thing the residents and elders of Karuthupuzha had to ensure was that the well-digger was never displeased with anything. He would need to be kept happy all through the digging process. His remuneration would need to satisfy him for if he felt shortchanged he could quite easily set free all the numerous evil spirits he had nailed to the Yakshippala tree, and then the whole exercise would prove to have been unimaginably counterproductive.

So, after the prasnam, word was sent out that Karuthupuzha needed a hardworking well-digger; one who could dig a well that was more than twelve times the depth of usual wells and also tether the evil spirits to the devil tree in the bargain. As predicted, a well-digger appeared soon, from up north. He was a strikingly handsome man, built like a statue, his body bronzed and his muscles like rocks beneath the earth. He spoke in very refined language, explaining that he had heard about Karuthupuzha's requirement from a friend and had decided to take up this rare challenge. He then laid down what was required from the townsfolk: special tools, help from the temple to locate the best spot and food eight times a day (he seemed to be partial to good food). He told them that he would not bathe or clean his teeth for the period of this digging but they were not to worry for this was only because of his commitment to his task. He spoke nothing of his remuneration and when they asked about it he said they could pay him as per their degree of satisfaction with his work.

The elders were relieved to find that the man was not greedy for gold or fine clothes or expensive gifts, but only asked for food. Then they asked him his name and he replied, 'Well-Digger'. They asked repeatedly, but his response was always the same: 'Well-Digger'. That was when they remembered that the astrologers had warned that it would be an insane well-digger who would fulfil the task. Looking heavenward to acknowledge the miracle, the elders agreed to call him just Well-Digger and to go along with his insanity in return for a permanent solution to their water problem.

Well-Digger, with the help of the priests of the temple, went out on a full moon night to find a site for the new well. He marked a spot to the west of Karuthupuzha, near a Yakshippala tree. The whole of Karuthupuzha prayed ardently at the precise moment Well-Digger brought his tool down upon the earth for the first time and began his colossal task. The omens all seemed good, the priests announced, with the stars all lined up the right way. There was no reason why another woman would ever need to be eaten by a panther.

Well-Digger worked alone, exactly the way he had told them he would; day and night, without pausing for a bath or to clean his teeth. The women of Karuthupuzha took turns to cook him the best meals they could eight times a day, bringing him the food themselves, lowering it down into the well using a rope. They watched him and whispered of his dedication to his work. He worked in his loincloth, sweating and bent over. Sparks sometimes flew as the iron wielded by his powerful arms connected with rock. At nights he used his powers to nail many an evil spirit to the Yakshippala tree; folks counted the increasing number of nails with admiration.

When the first of the moisture began to seep out of the mud and stones, it tasted as sweet as coconut water and everyone was happy!

Then, in his happiness, Well-Digger embarked on something new. Sitting deep under the ground in the semi-darkness, he began to carve figurines out of the rocks he had cracked. These were breathtakingly beautiful figurines—naked and finely wrought forms of men, women and children. (When she heard the figurines were naked, Priya had thought to giggle but she saw that Joby was very serious.) These figurines Well-Digger offered free of cost to the families, and soon every home in Karuthupuzha had some of them displayed prominently in their front rooms. People remarked that Well-Digger could easily rake in gold if he decided to sell the figurines; they were such fine works of art, but perhaps he was just too kind or too insane to think of business. The elders sent word out that people should not suggest too many business ideas to Well-Digger; he was their lucky find and they need not spoil his head with unnecessary temptations.

But Karuthupuzha ought to have paid the man decently. For the well was promising to give them sweet, cool water all through the summer, and the figurines showed that he was a fine, no, a great artist. The women fell madly in love with Well-Digger when they ran their hands over the figurines. They dreamt of his long, insane fingers that were strong enough to shatter rock and sensitive enough to carve these magical pieces. The men grew jealous because their women admired Well-Digger so. Some of them started suggesting that enough well-digging had taken place and whatever remained to be done could be taken care of by Karuthupuzha's own well-diggers. A jealous husband beat his wife to within an inch of her life. The elders, rather uneasy, told everyone to leave Well-Digger to his well-digging, throw away his figurines if they were causing quarrels, keep them if they liked them, but to stop seeing all this as anything more than a solution to their water problem.

All through, oblivious to the tremors he was causing in the world above, Well-Digger stayed in his pit that rapidly darkened as it deepened. He came out to the mouth of the well only to empty what he had dug up and deposit the fresh figurines he had created. But one day he felt a new hunger. He invited the girl who had brought him food to come down. He made the girl pregnant and then four other women in quick succession. Now the men of Karuthupuzha were uncontrollably jealous. And yet, because the well was only as deep as eight normal wells, the elders asked that Well-Digger's task continue. They further ordered that the man not be asked about his preposterous actions, for that might anger him and then—as per the predictions—disaster would strike.

Thus Karuthupuzha drank her bitter insult so she might drink sweet water forever after.

But the four husbands whose wives Well-Digger had made pregnant, and the father of the girl who had first gone down the well, could not swallow the dishonour so easily. As they looked at the same figurines that had entranced their women into infidelity the fire of hatred was stoked in them. As their anger grew, bound by a common desperation, these men drank themselves silly one night in a coconut grove.

The five men then walked drunk to the west of town. After a while they spotted the devil tree. They planned to pull Well-Digger out and give him a sound beating so that he would know better than to lead respectable women astray and destroy families. They told each other that the man would then flee Karuthupuzha and the well-digging could be finished by their own men. Perhaps, after listening to Well-Digger's cries of pain, they would even be able to forgive their women and pick up the threads of their lives again.

They reached the mouth of the well drunk and sweating, and listened to the scraping noise from within. In the moonlight they saw the mound of earth and rock that was piled up and, next to it, several fresh figurines. The five men looked at these—bewitchingly beautiful forms of naked men, women, gods, goddesses, spirits, children, nymphs, mermaids! There were also figures that were half-lions and half-men, birds that were partly fish. There were life forms unimagined. Each piece had a body carved in sinful detail. The older man, the father of the girl, was the first to pick up one of these and aim it into the darkness of the well. The figurine crashed harmlessly against a rock. The scraping noise stopped instantly. One of the husbands picked up another figurine and threw it in, and this time Well-Digger gave off a howl like an animal. The drunk men smiled at each other in the moonlight. Then they began throwing in the figurines, one after the other. Whenever one hit him, Well-Digger howled and that made them laugh. Guffawing hysterically the men continued to pelt Well-Digger with figurines; when they ran out of them, they continued to assault him with mud and rocks. First, they threw small rocks and little clods of mud. Then they grabbed fistfuls and threw it in. Finally, even as Well-Digger's animal cries rent the night, they began kicking the earth in in large and heavy mounds.

And thus they buried Well-Digger alive in his own well, feeding on his howls, laughing and clapping their hands in the mad intensity of their wrath. It took them all night, for they were sweeping up and kicking in mud and stones with their bare hands and feet. For most of the night Well-Digger cried out, sometimes scraping fruitlessly at the mud walls around him in his desperation to escape. But finally he fell silent.

In the morning, when the sunlight lit up their work, the men saw that the well was filled up with mud and rock. In fact it would be quite difficult to tell where it was, but for the freshness of the soil that filled it. The horror of what they had done sank in, now that the alcohol had worn off. Then they looked at the Yakshippala tree nearby, on the trunk of which the nails had been driven in to tether the banshees and evil spirits. Long lines of blood flowed down from the spots where the nails had gone in.

Legend has it that one of the husbands ran up to the puzha and drowned himself in it. The old man went raving mad and was seen crying and roaming the streets of Karuthupuzha for many days. His daughter said that he had got drunk one night and disappeared altogether. The other husbands also disappeared without a trace, one after the other. But the curse of Well-Digger did not end with the men who had buried him.

When more men and women disappeared, people eventually started to understand what was happening. The cursed well, the Wound in the Earth, could actually move about in the ground and suddenly open up under the feet of the person it wished to swallow. Whenever someone disappeared, an unimaginably beautiful figurine turned up at some spot in Karuthupuzha. 'This is true to this day,' Joby said, widening his eyes at Priya. 'When Mathukutty disappeared a decade ago, they found the figure of a small boy near the stone quarry. The little statue was stark naked and made of a stone found deep in the earth.'

At the time Joby told his tale, Priya had found it quite funny, especially the parts where women could get pregnant by descending into a well and people could find naked figurines so irresistible. But now as she stared across her arithmetic text she imagined a well, its mouth all bloody, appear on the floor and move slowly, haphazardly around her little room, to then rapidly take up position beneath her feet. She shuddered. She was suddenly glad that she had Joby and Lilly with her when she was on the road. She resolved never to go out alone even during the day.

Only Joby could have told her tales like this. Aunt Sharada would certainly not have done so considering she was only a child—tales featuring infidelity and murder would be a no-no. Uncle Paachu only told her the same stories of bravery and machismo over and over again. She was beginning to find them silly and predictable. She could not remember anyone else telling her such exciting stories.

When Joby told her a story he did not think about her being a child. He held nothing back, never choosing his topics too carefully, mixing myths with incidents, delivering his tales while drunk, although curiously this never interfered with the clarity and passion of the storytelling. He loved telling the stories as much as she loved listening to them. Joby told her stories because he loved to tell her stories and because he knew she loved listening and not because he wanted to teach her anything or to get her to do something.

That morning, when he told her the legend behind the Wound in the Earth, they were on a detour and sitting briefly under a coconut tree after giving the policeman Bubru the slip again. Once Joby had finished the story she had searched her own mind for a story that she could tell to reciprocate. Finally she told him of a very special afternoon in her life. She was at a fair in a forgotten city and she was terrified to go on a giant wheel, but her father had held her hand and taken her on it. She told him about how she had sat near her father on the seat of the giant wheel as it climbed straight up into the skies; it came down rapidly, making her want to vomit. She did not vomit only because she was clutching her father's sleeve. 'You must not run away from the giant wheel,' her father had told her. 'Experience it, and then maybe you will find it great fun!'

On another morning Joby had brought along a bottle of arrack, hidden under his shirt, because she had said she wanted to see him drinking. She wished to see how it turned him from a sober, sensible man into a drawling, sleepy drunk. So they detoured again and sat in the grove. There Joby took sips out of the bottle and began to sound very drunk. She could see that he was pretending for her sake and she felt like a princess being entertained in her court. But this turned to immense pity and concern when, as they began on their journey to school again, he vomited by the bushes.

When she asked him if he would die suddenly, like she had heard some people say he might, Joby replied that that wouldn't be a problem because before that he would take her to see the Wound in the Earth. 'Let's go together one of these days. Or nights,' he told her quite seriously. 'We'll find it near the Yakshippala, the devil tree. Though it moves from there when it wishes to swallow someone.... They say that when you go down that well you reach the land of the dead.' But, he told her, for an adventure as elaborate as that they might need to give her uncle, aunt, as well as Constable Bubru the slip. It would have to be on a school holiday. Perhaps she might need to come down her window at night using one of her aunt's sarees. Priya shivered with excitement at the prospect.

This led to a passionate discussion on ghosts and visits from the dead.

'Do you believe in ghosts, Joby?'

'What's not to believe? But I don't think there's anything to be scared of. People do come back after they die, but they come back out of some sort of love, some longing. They cannot bring themselves to part with this earth and their loved ones. Who in their right minds would otherwise leave behind the comfort of heaven and come back to this wretched world? If you hated a place and were lucky enough to be out of it, would you ever come back if you could help it? So those who return from death only do it because they love someone or something back here that much, no?'

Priya told him that it didn't matter if ghosts came back out of love or of hate; she was scared of them in either case.

Then she remembered that on another occasion Joby had told her that he found it strange that people only spoke of the ghosts of people. 'If ghosts exist, shouldn't our streets be crawling with *all* kinds of ghosts? I mean ghosts of dogs, bats, cows, snakes, cockroaches? They die too all the time, don't they? Some of them get crushed beneath people's feet and under wheels. Some are chopped up and eaten. Ugh, what horrible deaths! At least some of them should come back. Why are there only the ghosts of humans?'

And then he had said at another time, 'Even if ghosts exist, it's awkward to think they will scare and harm people, no? Because the people they intend to scare and harm will become ghosts too at some point, won't they? I mean, suppose I die and then come back as a ghost and drink up your blood until you are dead. Then you become a ghost too, don't you? Suddenly there's nothing scary about me. So wouldn't you walk right up to me in the other world and ask for an explanation? "Hello, what were you thinking, you idiot, drinking blood that doesn't belong to you?" That would be so embarrassing. Eventually all ghosts will stop misbehaving for fear that their "victims" will confront them when they become ghosts too. Don't you think so?'

Priya had laughed and now, sitting in her room, she could not really decide what Joby thought about ghosts. He could argue for or against their existence with equal vigour and logic. He was so clever!

Priya's mood darkened when she remembered how the morning when he had got drunk to show her what it was like had turned out badly. That fearsome and ugly policeman accosted them near the school. The man had angrily started to tease Joby for having given him the slip again, asking him what they were doing together that he should not see. Priya had seen, for the first time, Joby's eyes briefly flash in anger. In response Constable Bubru had pushed Joby about, slapping and hitting him semi-seriously on his shoulder. In the scuffle the bicycle had been dislodged from its stand and Priya had fallen down, scraping her palm and knee.

'Look what you've done,' Bubru had sneered at Joby. 'It's you. You have hurt the Yemaan's precious niece.'

She touched the knee now and it still smarted. She had told Aunt Sharada and Uncle Paachu that she had fallen down at school, so as not to get Joby in trouble.

'Eight eights are sixty four, eight nines are… er...eight eights are sixty four,' Priya suddenly sang. Even though it was arithmetic, she knew that her aunt appreciated it if she read out aloud once in a while, to show that she wasn't daydreaming or falling asleep.

17.

Sharada Corrects a Wrong

One day something happened in Karuthupuzha that made a deep impression on everyone. People spoke about it for long afterwards. As with all such incidents, everyone had a different opinion about what had transpired. Folks couldn't say if what happened was right or wrong. People weren't even sure whether the incident was funny or tragic. It was argued that this incident was quite a turning point in many ways, though some said it was just dramatic and nothing more.

Though it was a very bright morning, it seemed to have something in its air that incited discord or at the very least prompted people to act in ways that they wouldn't have considered acting on any other day. It was the sort of morning on which the moment you step out of your house you come across multiple instances of people being displeased or showing signs of irritation and you wonder why this should be so, because the skies are bright and there is a pleasant breeze and it's neither too warm nor too cold. The sort of day when everyone *ought* to be happy and yet they seem all ready to snap and shout and even fight!

That day, a couple of dogs had been growling at each other for some time over a silly morsel while plenty of edibles lay about. And then, even as the marketplace was coming alive for the day, someone had taken exception to the recycler Abu singing a parody that, on another morning, would have gone unnoticed. This man, a big burly giant who smelt of engine oil, was now chasing Abu around shops. While Abu was beaming with pleasure and continuing to make up songs as he fled, the man who chased him seemed to be growing steadily angrier.

But the star of the morning right at this moment was Joby, who lay in a ditch quite hidden from everyone's view, yelling abuse at the bright sky. No one knew what had made Joby angry. He had stopped sleeping in ditches and on doorsteps for quite some time now, so this was unexpected. Being a Sunday he didn't have to drop little Priya and so he had gotten heavily drunk the night before. In fact he still had a half-finished bottle of arrack beside him in the ditch. Barber Sureshan's shop was closed, not because it was Sunday (his weekly offs were Tuesdays), but because he was running a fever. That seemed to give Joby more leeway to shout ear-rotting abuse. Nobody paid him any attention but suddenly Paachu Yemaan and his wife Sharada were spotted. They had come to the market to buy vegetables and fish.

Paachu Yemaan appeared on the far end of the street, shaded by his umbrella, with Sharada following a little behind. The wife was never to walk by the side of the husband. She was always just a step behind him as was the custom. Every once in a while Paachu slowed to say something to her and it seemed that it would have been so much easier for them to just walk side by side. But when he stopped Sharada stopped, too, heard him out, replied, waited, after which they continued walking, almost in a line, Sharada right behind him, like they had walked around the sacred fire on the day of their marriage.

Seeing them, someone did the favour of going to the ditch and admonishing Joby, so that the drunk fell to muttering, except for the occasional extra-loud stink word.

Paachu visited the market less and less nowadays. He had, until some time ago, come quite regularly with his wife to buy fresh fish. When he was inspector, several vendors had offered them extremely good bargains. Despite Sharada's embarrassment and protests some had even given away certain things free of cost. Sharavanan, the dried fruits vendor, would offer them packets of dried Arabian dates 'for the sweet, precious little lady back home,' when Sharada knew that the man had several contraband items to sell and had his reasons to appease her husband. But Paachu would take the dates from him proudly and she would have to go along. Once Paachu Yemaan retired, Sharavanan had forgotten 'sweet, precious' Priya back home and the free Arabian dates had stopped coming. Several others, particularly the provisions and fish sellers, slowly stopped giving them great bargains. Many of them simply told them the prices everywhere had gone up and so they couldn't help hiking their own prices, and in fact Yemaan and Sharadechi were getting the same percentage of discount as before. Some shopkeepers did not even bother with such lies. They just charged more for the same stuff.

Surprisingly, Paachu had taken this well. For a while, he had continued to shop with his wife, mainly to chat with old acquaintances and make sure the fish she bought was the freshest.

Lately though, with him dropping things from his routine, it was only occasionally that he would drag himself to the market. He left the shopping to Sharada while he napped on his easy chair. He did not see much point in ensuring they ate only the freshest fish. One doesn't die if one eats fish a day old. As for chatting, he was quite aware that there were many who were laughing at him behind his back. Besides, when Sharada left for the market the house would be totally quiet and perfect for a nice, long nap.

But then Pariera had come over with a bottle of rum the previous evening, calling out to Sharada for some hot chips. 'But the chips will not go down well, sister, unless our throat is wet. So do get us some cold water and two glasses!' he had yelled towards the kitchen. In the course of their chatter Sharada had told Pariera that her husband was withdrawing more and more into himself.

'Hah!' the antique dealer told Paachu. 'Nonsense. Don't start getting lazy just because they spoil you with a fat pension, my friend. Go out and about. Walk around. Talk to people. You'll feel fresh.'

Between them Sharada and Pariera had managed to convince Paachu to leave his easy chair from time to time, and this market visit was the result. Sharada noticed her husband was indeed in better spirits as he walked. He was beaming and nodding to people. There were many people, especially some older ones, who actually touched their fingers to their foreheads in a bit of a salute when the ex-Inspector passed.

Then a fruit vendor tried to sell them bananas at a discounted price. The man had been shouting out his discount to all shoppers, saying 'Bananas at the price of matchboxes' and 'Bananas at the kind of money you drop into a beggar's bowl'. This was a particularly good-humoured vendor. Although he didn't do anything out of the ordinary, and only glanced at Paachu and Sharada when they walked up to where he was, his sales joke abruptly angered Paachu. He stood right in front of the man, chest thrust out in a belligerent policeman's pose, and told him that his bananas were in fact only fit for a beggar to eat. He said he wouldn't even use them as manure for the plantains in his orchard. He invited the fruit vendor to come over one evening and take a look at his orchard to see what real bananas looked like.

Perhaps Paachu Yemaan thought that the vendor was trying to slight him personally, talking to him about discounts to mock the times when the whole market had given him discounts because he was police chief. Maybe he did not notice that the vendor was a young fellow who seemed to not even know who Paachu was, far less be malicious to him. Whatever the reason, people began to snigger here and giggle there. One fat old lady who was selling loose underwear heaped on a cloth on the pavement began to laugh so hard that she was in danger of choking on her betel juice. Sharada finally managed to talk her husband away from the fruit vendor.

My husband has to make sure that they laugh at him, Sharada thought dispiritedly.

But Paachu's mood was salvaged when he met some old friends. He stopped to chat as Sharada continued to shop. Meanwhile, she saw a curious sight at the far end of the market near the bus stand.

Photographer Varky was standing there, his camera slung across his chest, almost perfectly camouflaged from view. One moment you could see him, the next you couldn't; he reminded her of a star in a cloudy night sky, tricky to spot. From time to time Varky would aim his camera at something, a vegetable, a passer-by. Sharada observed that people were in complete awe of him. The man would sometimes kneel dramatically on the ground to get a better shot of a cabbage that was sticking out of a pile of vegetables on a vendor's cart. On anthor occasion he would stretch upward to photograph a loose tile on a restaurant's roof. Or he would ask a vegetable vendor to pose and condescend to take a picture.

Sharada continued to observe him as she shopped. She noted his long, bony, cigarette-dried fingers as they fiddled with the big black camera. She observed the mole on his cheek under the checkered cloth cap and she thought that it was the mole that set him apart. Without it, his long, bony, rather sickly face would look most ordinary. It gave her a strange high to be observing Varky, unseen by him, because it was usually the other way around.

She looked around nervously for her husband, but Paachu was totally unaware of Varky. He stood with a couple of old people, looking around with gravity as if challenging anyone to laugh at him. She heard him say, '…and it's very different when you look at daily involvement. In the military you loll around, drinking and eating good stuff, and your role is only when there is a war. And how often is there a war? Very rarely. So you generally have a good life. Not so in the police force. No sir, the police have to be on their toes all the time: alert to mischief-mongers and gamblers in the day, burglars and bandits in the night…a policeman is on duty all the time, and….'

As she stood there observing Varky on the on the one hand and her husband on the other, it suddenly dawned on Sharada that Varky's photographs had actually captured Paachu's essence. For the first time she admitted to herself that the photographs told the truth. She looked from Varky to her husband. Perhaps Varky's camera had seen in Paachu what she herself hadn't in a lifetime. If you looked deep enough into any of Varky's pictures of Paachu, you could see, as she now saw, the cruel policeman who drove fists into stomachs, who fanned and benefited from a rumour that he was a killer, whom Sharada sometimes feared even today, the man who had insisted the police jeep be put in his service even after he'd retired, who hid his love for his niece so deep in his heart that the little one didn't even see it. Everything was so accurately—so mercilessly—captured in Varky's pictures, and blown up for the world to see. Naked. Paachu was naked in Varky's pictures.

She could not spot Varky anymore. She moved down the street, stopping occasionally to purchase something that figured in the shopping list she held, leaving her husband to continue chatting. She saw the photographer again, coming out of a little sweet shop, slinging his camera around his neck after taking pictures. The sweet vendor was trying to offer Varky a packet of condiments but he was refusing it.

Sureshan's voice echoed in her ears, telling her that this town was killing her husband. And one of the chief culprits was the photographer.

But of course Varky was only telling the town the truth about Paachu. Because a photographer is a person who can *only* tell the truth. Unlike a painter who could bring subtle, almost imperceptible alterations to reality with just a little more or less pressure on his brush, just a little less or more colour in each dab. A photographer could only choose what truth to capture with his angle. Varky captured the truth from a deft, rare and sharp angle. He revealed its nakedness with subtle, masterful lighting. He rode on the truth and that was his art. The angle was what made Varky a truly genius photographer, Sharada saw. He captured reality from a viewpoint from which even a wife had never really seen her husband.

Suddenly she heard a numbing expletive rise up from somewhere nearby. *Joby*! She hated the fact that several people actually seemed to look at her, and then at her husband, when the expletive was heard. Her husband was talking animatedly to a new bunch of people.

She had to grant that he looked like his old self now, not the sleepy pensioner he had been threatening to become of late. Admittedly only one of his listeners was looking at him and the other members of his audience seemed either forced or amused but at least Paachu seemed to be in fine form.

It would be extremely unfortunate if Paachu would discover Joby here, lying drunk in a ditch and yelling profanities.

She saw Paachu's tuft, just a stub where Sureshan had snipped it, and she wondered if Varky would capture him on film now if he saw him. Actually capture him, like a policeman captures a convict. She looked absently at the morning bus coming down the road, and from the periphery of her vision she saw someone walk up to the ditch to silence Joby again. She felt far away from what was happening around her, everything seemed to have turned into a dream. At the same time, she felt a strange impulse rise within her, perhaps it had to do with the air that morning that was making people behave in strange ways, perhaps a slow burning fire had finally reached the powder keg, perhaps it was the unusual clarity with which she saw her husband as revealed in Varky's pictures, perhaps it was a combination of all these, or something else altogether, but Sharada herself could never quite explain why she acted as she did. But we are getting ahead of ourselves.

She had just reached Poulose's grocery store. The grocer was greeting her when she saw that Varky was quite near. He seemed to look around him the way an eagle scans the grounds far and wide. Sharada placed her shopping bags at Poulose's counter and mumbled that he keep them for her for a while. She absently made way for Abu as he ran past her, singing something she couldn't hear. She walked, as in a dream, her eyes fixed on Photographer Varky, who was now drinking tea from a small stall in the central clearing of the market where the bus stand was. He had lit a cigarette and was exhaling the smoke in rings, occasionally taking a sip from his glass. The tea vendor asked him if he wanted a bun, for which he wouldn't charge, but Varky shook his head.

Varky was facing away from Sharada, looking at the bus as it approached. People had already started jumping off before it could stop. Everyone was in a hurry. Sharada could sense Varky thinking if he should shoot this bus; capture its busy little life on his film, freeze the everyday business of its journey, the heat of its engines and the glint of sunlight on its vivid new paint. She could sense Varky thinking that he could leave that for some other morning. She could see with dreamlike detachment his camera slung on his back and not on his chest, out of the way of his glass of tea. Quite some way away she could see her husband begin to look around for her even as he continued to be deep in conversation with his friends. Varky's head turned, sensing Sharada behind him. He nodded then, with some familiarity—the wife of that ex-Inspector—before he put the glass of tea back to his lips.

With one swift pull Sharada yanked the camera off Varky's back. The strap held it to him a moment longer, but then broke with a crack. People swore later that it happened in slow-motion, like in the movies. At the same moment that the camera came free of Varky and in Sharada's hands, the bus was slowly reversing into position. Sharada threw the camera under the tyres. Varky turned around and watched, first without comprehension, then in slowly mounting horror as the action unfolded. His hand had gone up to his neck, massaging it. The camera crunched explosively. Bits of it stuck to the tyre that had crushed it. The shattered lens gleamed like a million eyes. The bus sighed to a halt, resting finally and letting more passengers jump to the ground from its doors.

The glass of tea fell from Varky's hands, smashing on the ground. Sharada felt hot droplets of tea on her feet. Varky turned to her and his lips curled away from his teeth as his mouth opened. A most astounding shriek tore through the air. Varky was massaging the spot on his neck where the strap had cut into his flesh. This pain was to haunt him for the rest of his life. Even years later he would have to try different oils for relief from this; and hot presses, different leaf extracts and assorted allopathic pills.

But then people realized, and Sharada realized, that only air had escaped Varky's lips. He stared at her for a few more seconds in astonished silence and then turned and ran from the market without his camera, turning invisible one final time.

The shriek had come from Paachu. He stood transfixed in the distance. His friends stood around him stupefied. He was looking at his wife as she stood near the bus like a goddess appeased with her vengeance. A string of pungent expletives rose from the ditch nearby, but no one seemed to hear them. Perhaps the only sound everyone could hear was the loud snap of something breaking deep inside Paachu Yemaan's heart.

18.

The Anger of the Rain

The stars were still out when Paachu woke up the next morning. He lay there listening to Sharada's calm breathing and staring in the dim light at the rotating fan. He felt incredibly tired. He pretended to be asleep when Sharada woke up and went downstairs. Later, when it was the usual time for him to get up and get angry at the mirror, he continued lying on his back. He just couldn't bring himself to begin the day.

Sharada called out from below, telling him that Priya seemed to be running a fever. He reflexively touched his own forehead, and then felt low and ashamed.

He thought that what had happened yesterday had finally finished him off. It was the end of Paachu Yemaan, who once owned this town. His wife, the graceful and demure Sharada, had been the one to finally protect him. Protect him from that puny, good-for-nothing photographer! The angry God of Karuthupuzha, the wrathful and righteous hero who made his enemies freeze in terror, the only man in this town ever to have reportedly killed another man, had finally needed to be shielded, saved, delivered by his own wife. The truth was out in the open, and the whole marketplace had witnessed it.

And what did his wife think of him, that she had made so bold as to come to his defence!

Yesterday, after the incident they had walked quietly back home, Sharada walking a step behind him as always. Several times he had thought he ought to say something. Different things had almost burst from his lips:

'How could you! You have insulted me. I don't need you to defend me from that...that....'

'Thank you, Sharada. That Varky needed it. I should have done this myself long ago.'

'Don't tell little Priya what happened.'

'I didn't see Varky in that crowded place. If I had seen him you wouldn't have had to....'

But he had said none of it, because everything sounded absurd inside his head. He had just walked silently along, like a man numbed by snakebite and about to fall dead. He remembered being bothered by the thought that his wife might be looking at him from behind, watching the back of his neck or the tuft of hair on his pate.

And now, in his bedroom, he felt very tired because he thought that everything about him—the way he walked, ate, even thought—was hilarious. It drained him just to think about how he might prevent or stop this laughter. It was safe here, in his bed, but anywhere else he might be laughed at. Outside, a few baby birds made tiny gurgling sounds. Suddenly Paachu wanted to come down with a fever.

For sure, Sharada had put an end to that Photographer Varky and his illustrious tenure here. Everyone knew that Varky's soul lived in his camera. The man had disappeared from the market yesterday and Paachu knew instinctively that he wouldn't be seen in Karuthupuzha anymore. So no more blown-up pictures of Paachu Yemaan as he came out of his bath and jumped on one foot to clear the water in his ears. Oh yes, Paachu remembered that one. The picture had made him look like those offensive pictures of tribal women dancing, complete with heaving chests. He had dreamt the night he had seen that picture, that he was going deaf listening to the laughter of the entire town. He had dreamt that even the cows and the bats laughed at him.

And that was the Varky his wife had finished off.

He remembered the time when Pariera had told him, 'This Varky chap is way too much. You ought to have a talk with him. He cannot just shoot people and display them in absurd poses as advertisement for his work.'

At the time Paachu had tried to make light of the whole affair, had even been complimenatry about Varky, 'Oh, it doesn't matter, really. He is a talented photographer. Besides, nobody is really up to the task of insulting Paachu Yemaan, my good friend. I might be retired but at one time I ran this town. People still remember that.'

He sat on his bed and looked at the mirror. A tired old man stared back with droopy, watery eyes and a tuft standing up ludicrously at the topmost end of his head.

'Hmm, I wonder,' he muttered to himself, running his palm over the stub of hair. 'Maybe people always found me quite amusing. I *am* quite amusing.'

It started to rain and Paachu hurriedly closed the windows. Then he went back to look at himself in the mirror. He recalled how he had picked people up from under coconut trees while he was inspector; unemployed youth who had only been whiling away time playing a bit of cards. He used to sink his fist into their bellies, alleging they were gambling. He had also raided godowns, held up trucks with goods and beaten up drivers who were quite harmless. It seemed ridiculous now to think that this tired old man had done all that. It was laughable that he had, for years, maintained a scrapbook with pictures of angry film heroes. He wondered what his deputies at the police station might have thought if they had ever gotten hold of that book, with its cuttings of red-eyed, phenomenally muscled, prominently veined, dishevelled-haired, glisteningly sweaty men who seemed to leap out of the pages. What would his deputies at the police station think now if they saw how he struggled to hold back tears when he was at the cinema?

Maybe the thing he held in the greatest glory, his tenure as police chief in this town, was really nothing to get all that puffed up about.

He was quite sure that Sharada herself was not so proud of it; she didn't find anything inherently glorious about it. It was only he who thought highly about it.

All of a sudden he felt deeply ashamed about the fight for the police jeep, his high-handed conversations with Inspector Janardanan, his weighty letters to head office, his bragging to his acquaintances, his demanding a constable to trail his niece…everything.

Paachu smiled, in spite of himself, at the contrast between his humongous moustache and his tired eyes. Smiling through his moustache made him seem even funnier, and he giggled. How ridiculous that he had used this same mirror to practice his anger!

His mind flitted from one thing to the next, like a monkey that had sat on a wasp.

'The people of Karuthupuzha were never really afraid of me,' he mumbled. 'They were simply inconvenienced by my anger; maybe quite weary of my impulsive and free use of the fist, my use and abuse of power. That's not fear.'

From below Sharada called up to him. Paachu yelled something back but he noticed that the rain had so intensified that he couldn't even hear himself.

Now *that's* anger, he thought, looking at the giant droplets that were making his windowpanes shudder. So commanding, so lofty! The smell of wet soil filled the room and Paachu felt a sweet urge to surrender to the anger of the rain. Maybe he should just go back to sleep, and then maybe he shouldn't wake up at all.

He saw that the benevolent rain, the same rain that quenched the earth, had now turned unspeakably powerful. Its roar was far louder than Paachu's had ever been. He saw clearly now why people laughed at him today. How they were getting back at the puffed up, pompous turkey he'd once been. Probably even in his time as inspector they had laughed behind his back. Why, he might have laughed at himself, had he looked at himself the way he was doing now.

'Maybe I should just take my clothes off and walk in the rain,' he thought madly. 'Ha ha! Paachu Yemaan, naked as the day he was born. Oh, how that'll send them screaming.'

Turning into a buffoon made him think of Joby. He stared into the mirror and thought about Karuthupuzha's drunk buffoon who had won his little niece's heart. What great agony was eating away at the man that he was throwing his very life away and joking his way to death? In fact he did not know much about Joby at all, or even if there was some central reason that had broken him. He had met a lot of drunks in his career and tried to straighten them out with his fist. But about Joby all he knew was that the man was determined to drink himself to death, while being a comic through it all. For once Paachu did not see himself and Joby as being all that different. 'We're all the same,' he told the mirror.

But then he knew that he could never take the way out that Joby had chosen. It seemed an incredibly attractive and natural way to be, this tragic buffoonery. But he couldn't resign himself to that role, because of the weight of the life he had led which continued to propel him onwards. Whatever falsity he had nourished all these years kept him going, like a train that ran on the tracks for some distance even after its locomotive had shut down. He could never run naked into the rain. Joby could, any day.

He thought of all the years in service when he used to come home in the evenings proudly, like a player who came back victorious from the field. He remembered that it had irked him to see that Sharada did not often ask what he had done in the station that day, who he had vanquished, what mission he had accomplished, which crook he had taught a lesson. Instead, every evening, she had only yelled out to him, 'check your pockets before you put your uniform in for washing.' It sounded so banal and mundane when she yelled that same warning to him evening after evening.

And yet, after his retirement, it had hurt him that Sharada had stopped asking him to check his pockets when he came in from outside. It was as if there could be nothing important in his pockets anymore, now that he was old and retired!

No, he couldn't ever have run naked into the rain. But then he had to find a way out of the present state he was in. He walked up to the window and watched the world turn into a white haze under the deluge. Trees drooped and the soil was splattered about by the weight of the rain. No human was out there. He wondered what had happened to the little birds—they had probably died. When this was over he would find their nest shattered and their little bodies dismembered. He would find their mother, all wet and in shock, sitting frailly on another branch....

It's a different justice system out there, he thought with tears in his eyes, one that we cannot even begin to understand. That unspeakably cruel rain was yet so supremely righteous and confident. Bird casualties were part of the overarching scheme of things. Like the earth itself is so full of hills and valleys and dark wells and big monuments, but yet, seen from the perspective of outer space, it was smooth and shiny as it spun through the void. It was all just a matter of perspective to see things as they truly were. He just needed the right perspective. From there, his mind jumped to something else. As he looked out at the rain lashing down from his first floor window he wondered how it would be if he jumped. His head reeled and he was hit with a wave of nausea. He switched, instead, to thoughts of drowning himself in the river. Maybe he would get incredibly drunk on Pariera's military rum and then finish himself off in the puzha.

Even the way he was contemplating suicide was comic.

As he began to contemplate suicide he felt that that might be the way to sort out how he felt about himself, the way others felt about him. It made him feel better, feel victorious after all. There were a million ways to die painlessly and quietly. He knew that only his Sharada and little Priya would cry for some time. The rest of them would cluck their tongues and secretly find even his death funny. It wouldn't matter much to anyone and that was perhaps partly why he was crying now.

His tears were all over his face and moustache, and Sharada would come up anytime now! Paachu opened the window, the rain stinging his face as the wind blew the old curtains out of the way. He held himself up against the big droplets like a man facing bullets. He let the rain mix thoroughly with his tears so no one would know that Paachu Yemaan had cried.

'I will opt out. I will die my way,' he told the rain, braving it, watching it drench the neat uniform that Sharada had ironed and placed by the foot of the bed. He held his chest out and shouted into the din that he didn't care if it gave him pneumonia. And that in fact he hoped it would.

The cold and piercing raindrops drove him to again think of the many remarkable ways in which he could die—maybe he could use his old service revolver—that would be truly glorious (he had managed to hold on to the thing without surrendering it upon retirement). Perhaps he could climb up those hills beyond the river and jump off a cliff. He had a fear of heights, yes, but what did it matter when he had decided to die anyway? Another great idea was to get Chandy the constable to sneak him the keys of the police jeep so that he could drive it one last time into a tree.

'He was always a fearless maniac, that Paachu Yemaan,' people would say. 'Look how he went: violent and brave and mad!'

But in spite of how alluring thoughts of a glorious ending were, Paachu was beginning to feel disturbed to think like this. Though there had certainly been times in his life when he had thought about killing himself, the imminence and certainty of it frightened him. In his heart of hearts he feared physical pain and misadventure. He told himself that he was going insane. What had happened now, after all, that he was thinking this way? That sly photographer had it coming, and how did it matter that he had finally got it from an old lady who could bear it no longer? In any case, wasn't Varky the aggrieved party here? So why was he, Paachu, considering suicide? Varky should be the one thinking of drowning himself in the puzha. Ha!

He would never admit it to himself but it was a relief when Sharada opened the door and screamed, 'Wha-what are you doing?! Why are you…!'

She rushed and struggled to close the window against the rain and wind. He did not move to help her. Quite drenched by the effort, she finally managed to shut the rain out and began to dry his bald head, tuft and all, with the dry end of her saree. All she then said was, 'Stop this madness, please. Come down. Priya has a temperature.'

Paachu went down meekly, thinking that the one true characteristic of a born buffoon is that he would make the world laugh by earnestly seeking glory till his very end. It struck him that he must have a long chat with Joby—there was a lot that he wished to know about that drunk. Downstairs he placed his hand fondly on Priya's forehead and then went to call Purushan Vaidyan.

19.

Paachu, Joby and a Quarrel

It was just as well that Priya was down with fever, for that was perhaps the sole reason why Paachu Yemaan did not attempt suicide in the next few days. Although he probably would have lacked the courage to actually go ahead and kill himself but he was, on the day following the death of Varky's camera, desperate enough to try something nasty. There was also the possibility that he might have tried to kill himself but not gone all the way, losing his nerve at the last moment, as usually happens with so many. Imagine him coming out of the puzha spluttering and panting after a failed attempt to drown himself! Now that might have triggered more laughter. But thankfully you don't try such things when your little niece is burning up with fever and your wife is worried sick.

On the morning of the fourth day following the incident at the market, Paachu was standing by the road outside Joby's house, suicide temporarily taking a backseat in his head. He was thinking instead about how he wanted the conversation with the drunk to go. He didn't have anything specific to say; he'd just had an urge to walk with Joby down this lane to wherever the drunk went, perhaps to emulate the trips his little niece had every morning and evening with him, and squeeze himself into their world a little.

Joby came out of his house and began walking towards Paachu Yemaan, wheeling his bicycle beside him. Sharada had sent Joby a note through a washerwoman some days ago telling him that he needn't take Priya to school for a few days as she was sick. Worried, Joby had gone to Sharada's, using the entrance at the back that could be accessed from the orchard, so he wouldn't be noticed. When he enquired after Priya, Sharada told him the little one only had fever and would be all right soon, but that Paachu perhaps would blame him for it. Joby needed to be prepared. Paachu might say that Joby had allowed Priya to get drenched in the rain and that had given the girl the fever.

Now when Joby saw Paachu he started guiltily, wondering whether the Yemaan was here to berate him for allowing Priya to fall ill. His eyes flitted this way and that in search of an escape route. However, there was only one path and it led directly to where Paachu stood. Joby switched quickly to a very sickly smile and unfolded his lungi as a sign of respect and servitude. Paachu was surprised to see how emaciated and yellow the man looked. He looked far worse than he had on the morning he had stood on Paachu's porch. Now, his stomach was much more bloated than before. His fair skin was the colour of pale urine and his nose and eyes seemed more sharply outlined because of their emaciation. His eyes glittered—from a distance they made him seem very intelligent, but up close you could see he was, in fact, feverish.

'Yemaan was looking for me?' Joby asked, subconsciously putting the bicycle between him and Paachu.

'Not particularly,' Paachu lied. 'But now that you're here, why don't we walk together for a bit?'

'How's little Priya, Yemaan?'

'Oh, she's really down, but she'll be all right soon. She's taking Purushan Vaidyan's medicines.'

'Wouldn't it have been better to call Doctor Ambookkan, Yemaan?' Joby asked with concern.

'I think I can decide that,' Paachu said. 'I'm her uncle, and I *am* a little educated and all that, you know.'

The air crackled with tension. Thunder rolled somewhere far

away. Lilly the bitch joined them enthusiastically.

'I-it might start to rain,' Joby said in some time, walking a trifle slower. 'Would Yemaan like to come back to my home? If there's anything you wish to talk about, Yemaan....'

'I'm not coming to your home. Can't you walk?'

'Oh, I'm happy to walk, Yemaan. I just asked...,' Joby lapsed into silence. And then he asked: 'Is Yemaan displeased with me? Have I done something wrong?'

'Oh, why should I be displeased?' Paachu's tone was that of a hurt child. 'You're my niece's best friend. Why would I ever be displeased?'

I haven't come to fight, Paachu told himself. But part of him couldn't help thinking about beating this drunk up, making him bleed. It was the tired dream of a defeated sportsman who was mentally revisiting the various faulty moves that had cost him the game. They walked in silence for a bit.

'You know, Jose,' Paachu sighed. He had deliberately got Joby's name wrong. This was a technique of his—when he wished to demonstrate to the person he was addressing that he felt the other was his inferior, and that there should be no doubt about that, he would act like he had forgotten the man's name. 'We might differ vastly in our status, wealth, family background, achievements... everything. But, I was thinking, there's one thing we yet have in common.'

Joby looked at him. He seemed now a little more confident that he wouldn't be punched suddenly.

'This town laughs at both of us.' Paachu made this announcement like he was telling a joke. Joby looked at him curiously. 'We are both great strugglers in our lives (yes, I seem to think you are, too) and Karuthupuzha finds our struggles very funny.'

'I am a buffoon, Yemaan,' Joby said at last. 'I am known to be one. But you...you are widely respected, and...and feared.'

'Oh, come off it, Jose,' Paachu said, raising his hand to pat Joby on his shoulder and then deciding against it. The crackle in the air was diminishing. 'It's no great secret that I am the great clown here, maybe even greater than you. I didn't see it, quite deliberately, for years. I was in a lot of denial. But I cannot hide it from myself anymore. Everyone laughs at me. For God's sake, that's quite apparent.'

'Well, Yemaan, this town has nothing better to do. Some people will laugh at the very gods themselves; that's what idleness can do.'

'Maybe,' Paachu Yemaan said thoughtfully. 'Maybe. Maybe they would have laughed at anyone. But recently I looked into my mirror and laughed at myself! I *am* quite funny, I know that. Come on, Jose, being funny is not your exclusive territory, you know. My funny tuft up here (I've decided not to cut it anymore), my big blown-up pictures at that Varky's window, my tug-of-war for the police jeep, probably much everything about me...if you consider all of it, I *am* quite hilarious. Admit it, you needn't be afraid.'

'I don't laugh at you, Yemaan,' Joby said.

'Ha ha! Ho, ho, ho, that would have been the ultimate! One buffoon laughing at the other.'

They both laughed away at that and even Lilly seemed to be smiling, the black of her snout pulling back and her tongue stretching out almost to the ground.

'Well, Yemaan, you needn't worry about that Varky and his pictures anymore,' Joby ventured, relaxing a little now. 'I heard what happened at the market. I was lying in a nearby ditch.'

That made them rock with laughter until it hurt. Paachu began guffawing, then Joby joined in. Soon Joby had tears running down his cheeks. Paachu Yemaan was panting. They had to stop because Joby began retching, producing only air from the pit of his stomach.

'And by the way,' Paachu said abruptly, after they had started to walk again, 'I just want you to know that I know you and Priya have been violating my conditions from the start.'

'Oh, Yemaan,' Joby began, not knowing what to say. 'I-It's my fault. I thought the little girl....'

'It's just as well, I suppose,' Paachu said with mock moroseness.

'At least my girl has found a good friend. You know, Jose, I suppose it's because of you effortlessly breaking those rules that you won her over, really. You see, her uncle is a man of rules. Maybe she is fed up with rules. I think she likes it that her Jose so easily throws all rules to the wind and chats with her.'

'I am sorry, Yemaan,' Joby said.

'Don't be. I am not angry with you. In fact, I wish to learn from you, Mr Joby,' Paachu said, letting go of the wrong name suddenly. 'You are a drunk and you stink of liquor through the day, I know. I know, and Priya knows, that you are just not the usual sort of drunken wretch one notices passed out in front of toddy shops or by the roadside, but a smart man with a better than average upbringing. Yet, for some reason, you have taken up this way to live. We know all that. Yet I hired you to ferry my niece, and she will now not think of any other means to go to school. Oh, yes sir, it has gone that far! She really has taken to you. Not a day passes without her mentioning the stories you tell her. Of course, she confides all this only to Sharada, my wife, because she has so distanced herself from me. But I know what's going on. I know all about the Wound in the Earth and the legend of Aadityan up on the hills and all the other stories. It's clear—you have taken my place in her heart. I don't blame you, not at all, but it is time I admitted it. In fact, perhaps I should thank you, Mr Joby. She is a parentless child, and I suppose once I became so distant, she really needed someone to take my place!'

Joby saw the anguish in the man's heart but he could not think of anything to say. His mouth had dried up and his mind, not used to complicated thoughts, told him to get a drink fast.

'Were you going to the toddy shop?' Paachu asked as if reading his mind. 'Okay then, I will come with you.'

Joby looked at the man, stunned. The toddy shop was really no place for Yemaan, he thought. It was a rotten hole, really, visited by bums and drunks, the likes of himself. Joby remembered the last time Paachu Yemaan—Inspector Paachu—had stepped into the toddy shop. It was perhaps more than a decade ago when Inspector Paachu and a group of policemen had raided the toddy shop, declared it unclean, unhealthy and without proper documentation, and carried away loads of liquor bottles and food by way of compensation. They had even emptied the drawer in which cashier Rayappan kept all the earnings of the shop.

'I wish to come,' Paachu said. 'Take me to your toddy shop.'

Without a word, Joby took the road to the toddy shop, Paachu walking beside him. As they ambled along, Paachu went on talking, now morosely, now with painful honesty, now with loaded cynicism. He told Joby that he had only wished for the very best for his little niece, but she had grown so far away from him that at times they were almost strangers. After his retirement he had meant to focus a lot more on Priya's upbringing and see to it that Sharada's influence would not turn the child into just another small town girl, feminine and delicate, another Sharada herself. 'But of course,' he sighed, 'my wife is nothing like I thought her to be. That day at the market proved me wrong. Delicate lady? Ha ha! I was always wrong, my dear Joby, always. My life itself is wrong.'

Paachu was surprised at his own candour. It was as if someone else had taken control of his tongue and was making him pour his heart out to this drunk. But he had to admit that it felt good, letting it all out, keeping nothing back, even saying things he did not know were inside his heart. It was like pressing a hot wet towel upon a cheek swollen with toothache.

'But now I am beginning to think that it could only have ended like this,' he went on. 'There is always laughter in the end.'

'End, Yemaan?' Joby looked again into his eyes. 'End of what?'

'End of my life, of course,' Paachu said. 'I was actually thinking of killing myself, you know. It's just that I don't have the courage even to die....'

This was sensational news, Joby thought. Paachu Yemaan, the terror of Karuthupuzha, actually admitting to cowardice! He wondered if he was hearing things, if Paachu had been drinking. What was going on here? He felt he needed to say something.

'Oh, Yemaan, dying can't be too bad. Otherwise why would everyone do it?'

Paachu guffawed and Joby joined in. They walked on like that, laughing through their sudden bouts of emotion. Joby, too, began opening up as they walked along, his fear of Paachu Yemaan slowly dissolving in the sea of unexpected candour that was pouring from the lips of the other. He told Paachu all about Saraswati Teacher, his debates on whether he loved the voice or the singer, his dark and drunken days and nights in countless, nameless towns, his marriage with Rosykutty, how his wife kept things on the very edge of shelves and tables.... Confidences beget confidences. Paachu told Joby that he had purchased the orchard behind his house entirely out of money he had made through decades of bribes. It seemed each man was only awaiting his turn to reveal something or make a confession. When it started to rain they seemed unaware of it, though in the very remotest depths of his heart Paachu hoped he might come down with a fever that could end it all. But when he started complaining about his life's greatest agony now—little Priya becoming estranged from him—Joby stopped walking, held on to his bicycle as if for support, and looked directly into the Yemaan's eyes.

'I don't know if you know her, Yemaan. I mean, really know your niece? Do you know that she fears a white van, because they transported her dead parents in one when she was just a baby? Do you know that that evening, when the white van backed into the porch, will be the worst in her life even when she is eighty? My Yemaan, you should know her! She is beautiful.'

He told Paachu that Priya was terrified that her uncle would one day buy her a toy van that was white. She did not tell him directly because she felt that he would then definitely go and buy her the exact same toy van to help her overcome her fear. He told Paachu that she wasn't afraid of walking under elephants and that she could well go to sleep under one; what she was afraid of was lizards and the 'plop' sound they made when they fell to the floor. He told him she was convinced that she would one day become a giant wheel operator after all, in spite of everything her uncle tried. As Joby continued to tell Paachu all about his little niece it wasn't easy to see if it was just the rain or if Yemaan had started to weep.

They turned into the lane on which the toddy shop was located. As they approached it Joby yelled to Lilly to wait for them outside. He put his cycle on its stand and the two of them walked in, their clothes sodden with rain. People looked up stunned as they made their entrance, thinking the alcohol was playing tricks with their eyes.

◆

Cashier Rayappan looked up from his register. He felt a flash of anger when he saw that two men were trailing large, ugly puddles of mud and rain right into his toddy shop. His anger changed to awe when he realized that one of the men was Paachu Yemaan. And his awe became intense, eye-popping puzzlement when he realized that the great man was in the company of the drunkard Joby. As these thoughts unfurled in his mind, all Rayappan could do was stand up like an uncoiling spring, the way a constable at the police station might have stood up when the inspector walked in. Paachu nodded to him in absent acknowledgement.

The smell of country liquor, hot food and perspiration vividly brought to Paachu's mind the afternoon, about twelve years ago, when he had raided this place. He felt the urge to shout at the drinkers, get hold of Rayappan by the collar and break a few bottles. Instead he meekly let Joby lead him to a table and bench. He sat next to the drunk, wondering if he should place his elbows on the greasy wood in front of him, and then went for it.

The other drinkers gradually began to be less awed and more amused. Someone loudly whispered that perhaps Yemaan had at last found his true calling for his pension years. A fat man, who seemed to have taken a bath in his crab roast, wondered aloud to Rayappan why the police raided this place every decade or so. Paachu looked directly at the man and smoothed his wet moustache slowly and deliberately until the man finally looked down at his crab roast again. Two old friends in the far corner silently placed bets that Paachu wouldn't pay for his drink since he had once been a police inspector. The rain outside slowed to a drizzle. Paachu looked at the dreamlike field outside that was bathed and fresh and he felt like a lost traveller who was tired of searching for home.

Meanwhile Joby rapidly settled into the place with the ease of an animal set free into the jungle. Rayappan himself came over to serve them, acknowledging Paachu Yemaan as a special guest. Joby promptly ordered a pot of fresh toddy for his friend and benefactor, and good old arrack for himself. Paachu realized that Joby's tone and manner were changing; his voice was unnecessarily loud and his mannerisms became caricatures of his normal ones. It was the toddy shop and Joby was putting on the garb of a comedian.

'The crab roast is today's special, Yemaan,' Rayappan said. 'Would you like to try it?'

Paachu controlled his urge to snap back that he had better things to do than to try out filthy dishes at dirty toddy shops. 'Sure,' he said instead, wondering what Sharada might have thought of all this.

All eyes were fixed on every move the two men made. Paachu felt a moment of awkwardness when the drinks came and the food was served. But, determined to make a day of this, he pretended to enjoy himself. He planted his elbows deliberately on the greasy wood of the table and dug into the crab roast. He downed toddy like a seasoned drinker and was quite surprised that he liked it. He couldn't help thinking of the effect it would have on his digestion, and whether crab caused constipation.

Maybe I should come here with Joby every day, Paachu was thinking. Maybe I'll come back this very evening. Slowly I'll start to joke with them and drink with them. They might even begin to accept me here and I won't have to feel so bereft, so unwanted, so useless in my retirement. I might even introduce Pariera to this place!

Joby began drumming on the table. Even though he didn't quite realize it, he was still quite wound up by his unexpected encounter with Paachu and the flood of confidences that had poured out of the ex-Inspector that after his first swig or two he got terribly drunk. He began to sing:

> 'Mother gave me tamarind
> Sister gave me fish and kind;
> Father gave me very cold ice,
> And aunt gave me every spice.
> But I wanted a bottle, ah one of those,
> To take away my many woes!'

He sang loudly, in the tone of a fisherman song, clapping and tapping on the table. But even though Joby was making such a din, the attention of the drinkers was still on Paachu.

'You needn't sing, Joby,' Paachu joked, looking around for approval. 'I'll pay for your drink anyway.' He made the caustic remark in the hope that it would win him new friends. Perhaps they would join in with a snigger or a snide remark. But the stupid drunks did not seem to hear him. They just stared at the dribble of toddy and bits of food on his moustache, the tuft that had begun to free itself of the rainwater and was trying to stand erect on his pate, the wet shirt that still clung to him and revealed the hair on this chest and the restlessness with which he moved his short, stout legs under the table. They found *him* funny, not what he said to Joby.

I'm as different from them as oil from water, Paachu thought. The trouble is, these are absolute idiots. They do not even get an intelligent joke. They only laugh at people's tufts and moustaches. And they can laugh tirelessly at the same tuft and moustache for their entire stupid lives.

They might still have enjoyed that morning—Paachu with his toddy and Joby with his arrack. They might yet have had the hope of a new beginning, as they ordered a fresh plate of crab roast and Rayappan suggested some boiled tapioca and sardines to go with it. Even the other drinkers were slowly taking their eyes off Paachu Yemaan. The clouds might yet have gathered above them and put an end to the dryness in the air, had everything not been disturbed by a sudden metallic clank at the door.

'Aaaah, there you are,' thundered Constable Bubru, seeing no one but Joby at first. 'I've been searching for you all over town, my friend, my best, best friend. And where did you go without me—' Bubru stopped his histrionics abruptly when he noticed Paachu. But then being the crude, moronic bully that he was, he decided to see how far he could go. His stupidity was bolstered by the fact that he had been drinking from quite early in the day and this made him even more vicious than usual. 'Oh! Yemaaaaan! The town's own Yemaan!' he cried, 'Well, I can see that the two of you have joined hands and given poor Bubru the boot.' He turned to Rayappan and said in a cruel, mocking tone, 'You know, Cashier, this Joby here, is my best friend. There was a time when he couldn't down his arrack without Bubru by his side. That was when this Yemaan, Karuthupuzha's boss, had needed Bubru to safeguard his precious niece from Joby, my best friend. Now they have begun to drink together and they did not even think of asking me to join them. But I am not one to take offence! Ah, no sir, Bubru doesn't take offence at all! Cashier, bring me something quickly, so that I might drown my sorrows.'

With a clank of his boots he came over and sat down beside Joby, and began to dig into the crab roast, uninvited. He then made a big show of putting his arm around Joby, leaving the marks of gravy on Joby's shirt. People later wondered whether someone who had seen Paachu and Joby walking together had reported it to Bubru, who had then immediately stomped off to the toddy shop. It wouldn't do if Joby had joined hands with Paachu.

'Hello Bubru,' Paachu greeted him. The muscles at the corners of his lips quivered for some reason, making his moustache move tiredly, like a slowly dying centipede.

'Karuthupuzha's Yemaan, salutations,' exclaimed Bubru, standing up suddenly, nearly upsetting an empty bottle on the table. 'Constable Bubru reporting, sir! I have been faithfully trailing your target for months now, perhaps for an entire year, and here's my report. He vanishes at times with your little niece, a growing girl who seems herself to enjoy these brief elopements. . . .' He drank from Joby's bottle which was half empty. By now, it was clear to everyone that Bubru was already quite drunk. He kept a stock of foreign liquor at home that he had extorted from lorry drivers, and this morning he had already taken several generous swigs from a bottle of McDowells. 'And then the target went missing again this morning, sir, and I traced him here, in Karuthupuzha's toddy shop, arm in arm with Karuthupuzha's Yemaan, your honour himself!'

The man who was bathing in his fifth crab roast began to snigger appreciatively. Rayappan came over and placed Bubru's arrack before him, hoping that the distraction might deter the man from continuing. The clouds had totally cleared away now. Sunlight and heat streamed in from the windows. The lone waitress of the shop, a very huge woman wearing a lungi and a dirty blouse, switched on the ageing radio on a shelf and carefully pointed it west. She turned up the volume.

'Switch that bloody thing off,' Bubru thundered. 'Bitch, don't you see that Constable Bubru is reporting to his all-time boss?' The woman immediately switched off the radio and, by way of registering her compliance, even turned it back to the east. She walked out of the place and into the kitchen, deeply insulted.

'By the way, dear Karuthupuzha's Yemaan,' the constable continued, speaking to Paachu but looking intently at Joby and poking the drunk with gravy-laden fingers, 'the target here, my best friend Joby, seems to be dying, don't you think? A little of the man vanishes every day. Why, my friend, you are all yellow now. Soon there will be nothing left of you but your funny songs. And then what will I trail? And dear Yemaan, your niece's first ever lover will be gone! Dead, whoosh!'

At the other end of the bench Paachu Yemaan was seething with real anger, not the put on one he used for practice. And then, just as something had snapped within him the day Sharada had murdered Varky's camera, he felt something give within him. He recognized a bitter truth for exactly what it was, and it wasn't pretty. He was a coward beneath his bluster, he realized with a cold finality. Everything that he had worked on all his life, his toughness, his bluster, his attempts to terrorize the inhabitants of Karuthupuzha had only served to mask the fact that he was actually a timid bully who shrank away from confrontation and those who dared to oppress him. He should have killed Bubru for insulting his precious niece Priya. He was unable to do anything with it. He swallowed his anger the way little Priya might have swallowed Purushan Vaidyan's bitter kashayam.

Joby didn't seem to be put out by Bubru's unruly behaviour. He even poured the constable a drink, presumably to appease him into silence. He downed his own arrack fast, stopping for a moment to make a gulping sound, so that it looked as if he might throw up. But he killed the feeling by licking some lime pickle off a very dirty plate.

'Even Karuthupuzha's Yemaan's wife will be very sorry when Joby here dies,' Bubru continued, drinking from the glass Joby had filled for him. 'Oh, they all love him; all except Karuthupuzha's Yemaan himself. What am I saying, even the lord is now friends with my friend! Though until recently he had paid me to trail him. I am fired now, I suppose? How do you do this, Joby?'

All the drinkers were giggling and winking at each other, egging Bubru on. So Bubru became even more insulting, and with each passing comment Paachu's eyes reddened the more and Cashier Rayappan winced harder. Only Joby continued to drink and lick at the pickle indifferently, stopping every once in a while to fill Bubru's glass. Even through the shame he felt at his own cowardice, Paachu couldn't help but feel disgusted by Joby's behaviour. Among all the reactions in the shop, Paachu found Joby's the most disgusting. To try to appease the constable even now was utterly shameless! This man is already dead, Paachu thought.

Bubru drawled on about how the head office was thinking of buying a special jeep for Karuthupuzha's Yemaan, how some of the policemen were thinking of building a temple where the honourable

Yemaan was God, about how they ought to start a new, five-star toddy shop now that Yemaan had taken to this fancy. And since Joby and Yemaan had now become friends it seemed that he, Bubru, would have to take to farming or something like that. It seemed to Paachu that Joby was at times even amused. Rayappan went on supplying arrack for Bubru and Joby, and fresh pots of toddy for Paachu.

Bubru turned to what had happened in the market the other day. 'Oh, that poor Photographer Varky! To have crossed paths with the high and mighty of Karuthupuzha. I told him once that he was digging his own grave with those pictures of his. Well, the glorious lady, the wife of our lord here, she rose to the occasion and crushed the stupid photographer's camera!'

Fresh sniggers did the rounds. Joby ordered another crab and boiled tapioca. He seemed to have resigned his position as chief entertainer because Bubru's performance was more than enough to keep everyone entertained.

'It's just as well that Varky disappeared, you know,' Bubru went on. 'It's not as if he could have stood up and fought. No, not against that lady; the goddess herself. I mean, what do you suppose he could have done? Placed a complaint with the police that his precious camera had been crushed? Ha ha! That wouldn't have worked, and I will tell you why.'

Now Bubru directed his gaze at the fat man sitting at the table across him, because he seemed the most amused by his crude insults. In a confidential tone he continued, 'This is for your ears alone, brother. The new Inspector Janardanan, you know him, right? Well, Inspector Janardanan has a certain weakness for the old Yemaan's wife, you know. And she knows that too; that's why she was so bold in front of that entire market that day! Inspector Janardanan calls our Sharadechi a goddess, nothing less. He says Karuthupuzha's Yemaan here could do a lot more justice to such a wife. Thanks to Janardanan's weakness for our Sharadechi, poor Varky could not even have filed a complaint.' He paused to gulp directly from the bottle. 'Janardanan loves and worships beauty, I tell you folks, especially if that beauty is married to a retired inspector who does not believe that he is retired. Ha!'

'Oh, Paachu Yemaan believes that he is retired all right,' Joby interjected quietly, clearing his throat. 'If he still believed he was Inspector, this is what he would have done.'

In a flash Joby picked up an empty bottle and brought it down heavily on Bubru's head. The crack of bone and glass came together. The sound was heavy and conclusive. The constable fell the way a huge pillar would—he slid off the bench one inch at a time, and on his way to the ground, Joby smashed a second bottle to the side of his head. And then, as the fat man across the room slowly stood up, crab roast dripping down on a band of saliva from the corner of his lips, Joby vomited on the unconscious constable.

Paachu sat there as though nothing had happened, lifting a pot of toddy to his lips and taking a piece of crab off the plate. It seemed as if ages passed just like that, after which Rayappan and the others came over to hold Joby back. But the drunk was totally in control of himself and didn't need any holding back. He wiped his mouth.

Then someone remarked, 'Is the constable dead? If he isn't, then Joby is. We won't have to wait till his liver kills him.'

Bubru wasn't dead. He was breathing shallowly and grunting. After a while they carried him out of the shop and down the narrow pathway to Eepachan Mothalali's car that had been summoned to take Bubru to the hospital in the nearby town. Everyone agreed that Joby would be killed soon. 'Just you wait till Bubru comes back from the hospital,' the fat man said as though Joby wasn't around to hear him. 'You can't hit a policeman and get away with it. There won't even be a case when Bubru has his revenge. He will smash the buffoon's brains in.'

Silently, Joby walked past a very drunk Paachu Yemaan and vomited out of the window.

20.

Bad Dreams and Good

He was teaching her to cycle. Both of them knew that she was too little for such a big bicycle, but that made it even more thrilling. She was beginning to balance herself on it. Gradually, she was able to even out her weight on either side, just as he had taught her. She thought that at the rate they were going she would know to cycle by the time she woke up from this dream. And that would be a miracle!

'You must not run away from the bicycle,' he had told her. 'Experience it, and then maybe you will find it to be great fun!'

He had taught her to park her fear aside first and to keep looking ahead—not at the ground or the handlebar. She had done just that. Now she was balancing the cycle and it was sliding down the road, on either side of which were endless fields. Even if she erred, she knew that he would not let her fall. He would hold the bicycle straight and compensate for the fact that she was a little girl and she was still learning.

But the trouble with such dreams was this. If you were having them during a deep, trouble-free and happy slumber, they go along predictably fairy tale-like. But if you were running a fever, if all the joints in your bones were slowly throbbing, and if you had just had some bitter kashayam and its bitterness still lingered, then the dream would invariably turn into a nightmare. She knew this, and this is what she was dreading. But it helped to know that Joby was in the dream too, and that he was right behind. Even if it turns into a nightmare it is fine, she thought. Because he is with me.

But that was not to be. Because, as the bicycle picked up speed, the smell of arrack and sweat fell away behind her. With a painful flash, she realized that she was going too fast for Joby to keep pace. Why, the bicycle was now speeding along the dirt track, and the fields on either side were a blur. She turned to look over her shoulder and the bicycle began to sway. She couldn't see Joby anywhere. She was on her own. In her terror she saw the road dance in front of her, first to the left, then to the right, then to the left again, each time swaying more and more, like a swing that was about to come off its hinges. She screamed, first for Joby, then for her father.

The cycle skidded off the road and into the field, moving impossibly fast. When she fell she felt a strange and terrifying tingling at the tip of her nose, as if it was bracing itself to thud painfully against the ground.

This has gone too far, she thought. Too far for me to wake up now.

She fell and closed her eyes as the ground flew up to meet her face and nose. But there was no painful thud at all. The bicycle disappeared from underneath her and she continued to fall. She heard a voice say that to this day some women, pregnant women who'd gone to fetch water from the river, were eaten along with their unborn babies by a panther. She opened her eyes a trifle and realized, in unspeakable terror, that she was falling down an endless vertical tunnel with crude, circular walls of earth.

Soon the speed of her fall began to decline, as though she were a particle fallen in liquid. But this was not any less terrifying, because in her slower movement she could make out in the earth and rocks around her little hollows left from which beautiful naked figurines had been wrenched out. She realized that she had been hearing the tapping of metal on stone for some time, which was now reduced to plops, like sound travelling through water. She knew it was Well-Digger in action, as he worked his way into the earth. She could imagine him digging the earth for water while also carving out those figurines, an unutterable curse trapped in his insane heart. In her nausea and panic, she called out to Joby again, but her voice sounded too faint even to her ears.

On the sides of the well she saw rusty nails driven into the hard rocks, and blood trails beneath them. She said aloud that the ghosts were not to hurt her, for then she would die too and become a ghost herself, and then ask them what their business was. Joby's cold logic comforted her. But she was still too scared to try to grab a creeper or root or rock on the spooky wall and arrest her fall. She could then have crawled her way back to the surface and then run, run back to her bed and hugged Aunt Sharada! At this she felt sorrow deep in her and could even taste its bitterness in her mouth.

The tapping of Well-Digger grew louder as she descended, though she wasn't surprised when she couldn't see him at all when she had finally landed on the uneven floor of his well. The thudding sound came from all around now, perhaps the mad digger was buried in the earth and was trying to work his way out.

She looked around and, to her surprise, saw that at the bottom of the Wound in the Earth there was a door on one side. It looked ancient, yet it wasn't dilapidated or rotting. Her feeling of dread grew and now there was more sorrow than fear in her heart. She almost knew what was going to happen.

She cried out painfully, cursing the fever and telling Aunt Sharada that she wouldn't ever fall asleep when sick again, because it gave her such horrible nightmares.

And then the ancient door slowly opened. She looked around for Aunt Sharada, or Joby, or her father…anyone! But she was alone, and the mouth of the well was impossibly high above her. The thudding of her heart was now indistinguishable from the sound of Well-Digger working. She stared with dread at the open door and the darkness beyond it. Then a white van backed up through the door and its rear doors began to open. She screamed silently into the liquid air, and shut her eyes because she could not take another look at her dead mother and father even though she knew that this was a dream. But when she opened her eyes a fraction, horror and sorrow hit her hard. It wasn't her parents lying dead inside the van this time.

It was Joby!

She looked at his dead face, calm, smiling, yellow, silent. Priya cried. It was a relief because it finally seemed to release her from the clutches of the nightmare. Her room came into view. Outside a slow drizzle was pattering at the closed window. It was evening.

'You're sweating,' Aunt Sharada said, smiling and holding her close. That was when Priya was certain that the dream was over. 'This means the fever is starting to leave you.'

◆

Paachu Yemaan could not be sure if he was asleep or awake as he watched the sheet of water in front of his eyes. The drizzle had intensified into a hard rain and fell in a steady pattern as it cascaded off the edge of the roof. He was mesmerised. If even a single drop in that sheet is missing the pattern will be broken, he was telling himself sleepily. How irreplaceable each drop is, though it stays put for such a fleeting moment!

A week had passed since the quarrel at the toddy shop when Joby had nearly killed Constable Bubru. Reports had begun to come in only sometime after they had rushed Bubru to a hospital in the town. At first people said that Bubru had died on the way. The car on which he had been taken belonged to Eeppachan Mothalali, and its driver Velu had said that somewhere along the way, when they were well outside Karuthupuzha, Bubru had opened his eyes and then gone into a fit. They had to stop the car and watch as he frothed at the mouth and his eyes became white globes. It was frightening. Purushan Vaidyan, who had been with them, had looked towards the heavens and prayed. But later Bubru had lain very still, burning with fever for some time and then gone cold. He had bled a lot and it did not seem that he would really ever wake up. Velu claimed that the hospital had only admitted him to make some money.

At the time Paachu Yemaan had wished—no, prayed—that Bubru wouldn't die. He did not know why but he wanted that constable to come back alive. It wasn't as though he wanted to give him a hiding or anything, he knew now he was not capable of that, but he did not seem to want anyone dead. He worried about what Bubru would do to Joby. He pushed that thought aside for a bit. He had worried about that problem ever since the incident in the toddy shop and he would give it rest for a bit. Now, watching the trees with their branches nodding in the rain, he hoped even Photographer Varky would return. He dreamt that he had bought Varky a new camera, using up a good part of his savings, and told the photographer to put up his funniest pictures. It was a new form of resignation, this, and he felt content and rested. He even smiled as he dreamt that he was posing in all manners of comical poses for Varky, jumping on one leg or pulling at his own tuft. He wished he had sat near his niece the whole day, watching her dream in her fever. He had been dreaming of all sorts of things lately—of ferrying his little niece on Joby's cycle, drinking whisky and soda with Janardanan, Pariera and Bubru, discussing art with that Hariharan in a way that neither knew what was being said, buying fresh fish at the market with Sharada and arguing about the price, bathing young calves and goats, bathing his little niece and more. He dreamed of life, to put it simply.

But to return to Bubru, it seemed in a day or two that the hospital in the city would be operating on him. It could only mean that Bubru was in critical condition, but still alive. This was just when folk were wondering whether to declare Karuthupuzha's buffoon a killer or not. They held on, and it was just as well, because the news arrived shortly that Bubru would indeed live and would, in fact, be home soon. People observed Joby's face as he went about his buffoonery, but could see no signs of fear. The man went on singing his silly songs and clapping his hands, curiously getting drunk on less and less arrack. In fact, many claimed he had stopped drinking and was mostly only going through the motions. The other drinkers now only clucked their tongues in sympathy, deciding not to enjoy humour from a dying man for fear of inviting the wrath of the gods.

The only one who was truly afraid for Joby was Paachu. As he continued to watch the sheets of rain slide off the roof he thought that even though he didn't want Bubru dead he was very fearful of what he would do to Joby. He was certain the constable's first act upon his return would be to kill Joby; not punch or beat up but kill. He knew Constable Bubru well enough to be certain of that. And it wouldn't take the man much. Joby would be drunk and outdoors at night as usual and Bubru would kill him with his bare hands. Joby had brought this upon himself by avenging the insults Bubru had heaped on Paachu Yemaan. That made Paachu feel very guilty. He had told Sharada, 'I cannot just watch that brute come back and kill the drunk. What do I do?' Paachu thought about Joby's wife, who would be widowed. He thought of little Priya and how her heart would be shattered by this. She would feel twice orphaned. He thought about what an unequal fight it would be. Joby would go quietly and the police wouldn't even register a case. Everyone would say the man deserved it. They had already begun saying it.

And then, as he lay there watching the rain, the fear dissipated. He wasn't tormented anymore. He had come up with a few vague ideas of how he might protect poor, brave Joby from Bubru—he could perhaps talk to Inspector Janardanan, pull a few strings, have Bubru transferred.... He smiled now. None of that would be necessary. He saw that now. The power that keeps the wheel of life turning, no matter what we do and however much we are convinced we are turning it, would take care of this too. All he could do was sit here and breathe in the smell of the rain. He thought of his walk to the toddy shop with Joby. Of how the ice had gradually melted between them and they had begun laughing like old friends. He remembered thinking that it was no wonder his little niece had been won over by this drunk. He had then connected some of the stories of Joby that he had overheard Priya tell Sharada, with the man who walked beside him holding his bicycle close, as though for protection. It was the same man who had brought the bottle down on Bubru's iron head, caving the constable's skull in.

He wished Joby didn't have to die, but he knew that there was nothing he could do about it. He might as well be realistic—Joby would be killed by Bubru very soon. And they would linger around the dead man—Joby's wife, little Priya, Barber Sureshan, Sharada and himself—the way zebras hang around for a bit while the lions were eating their young one. He felt calm in his powerlessness, just like the earth lies passively under the lashing rain.

The Yemaan started snoring with his eyes open, observing the rain and thinking and dreaming at the same time, doubting if he had really heard his wife shouting above the sound of the rain that Priya was sweating and that the fever seemed to be leaving her at last. It was only a routine fever that she had, so he was surprised that the announcement that she was getting better brought him such immense joy. But perhaps, this was just another aspect of the massive transformation that had swept over him ever since that day when Sharada had taken on Varky. As he had looked within himself and discovered what he was really like, the knowledge had been almost too much to bear. And it manifested itself in all sorts of strange ways. Now, the joy that welled up within him upon hearing of Priya's recovery began to blossom into an immense love for the world and everyone in it. Uplifted and transformed by his newfound love for all mankind, Paachu fell asleep to the drumming of the rain. From that moment, Paachu loved everything and everyone. He wished to change nothing and no one.

21.

Drunk Without a Drop

Joby looked at the jar of mango pickle perched on the very edge of their ancient, shaky dining table and thought for the umpteenth time that it would be brilliant if there was an earthquake now. Not a big one, just a tremor. This jar and a million others like it would come shattering down all over the house like the rain outside. It would be quite a riot.

He watched as Rosykutty came into the room and set down a pot of buttermilk, its bottom hanging in the air. He smiled. They sat down to dinner and he drank some water because his throat was dry. He hadn't had a drop of arrack for some days now; probably four, maybe more. In fact he did not remember having had much to drink since he had smashed those bottles on Bubru's skull. It seemed he just couldn't handle liquor anymore. He had tried toddy and he had tried some whisky, but it was all the same. The moment he smelt liquor of any kind his stomach churned. His body was rejecting the stuff that was killing it, though his mind (and apparently just this little patch at the back of his throat) still craved it. He felt restless, his head and joints hurt and he kept wishing that the world would end, as Rosykutty served him his dinner.

Of course, he wasn't surprised that his wife hadn't asked him why he had stopped drinking all of a sudden. He did go out during the daytime, but he came home without reeking of arrack every evening, which was something very new in their lives. He watched her as she ate in silence, thinking it would be really interesting if she suddenly looked up, like normal people did, and asked him why he was staring at her. But of course she only focused on the plate on the edge of the table before her. He felt her movements now resembled her sewing. Her fingers moved with unconscious deftness, her fine hands coordinating perfectly with each other, and her eyes seemed to see the sewing machine in front of them at all times, as she followed the movement of the thread and the patterns she was creating.

She was an orphaned girl, he reminded himself. Maybe as a little girl she had insulated all her feelings, buried them irretrievably deep inside her so that she might not die of a roasted heart.

A roasted heart! What a fine expression that was! He remembered when he'd heard it for the first time, although the reference had been made to some other organ. He had once asked Barber Sureshan why he needed a nap every afternoon. The barber simply had to steal a little nap—even if it lasted only ten minutes—after his lunch. He put up his CLOSED sign and rested, even if he hadn't had business worth a single rupee that day. Joby had asked his friend if this wasn't a sign of growing laziness. And Sureshan had replied, 'Anyone who experiences reality with enough intensity needs his afternoon nap. Or your mind will be roasted.'

Maybe his Rosykutty was having her nap all the time, all through her life, with her eyes open. An orphan's reality would be unbearable to bear in all its intensity, he thought.

He suddenly felt the urge to have a conversation with her and said, 'You know that little girl I ferry to her school and back? I once told her that her uncle had a really big dream: to make her into a police inspector. And she said that a giant wheel is bigger than a police inspector. Much bigger. Ha ha!'

Rosykutty looked up from her plate, her large eyes not displaying a hint of emotion. She just mumbled, 'Hmm' and was about to look down at her plate. But then she looked up at him again and said in her quiet, understated manner, 'I heard that constable, Bubru, is back from the hospital. He returned this morning, it seems. Be careful when you go out.'

His heart leapt in joy. He wondered if he shouldn't just pick up the jar of pickle and smash it against the wall opposite in celebration. It was incredibly uplifting to have Rosykutty show some emotion, express concern for him.

'Oh, I don't fear him at all,' Joby said quietly, moving the rice about on his plate. 'He is just a filthy bastard who thinks ugly thoughts. You should have heard him go on and on that day! You would have smashed his head in too.'

For a moment there they were talking like a normal husband and wife, he thought. Talking shop. Talking about some concern of hers, some problem of his. He felt happiness and life beckoning to him, although he knew that this would last only for a moment. He wondered what it would be like to begin his life all over again. Would it be any different?

They ate in silence, listening to the rain pick up outside. It was almost dark now. It turned dark early now, thanks to the heavy clouds. Joby felt the irresistible pull of alcohol. Now, he wanted was to get some arrack in, feel the burn making its way into him, melting away all his chaotic thoughts. He felt the old metallic taste in his mouth. The food was tasteless.

Then the power went and all was dark. They would still give you uninterrupted power despite the rains, if you bribed the electricity office through Electrician Chacko. Chacko was a friend, yet he couldn't give Joby uninterrupted power because his higher-ups would insist on a bribe. If you didn't pay up they simply said the rains required them to cut power for safety. It was cheaper to light candles. Rosykutty got up, washed her hands in the kitchen and came back with a lit candle. He watched her form, remarkably elegant and straight, as she came and fixed the candle on the very edge of the table. Her skin appeared white in the candlelight, her eyes big and clear. He wanted to look down at her feet to see if they touched the ground. Instead, smiling, he served her some rice, putting it shakily on her plate, almost lovingly.

It was the first time that he had ever served her, though she failed to show any surprise, of course.

After dinner Joby looked around the house to see if he could find some arrack, though he knew there wasn't any. He hadn't kept any here, he was sure of that. Yet he looked inside the dusty cupboard and in a cloth bag that he hadn't used in years. He was hoping that merely looking for liquor would give him momentary relief. After all, he only needed a tiny drop right now. Perhaps the craving would go away if he fooled himself.

He poured himself a glass of water, put a piece of mango pickle on the lid of a jar, drank the water quickly, with a wince, and licked up the pickle. For a moment he actually felt the familiar burn in his throat. He even thought his head swam a bit. The candle cooperated by fluttering its flame slightly, wanting him to think that his vision had blurred with the arrack. Joby smiled towards the kitchen where Rosykutty was washing the vessels.

'Drunk on water,' he yelled, his voice full of happiness. He wondered if it would be even more effective if he filled an empty arrack bottle with water and poured it out into a dirty toddy shop glass instead of this clean steel one.

He could see flashes of lightning through the window. But soon the rain thinned to a drizzle and Joby decided to go out. The toddy shop wasn't his destination, but he thought he might just go out, perhaps for a walk. And, if the toddy shop was on his way....

He put on his sweaty, dirty shirt, grabbed his wallet and yelled to Rosykutty that he would be back soon.

'Be careful of that Bubru,' she said again, coming out of the kitchen. His heart swelled in brief joy again and he grew greedy—he hoped that she would ask him if he absolutely must go out now, in the dark and when it was raining. If that was too much to dream of, maybe she would at least remind him to take his umbrella, like some other wives did. But she just watched as he went out in the drizzle, still buttoning his shirt, his forehead warming with a fever.

◆

The rain hit him, first cold, then warm and comforting, seeping into him through every pore. He turned his face up, glad that he wasn't carrying the umbrella, and drank directly from the sky. He again felt the burning trail down his throat, like life filling up inside him. He felt a little lightheaded again.

Joby walked down the lane and soon Lilly jumped over a fence and walked beside him, not minding the rain either. 'You're growing old,' he told her, watching her fur stick to her.

He heard movement by the side of the road and saw that it was Surendran, the dosa vendor, shutting shop.

'Looking for a nice warm ditch?' called Surendran out to Joby who immediately began walking unsteadily, as though very drunk. But the miracle was that as he acted the part Joby did feel even more lightheaded. He drank more rain compulsively. Then Surendran called out again, 'Watch out for that policeman you knocked down. I heard he is back.'

Joby waved to the man and walked on, genuinely struggling to keep his feet steady.

As he walked on with Lilly, people going back to their homes gave him curious, pitiful looks. Some yelled, 'Hey, buffoon, that Bubru is out. Go home, quick!' Others whispered to each other of the gruesome fate that lay in store for Joby. Somebody tried to give him an umbrella, saying he could return it the next day. Sundaran the mahout, returning home balancing a parcel of jaggery in one hand and a big black umbrella in the other, yelled to the world in general that perhaps somebody should call the police; there would be violence tonight. Someone else laughed nervously from a shop window, saying that it was the police that Joby ought to be fearing now. Someone wise, a little further up where the lane diverged in two, remarked that Bubru wouldn't be able to find Joby, as he would be hidden in some ditch very soon. As he said this, the man crossed his heart and looked at the drunk fondly. Women held on to their children as they stood in their candlelit homes—they wanted no part in this. Many blamed Rosykutty for not keeping Joby locked indoors tonight.

Why does everyone love me all of a sudden, Joby asked himself, his mind intoxicated and his forehead burning up with fever. The way people were behaving, it was almost as if the show was drawing to a close. It was as if all those he was encountering as he made his unsteady way down the road were watching a comedy movie in which all the action was funny but tinged in sadness. Also, the movie was coming to an end, and as the audience had begun to genuinely identify with and like the comedian in it, they were feeling bad that the show was over.

In a fit of reciprocity Joby wondered if he should also not love his audience a little. Many of these were men he had sung and clapped his hands for in the toddy shop. To make these people laugh, he had had to endure slander on his own wife, his work from time to time, what he wore, how he walked and so on. To many he had painted the most intimate details of his life in a funny manner; he had turned his tragedies into comedies so they might laugh. In a sense he had given them his all. He was discovering that there was nothing more to him than what they had seen and laughed at. If they loved him and offered him their umbrellas, now that the curtains were going down, it wasn't without reason.

In a fit of emotion he wondered if he should not find Barber Sureshan and thank him for everything. He thought he might walk over to Paachu Yemaan's house to see how little Priya was doing. 'You would like that, wouldn't you,' he asked Lilly, giving her a gentle shove with his feet. But he immediately told himself how distasteful that would be. He would be nothing more to them a drenched beggar burning up with fever and needing help. No, he wished to meet no one right now. All he wanted tonight was to drink up the rain and keep walking until he dropped.

◆

By the time he reached the marketplace almost all the shops were closed for the night. He realized, his thoughts loose and fluffy like wisps of cotton in the wind, that he hadn't headed in the direction of the toddy shop after all. The rain had eased to a loud drizzle. He vaguely felt, in a far corner of his head, a longing for lime pickle and more rain.

'More rain, with larger drops,' he ordered as if to Mandakini, the waitress at the toddy shop. 'Along with some free lime pickle.'

He spotted, in a dimly lit alley covered by a thatched roof, the recycler Abu oiling the wheels of his bicycle, looking towards him. By the way Abu's lips moved (Joby could not hear him over the sound of the rain), he could gather that the man was singing a parody, probably about revenge or a skull being cracked in. It would be cynical, for Abu knew no other way. Now here's a man, Joby thought, who doesn't really feel much for anyone. He does not feel any love for me at all, even now. Unlike all the others, I think he just watches everything, amused, glad that he is getting enough entertainment for his ticket's worth.

Licking his lips, Joby moved on, away from the light and activity of the market. He reached the jackfruit tree and slumped down at the base of its trunk, among the roots that jutted out of the ground. It was surprising how cosy this dark, hardened, wild corner of the universe felt. The protruding roots and stones did not hurt him at all. He made himself comfortable beneath the tree, feeling like a giant sleepily settling into a mist-filled valley, its trees bowing to cushion his colossal shoulders. The only discomfort was when the lightning came, displaying the marketplace and the streets in brief flashes of unsought revelation. In the flashes of lightning he could dimly see the smooth curve of a snake as it slept on one of the branches. He could see the jackfruits overhead, perennially pregnant, waiting for whoever might be hungry. He felt something slightly thorny tickle his feet, but as he moved it slid away. He smelt the damp nests of the birds above and imagined the worms burrowing in the earth beneath him.

Some nights of his childhood, when he was unable to sleep, he would lie on his side and look at the patterns on his bedsheet. They would come alive in the moonlight pouring in through the window—big and small leaves, flowers, pods, nameless wisps, clouds.... Gently the leaves would begin to move, fanning his face as he walked among them, exploring. Soon giant, friendly insects made their appearance—ladybirds and butterflies, mostly—upon whom he knew he would soon be riding and flying. There were no enemies in this world, and he was king of it because he had discovered it. He could sink into the tall grass here and he knew he would find no scorpions or poisonous spiders at all. He needn't even think about them, because this was a world he had created.

He ran his fingers through Lilly's wet fur. He felt safe now. He had succeeded in conjuring up a world for himself under the jackfruit tree, just like the glorious world he had wandered through as a child. He could feel Lilly lick his fingers, enveloping him in her unconditional love. The skies contributed to the magic at last by shutting out the lightning and pouring down rain.

It was strange, you might say, that Joby did not once think of Saraswati Teacher or Rosykutty at all. But who is to account for one's thoughts at such a time? He did think of little Priya, about the time he had first met her and of her watery eyes. He worried about her some, but even the worrying seemed pleasurable. He felt proud of his relationship with her. He sighed, knowing he would never see her again.

In that darkness he thought he heard the repeated clank of metal on stone. Several times he thought he felt an unfriendly breath in the air, but he couldn't be sure, neither did he make an effort to be sure. Nothing bad could reach him here.

He shut his eyes, his nostrils filled with the aroma of the eternally bounteous jackfruit tree. He drank in the rain and got more intoxicated on it than he had ever been on anything else. Later, when it had stopped raining, Lilly came out from where she had snuggled into him and began howling into the night.

Epilogue

The events surrounding Joby's death were unclear. No one could say for sure that Bubru had killed him. Joby had been discovered dead under the jackfruit tree by people who had come out to investigate what the bitch Lilly was howling about. They had found the drunk leaning against the trunk of the tree, apparently uninjured, in the fulfilment of death. A large jackfruit, its knobbly green skin shattered and oozing seeds and pulp, lay by his side. Many said Bubru had smashed it on his skull, but it could have just as well have fallen on him directly, killing him instantly. Or he might have been long dead of an arrack-injured liver by the time the fruit had fallen on him. In any case a smashed jackfruit beside a dead buffoon was comical and some people even found it worth smiling about.

Even though it was uncertain what had caused Joby's death, people now stood up respectfully on their feet when Constable Bubru passed. Bubru had a heavy plaster on his head for some time, which made him look even more frightening. Was he connected to Joby's death? Bubru admitted nothing and denied nothing. Tailor Manikyam took the first step and stopped charging him for the khakis he stitched for him. (Bubru had always enforced a severe discount, but now he didn't have to pay at all.) At the toddy shop they spoke in low tones when he was drinking. Sometime later, it seemed that the businessmen had started paying him a regular bribe for his goodwill. In return he 'protected' them. One after the other all the politicians began to claim that he was on their side. It was rumoured that Inspector Janardanan had written to head office recommending

Bubru for a double promotion. People predicted Bubru would soon be growing a mammoth moustache.

About a year later Priya began taking music lessons from Saraswati Teacher. She was now an old woman with a sweet, youthful voice. The girl often fancied that she saw a young Joby standing at the window, smiling, putting up both his hands to say that he hadn't brought his bottle of arrack along.

Paachu, the erstwhile Yemaan, had convinced Eeppachan Mothalali to sell him his old Ambassador car, in which he now took Priya to school and for her music lessons. He bought the car with the money that he had kept aside to buy Varky a new camera if ever he came back. But it seemed clear that the man would never come back. Paachu sometimes pretended that the Ambassador was the police jeep and even heard the siren in his head. But it wasn't like a fever anymore. He was only mildly amused.

Barber Sureshan often told the tale of his friend Joby, the man who was a drunk but pure of heart, who wasn't meant to fall down in ditches but fell down in life for some reason. He eulogized something about pulling a flower apart, petal by petal, which was when people stopped listening to him, not understanding what he was trying to say.

The one person to prosper after Joby's death was his wife Rosykutty. With none of her savings draining away anymore, she soon bought a shinier and faster sewing machine. A lot of people, led by Paachu, went to her for tailoring jobs, mostly out of pity. Sharada spread the word among maids and labourers that Rosykutty was the best tailor in town. So Rosykutty sat up day and night, working to meet the never-ending demand, her output always accurate to the last specification. People predicted that in a few years the dead buffoon's wife would buy the land adjacent to their small home and set up a professional tailoring shop there.

But we're getting ahead of ourselves. There's a little more that needs to be said of the morning after Joby's death. After they took her Joby's body away, Lilly had loitered around the place for some time, sniffing at the ripe fruit and flies, taking in the last of his smell, trying to come to terms with her loss. She had then taken a short nap under the tree, after which she had stood up, put her tail between her legs, and walked right up to the little girl's house, hoping for another glimpse of her master.

Now, as she took short naps again at Paachu's gates, Lilly once again dreamed—like she had under the jackfruit tree—that Joby would shortly come out with the girl on the carrier of his bicycle. But when she opened her eyes an unbearable sense of loss hit her again and she began howling with all her might. Once or twice the man with the big moustache came out and looked at her. He seemed to understand her pain, she thought she could see that in his big sad eyes.

When passers-by heard Lilly howl, for some reason they did not say, 'You know that drunkard and buffoon Joby? That's his dog, howling. I think he's dead.' Instead, what they said was: 'You know that brute policeman Bubru? I think he's killed that drunkard and buffoon Joby. That's Joby's dog, howling.' No one cried for Joby but they all whispered about his death. The news rode on Lilly's howls, spreading like quiet seeds in the wind.

Paachu Yemaan had been told about Joby's death by a couple of labourers, smelling of arrack, fairly early in the morning. He might have known earlier had the telephone lines not been cut in the night's rain.

'That's sad,' he said, shaking his cannonball head. 'Really sad.'

He went into the house through the back door, his legs shaky and his mind confused. Reflexively he wished to hide the depth of his sudden, embarrassing sorrow. Why, I hardly know that drunk, he told himself. Jose or Joby or whatever. Just spent an evening at the toddy shop with him once, that's all. He wished the house was dark like the inside of a cinema theatre so he could hide his face. He heard the drunk's dog howl in front of the house and realized why Lilly sounded so sad.

As soon as he told Sharada she voiced his root fear, 'Oh, how do we tell her?'

'We cannot tell her now,' he said. 'She isn't well.'

'She has almost recovered. Her fever has left her. And she's asking about that dog howling in front.'

'Oh!'

They went out of the house again and sat on the back porch. Sharada said, 'I used to give him freshly fried banana chips. It took so little to make that man happy!'

'Sharada, how do we tell Priya?'

Paachu was more desperate than his wife about how they would break the news to the little girl. They spoke about it for a while and then when they were unable to agree on a way forward Sharada calmly got up and went inside, where he discovered her reading one of her sacred books. She could find peace in any situation.

He brooded, wandering through the orchard, absentmindedly checking if the mangoes were ripe and examining the rust under some pipes attached to the water pump. He went on mumbling to himself, nodding and wrinkling his brow. He sat down on the ground, dug up some wet soil with his fingers and inhaled its aroma. He nibbled the tip of a blade of grass. Then he got up, washed his hands at the pump and hurried indoors.

He ran up to his bedroom, put on his shirt, looking briefly into the mirror. His tuft stood upright like a lone cactus in a desert. He fingered it and murmured under his breath: 'Now it'll be me. *I* will take you to school and back, okay? Like before.' Then he left the house, yelling to his wife that he was off to the market and would be back before lunch.

He returned in some time with a big parcel under his arm. He was puffing and panting, thanking God that it hadn't started to rain as he had forgotten his umbrella. On any other day Sharada would have reminded him, he knew. He saw Joby's dog was sleeping again by the gate and walked quietly inside.

He looked out of the window and saw that Sharada was rubbing little Priya with a wet cloth in the backyard, and for a moment his heart thumped painfully. Had she told her yet? But then he relaxed, because he saw that Priya looked chirpy and eager to go out and play.

He placed the parcel on the dining table and watched the two through the window. His heart swelled with love when he saw how frail Priya was under her petticoat. 'Why, you're still only a baby,' he exclaimed to himself, looking at her spindly limbs. He noticed how peaceful his wife was, as she cleaned the little girl. The scene reminded Paachu of a cow licking her calf. Sharada had heated the water after dropping in some medicinal leaves that she had carefully picked from the orchard. She had then chosen a fresh, unused towel from the cupboard, because Priya was convalescing and she had to be careful.

When they came in he told Priya, 'My mouse, I have some bad news for you, I'm afraid.'

But Priya was in no mood for serious talk and said exuberantly, 'Am I going to die, Uncle?' At some point during the nightmare she had dreamed that Purushan Vaidyan had told her uncle that she would die soon. Now, in her wakefulness and relief, the dream had become a joke. Then she said, 'I dreamt I heard Lilly call me. Lilly is Joby's dog, you know. Girl dog. I'm not sure it was a dream.'

'You are not going to die,' Paachu said, grabbing her hand and pushing her down on the sofa. 'I want to give you something. And then tell you something.'

He took the parcel from the table where he'd placed it, sat down on the sofa and pulled his niece on to his lap. She felt warm. Was the fever still lingering or was it because she had been rubbed with warm water? Or maybe he felt that she was so warm because he hadn't put her on his lap now for a very long time. She looked at him shyly, wondering what all the drama was about. Sharada made herself busy laying out their lunch.

'I want to give you this,' he said, putting the parcel in Priya's hands.

He had decided he would tell her the news of Joby's death as she undid the wrapping. But then he put it off for a little longer. Priya's face glowed with surprise when she saw that her uncle had at last gifted her a big, beautiful doll, the kind every little girl would be proud to own, the kind that shut its eyes when you laid it down and opened them again when you stood it up. She laughed, delighted, her eyes shining.

Acknowledgements

My special thanks to David Davidar who, with a deft touch here and a tap there, has given this novel a finesse that I'm proud of.

Thanks also to his editors at Aleph, Simar Puneet and Rosemary Sebastian Tharakan, whose close reading and hard work have made this a smooth read.

I am deeply grateful to the small village of Cherupoika in south Kerala and her inhabitants. The magic of this place seeped into me decades ago and keeps me dreaming to this day.

I owe a great deal to my college mate, Ajayan T. R.: our long chats in that dingy little hostel room have given me more fresh perspectives than any of life's other tragicomedies.

And talking of friendships, I consider myself fortunate to have a friend like Surej Kartha whose views and struggles have always made me think and sometimes helped me create.

Much thanks to my sister, Maya. She is special to me and she is the most resilient person I know. Her silent strength has awed me. One day, when I've mastered my craft, I hope to write about her.

My cousin, Ritwik, and I have shared so many anecdotes since childhood that I wouldn't know how many of them found their way into this book. Let's never run out of them, brother.

My daughter, Sruthi, has been a source of happiness and calm through the difficult phases of my life. In moments of clarity I can see that it is to her that I am telling my stories.

As always, I haven't words enough to thank my wife, Rasmi, who has accommodated me, inspired me, corrected me and most of all nourished me. But for her this would be a novel I mightn't have bothered to write.

My deepest gratitude is for someone who hasn't yet learned to read this: my best friend, my pet Labrador, Yippee. It was through his struggles with life and death that this angel taught me the importance of keeping at it. So I kept at it, and here's what I got.